RISE OF THE DEAD

ANTHONY GIANGREGORIO

RISE OF THE DEAD

Gentle waves lapped the side of the yacht, as it sat moored five miles off the coast of New England, Massachusetts, which was the closest outcrop of land.

Where this yacht should have been used for sunbathing and fun cocktail parties, the ocean-going craft was being used for more sinister motives.

Deep inside its decking, a man named Dr. Walter Stanton worked feverishly to bring the dead back to life.

Ridiculous you say?

Perhaps, but every great scientist was called ridiculous or crazy before they made the breakthrough that revolutionized the world.

And Dr. Stanton was no different.

His parents had died when he was young, and after spending half his life in the foster care system as an orphan, he dedicated himself to be on the honor role, thus earning a scholarship to the college of his choice. He was a dedicated man, yes, but he was driven with the need to excel far beyond his peers.

Which brings us to the present situation.

A seagull walked along the bow of the ship, searching for a scrap of food. Where normally the large ships it found were a wealth of sustenance, this one was woefully inadequate. Still, the bird had nothing else to do, and so ruffled its feathers and waited for some source of food to appear.

A scream and a moan came to its hearing and its head shifted in the direction of the noise. Not knowing where it came from, the gull walked a few inches and then stopped.

Then another moan sounded, this one mixed with pain and a shriek of agony that pierced the air and sent the seagull flying away.

It didn't know what was happening on the yacht, but in its small brain it decided there were other, more lucrative places to find food.

Yet another scream filled the air like a siren, and suddenly the waves didn't seem so gentle.

In the aft section of the yacht, the door to the lower levels burst open and a naked man stumbled out. His skin was pale white in the harsh sun, and if one was to move closer, it would almost seem like dried leather. There was a slick coating of ooze covering the body, and the skin on the torso seemed to slough off the bones like sagging clay. If one was to move closer still, they would see something even odder than the man's complexion.

They would see the V-shaped stitching on the man's torso, which looked deceptively like an autopsy scar. The man flailed his arms in front of him, his mouth open wide as he released another guttural scream.

The oddest part of the macabre sight was the man's eyes, which were filled with an unearthly pain that would fill any human with compassion for the pitiful creature.

The man had two small electrodes on each side of his forehead and two more on his neck. Added to the two on his chest—one directly over his heart—and it was easy to see they were electrical contacts for his body. Both arms still had the remains of IV's in them, the odd color chemicals in the tubes unknown to any but the most expert in the field of chemical biology.

The man stumbled around the deck, bouncing off the walls and almost falling over the side more than once, when another man appeared through the doorway from below.

This man wore a blood-soaked lab coat and his acne-filled face was almost as pale as the naked man's skin. His small, wire-rimmed glasses were askew on his face, and there was more than one streak of crimson splashed on his cheeks. His small, beady eyes were wide with worry and fright as he tried to wrangle in the naked man. Then another man appeared, this one wearing the green scrubs of what would be found on a hospital orderly on any given day, and the name **SMITH** stenciled in bold thread on his left chest, right above the pocket. The man had bright red hair and freckles all over his face, making him look much younger than he was.

"Get, him, Smith, before he falls over the side!" Dr. Walter Stanton yelled to his assistant as he tried to stop the naked man from getting past him. If the man saw the doctor, he showed no sign, but instead charged forward, Dr. Stanton moving out of the way at the last instant before he was knocked into the water ten feet below.

"Why, Doctor? The experiment is a failure anyway. Just let the poor smuck go over the side and be done with it."

Dr. Stanton spun on his assistant with venom in his eyes. "A failure? Are you serious? Surely you jest. How can it be a failure when the proof is right before your eyes? I've done it, Smith. I've done what no man has ever attempted and succeeded in the past. I've brought the dead back to life! Those fools at Boston Medical laughed at me, shunned me, well, when I bring back proof they'll be kissing my feet to get a chance to look at my research."

As he spoke, his eyes were wide with madness, a touch of insanity thrown in for good measure.

"How can you call this a success, Doctor? Look at the poor jerk. He's nothing but a shell. Whoever he was before is gone. Whatever is in there is nothing but instinct. Accept it, Doctor, you failed. You haven't created life; you've created a monster....a zombie."

"No, I did not, Smith, and if you don't help me with him I'll see you never work again!"

The naked man was in the corner of the bow now, his legs caught in some netting left over from the last occupant. He was struggling to break free, but at the moment he was trapped. If Dr. Stanton had moved closer, he would have seen the eyes of the zombie had changed slightly. Where there was once pain, now there was something else.

A hunger for something he could not possibly imagine.

With a weary sigh, Smith did as he was told, slowly moving towards the naked man. Dr. Stanton did the same, and as each man came at the zombie, the newborn ghoul spun around, its head jumping back and forth as it stared at the two men who wanted to trap him.

Just as Smith was about to reach in and grab the zombie, he stumbled over his own two feet, causing him to lose his balance. He fell backward and his head cracked against the anchor with a thickening *thump*, the man's eyes closing in death almost immediately.

Dr. Stanton barely noticed, his eyes only for his zombie.

As he tried to grab his creation, the zombie broke free of the netting, lunging at Dr. Stanton with its mouth open wide, as if it wanted to bite him. Dr. Stanton didn't expect to be attacked by his own experiment and he promptly recoiled in fear. The zombie ran past him, continuing on until it struck the waist high railing lining the deck. With no hesitation, the ghoul hit the railing and the top half flipped over, the lower half soon following.

Dr. Stanton could only scream in frustration when the ghoul slid over the side and splashed into the water. Dashing to the railing, he watched his work of ten years sink to the bottom of the ocean like a lead weight.

He squeezed his fists in anger and yelled to the clear blue sky. "No! This can't be happening?"

That was when he realized Smith hadn't gotten up yet. Glancing to the prone man, he saw the bright pool of blood seeping from under his head. Moving towards him, he leaned down and checked for a pulse.

There was none. Grabbing the man's wrists, he pulled him forward and gently laid him on the deck. Rolling him over, he saw the large gash in the back of his head and the white of bone protruding from the wound.

Smith was very dead and now not only had he lost his test subject he was also down one assistant.

Standing up, he moved to the railing and gazed across the water. He had chosen to come out here away from shore to escape any prying eyes. Out here in the ocean, he could be free to do whatever he wanted without fear of being discovered.

He glanced down at the churning ocean at the exact point his zombie had disappeared, then he looked at Smith's corpse.

The man was dead, yes, but he was still of use to him. In fact, he may be more use now than he was before.

With a serene look on his face, Dr. Stanton dragged Smith's body across the deck, a trail of blood being left behind, the effort causing him to wince in pain while he struggled to move the body into the lower levels of the yacht.

True, he had lost one body, but God helps those who help themselves and he now had another.

His experiments would continue and this time he would make sure to get it right.

He would break the divide between life and death, and if he failed again, well, he could always toss Smith over the side, and then just go out and kill someone else, trying all over again.

* * *

It was a beautiful summer day on Nahant beach on the northern tip of Massachusetts.

Everywhere you looked people were enjoying the sun. Bathers swam in the ocean while walkers strolled along the shore. Mothers sat with umbrellas while toddlers played in the sand, a few eating a handful every now and then.

A young woman in her mid-twenties was swimming about twenty feet from the shore. Her arms and legs were moving smoothly as she propelled herself through the rolling surf.

Suddenly she felt something on her leg and then a small pain filled her body. Panicking, she kicked away from whatever had bitten her and then stroked for the shore.

Stumbling out onto the beach, she leaned down to examine her leg.

She was shocked to see a small bite wound on her calf, and when she examined it more closely, she could have sworn there were teeth marks there.

The wound was about an inch wide, circular, with blood seeping out of the indents to pool in the wet sand by her ankle.

Turning, she gazed back over the surface of the water. Other people were swimming, too, and she was about to yell out a warning that something was in the water when she saw a small boy of no more than ten get pulled under the water like a shark had gotten him.

It was like magic. One second he was there and the next he was gone.

The woman stared at the spot where the boy had gone down and a second later she saw a dark stain color the water.

She wondered what could stain the water like that when the boy's head popped back up. Only where the head should have been connected to a body, it was alone, bobbing on the surface like a beach ball. Then the head began to sink again to disappear once more.

She screamed then, long and loud, and everyone within earshot turned to look at her, wondering what was wrong with the woman with the bleeding leg.

She was the first to see the naked man with a V shaped scar on his chest step out of the water exactly where the boy had disappeared.

As she stared at the man, her eyes couldn't help but go to his exposed groin, but only for an instant. Because when she saw his face, she knew the man wasn't right. Plus, the way he had walked out of the water it was like he was going for a walk on the ocean's floor; as if he didn't need to breathe, his bloated body resembling one of those floaters she had seen in an episode of CSI.

A man in his late sixties wearing a European Speedo moved to the naked man, yelling at him to get some clothes on, that there were children on the beach and that if he didn't, the old man would call the cops.

It was when the old man was within arms reach of the naked man that the woman realized things were worse than she could have ever imagined in her worst nightmares.

The naked man reached out and grabbed the old man by the shoulders, and as the man began to protest, the naked man leaned forward and sunk his teeth into the old man's neck. Teeth clamped tight, cutting into the wattled neck, and when the head leaned back, three inches of the old man's flesh was in the guy's teeth.

Whether it was dumb luck or fate, the old man had his carotid artery ripped out and the blood shot from the open wound like a geyser, spraying five beachcombers who were watching nearby. Screams and panic were now the nature of the day as some ran away while others tried to help the old man.

Chewing merrily, the naked man moved off, the old man going to his knees while he gasped and spit blood.

A lifeguard arrived and went to the old man's aid, laying him down while she tried to compress the wound. But it was hopeless and in seconds the man had bled out and was dead. The guard closed his eyes, feeling sorry she couldn't have done anything more

The lifeguard stared at the old man for a moment and then gazed through the crowd of people, looking for the naked man.

People were pointing the way he had gone and the lifeguard knew she needed to catch the guy before he attacked anyone else.

Just before she stood up, however, the old man's eyes snapped open and before the lifeguard knew what was happening, the old man sank his dentures into the lifeguard's forearm, the young woman screaming in shock and pain. The old man worried at the arm, and when his head came back, there was a large piece of the woman's arm missing. The old man chewed happily, like he had just plucked the greasy skin off a chicken breast, while the lifeguard punched the old man in the face and rolled away screaming.

From a hundred yards down the beach, more screams filled the air, and as a few watchers turned to look, they saw the naked man attacking a woman who had been sunbathing. The man was on top of her, his teeth buried in the back of her neck and the woman's legs were kicking up and down as she tried to escape. But the man was heavier than her and she was trapped as he dove in again and again, eating her inch by gory inch.

The first woman who had been bit on the leg felt faint, and before she knew what was happening, she collapsed to the water's edge. As she lay oblivious, the wound on her leg began festering at an alarming rate, a blue and black ooze seeping out of it to replace the once red blood. The woman stopped breathing and people gathered around her, not understanding what was happening. While some tried to help her, behind them the lifeguard felt faint and dropped to the sand, her face becoming buried in it, her last breaths sucking in the small crystals.

There was more panic as some tried to figure out what to do and a dozen cell phones appeared as the authorities were called for help.

The young woman's eyes snapped open as suddenly as they had closed and the two people leaning over her trying to revive her were assaulted before they could do more than scream. Teeth flailed and sank into exposed flesh, the fact almost everyone was wearing nothing but bathing suits making the feeding all the easier. It was just so nice not to have to fight your way through cumbersome clothing to get at the meat underneath.

With the young woman attacking her helpers, the lifeguard stirred. Coming to her knees, her face was covered in sand and though the crystals were in her nose and mouth, none were blown away from her exhalation.

It was like she wasn't breathing in or out.

The lifeguard turned with dull eyes and reached out to the first victim she found. An old woman with a flowered hat and a one piece bathing suit had wandered too close to her and the lifeguard pulled her to the sand and sank her teeth into the woman's wrinkled right cheek.

The old woman shrieked in pain as the lifeguard tore her skin from her skull, the flesh stretching like elastic. With blood squirting out, the lifeguard reached in with two fingers and scooped the geriatrics' left eye out of the socket like she was having an appetizer before dinner. The orb was pulled free and the viscous nerves dangled and then broke free as the woman popped the eyeball into her mouth, crunching merrily like she was chewing on a whole, cherry tomato. A pinkish-white ooze trickled out of her mouth to sluice down her chin, where it then dripped like saliva to the churned up sand at her feet.

Swallowing the eye, she leaned in and took the other one, swallowing it like an undercooked hardboiled egg. The old woman, now blind, screamed and kicked as the lifeguard continued to feed.

When the eye was consumed, the woman went in and sank her teeth into the old woman's sagging left breast. Blood-red teeth clamped down on a wrinkled nipple and tore it free, scarlet shooting up into the air while the woman chewed merrily.

Across the beach, the naked man had left the prone woman and had gone for easier pickings. A toddler had been left unattended when the mother had gone to investigate the screams. The man reached down to the toddler, and with one bite, severed the child's jugular. The child screamed and kicked its tiny hands, but the naked man was oblivious. Warm blood filled him with its essence, and when he was satiated, he dropped the small body to the sand and moved on for more.

Like a domino effect, the victims became the attackers until more than half the beach was filled with ravenous dead people who now wanted only to kill and feed on the living.

When the police finally arrived, they had no idea what was happening and soon the first officers went down under a hoard of bodies, then, they too, joined the fray. Every person was wounded in some fashion, but was still more than mobile. When the entire beach was assimilated, the undead moved out into the parking lot and slowly began walking towards the nearby town of Marblehead.

Whatever was driving the newly born zombies on, the main ingredient was hunger, and deep inside their dead brains, they knew there would be more prey in the town.

The zombie invasion had begun, and God help everyone who lived on this green earth.

* * *

Jeremy Tyler was a slacker.

No, wait. Calling Jeremy a slacker would have been a compliment.

Jeremy was in all reality a loser.

At just a month over nineteen, he had no job, almost no friends, and of course, no girlfriend.

But despite all this, he still managed to get drugged up, stoned or just plain hammered almost every night of the week. It didn't hurt that his parents were both very successful. His mother was a pediatrician and his father was a corporate lawyer and the two had made quite a nice life for themselves. He knew he was an accident, a hole in a condom or perhaps one night his father hadn't pulled out in time. No, his parents had never said this, but he could always feel as if they didn't truly want him.

Of course, being passed off from nanny to nanny, babysitter to babysitter, helped him to come to this realization early in life.

So with no parental love and not a lot of confidence, Jeremy had never felt the need to excel at anything. He received a modest allowance from his parents, and as long as he promised not to get arrested or get into too much trouble, they would overlook his indiscretions.

This was why it was almost noon on the day after the outbreak on the beach and Jeremy was still sleeping in his bed on the second floor of the Victorian house his parents called home. Though he had lived there all his life, it was never home to him. He had always felt like a guest who was just staying until he turned twenty or so.

He knew his time of sucking on his parent's teat was quickly running out, but he didn't care. If he had to, he would live on the street.

So when the sound of metal rending metal in a cacophony of horrendous impact flooded into his bedroom, he snapped awake with a snort and a grunt.

At first, he didn't know what had pulled him from his alcohol/drug induced slumber, but after a few seconds he heard the sound of car horns blasting at his eardrums like tiny musicians had taken up residence in his head.

Someone was really angry and didn't seem to want to let up on the horn, and with a few choice imprecations at being disturbed, Jeremy rolled out of bed. His left cheek was a mass of indentations and wrinkles from the bed sheet, a testament to how hard he'd been sleeping.

Swaying slightly, and still feeling a little buzzed, he slid into his pants and put on a shirt.

He was proud of himself with that one.

He had actually taken his clothes off before going to bed. There had been times when he'd woken in the morning fully dressed, right down to his boots and leather jacket.

The car horns were still sounding and he felt a headache coming on so he headed for the bathroom. As he moved through the house, he remembered his parents were away on vacation. Club Med or some such place. Frankly, he didn't know or care.

After grabbing some aspirin and relieving himself of the beer he'd consumed the night before, he stumbled down the stairs and into the living room. The shades were open and the noon day sun blasted his irises, making him wince in pain.

His leather jacket and boots were where he had dropped them the night before and he slid into them with infinite care, his head still hurting as he waited for the pain reliever to kick in.

Before he went outside to tell the idiot with the horn to knock it off, he took out a pair off dark sunglasses from his coat pocket and slid them on. With the brightness of the day reduced, he already felt better.

As he moved to the front door, he paused by the mirror in the foyer, inspecting himself. After all, you never know when you might meet a cute little honey.

He fixed his black curly hair and made sure everything was buttoned and zipped. After that time he had left his fly down and had forgotten to wear underwear, well, that was a story for another time.

He looked like a hard rock musician and he worked hard at keeping the look in place.

Satisfied with his appearance, he opened the front door and stepped out onto the front walkway.

The horn was coming from his right, and he couldn't see anything until he cleared the small walkway, the tall hedges hiding the street from view.

As he strode down the walkway, he caught the distinct odor of fire. And not fire like from a fireplace. No, this had the distinct flavor of wood mixed with plastic and insulation.

A house fire.

For the first time as he moved down the stone walkway, he realized it wasn't as bright outside as he'd thought. The sky seemed overcast and he realized it looked like smoke.

Wow, must be some fire, he thought, as he stepped out onto the sidewalk and onto the main street that his house was on.

As he did this, he stopped short in utter shock, his mouth slowly falling open like he was a triple-stupid idiot. His eyes panned across the once placid scene of manicured lawns, painted homes and expensive cars lining the streets.

All that was gone now.

He didn't know exactly what had happened, but from the time he had gone to bed last night, slept the sleep of a drunkard and dope fiend, and had woken up the next day, the entire neighborhood had gone straight to Hell.

His eyes tried to take in everything around him and for a second he wondered if he was still dreaming. The house across the street was in flames, the orange and red tendrils licking up to the gray sky. Three houses down, he could see the rear end of a Cadillac sticking out of the home's living room, the picture window shattered when the car had driven straight through the outside wall. To his left, another home was burning and he saw what looked like two bodies on the front lawn. And when he squinted to get a better look, both shapes appeared to be covered in red.

Blood? Could it really be blood?

What was going on? Did a meteor hit while he'd been sleeping and the world had fallen into chaos in a matter of twenty-four hours or so?

Though the people had been there the entire time, he was so busy staring at the devastated neighborhood he didn't realize there were people walking around in the street and near some of the homes.

At first he did nothing, just watched them. They all moved listlessly, like they had worked all night and were moving on autopilot.

Jeremy began crossing the street, wanting to ask someone what exactly was happening. He slowed when he got a better look at the accident that had woken him in the first place. Two cars had collided in the middle of the road.

One was a large F-150 truck, the other a small Fiat.

Guess which one won?

The owner of the Fiat had been catapulted through the windshield, the bloody and broken corpse lying on the hood of the car. The front of the car was crushed, reminding Jeremy of an accordion.

As he moved closer to the accident, he could see the man on the hood was definitely dead. His head was at an odd angle, well more precisely, his face was in the wrong direction. If the man had been standing up and was facing Jeremy, he would have only seen the back of the man's head.

Moving closer, shocked at all the blood on the hood of the car, Jeremy gazed into the F-150. There was a woman inside, but she hadn't been wearing her seatbelt and her head had struck the windshield so hard she'd cracked the safety glass. Her head was leaning on the windowsill of the driver's door and her eyes were open, staring at nothing. Her left arm hung out to droop like a piece of spaghetti and he went over and touched her wrist like he had seen the doctors do on television. After more than a minute passed, he couldn't find a pulse, though that just might mean he didn't know what he was doing.

Muttering a few more choice curses, he turned around and was going to go back home, wanting to call the police when he realized all those people that had been moving around listlessly were now staring at him.

He moved his head from left to right and counted more than a dozen people, all staring at him with wide eyes. To say it was an eerie feeling would have been redundant.

Not knowing what to do, he began walking back to his house, careful not to look at any one individual for more than a second. They say you don't make eye contact with someone if you don't want trouble, and brother, he didn't want trouble.

He'd crossed no more than ten yards when the first guttural scream filled the air. But it wasn't the last. As a man on his right yelled and began coming at him, wearing nothing but a bathrobe and one slipper, the others took up the chant.

What was odd was they weren't moving very fast, almost like they were running in slow motion, like no matter how hard they wanted to reach him, their bodies, their limbs, wouldn't let them.

But there were a lot of them and even with their treacle-like movements, he was going to be surrounded.

Dancing to the left, he tried to get past the man with the robe, and as the man lunged for him, he ducked and ran forward. But there were others waiting for him and when he stopped short, knowing he was trapped, he put up his fists and got ready for a fight.

"Okay, you assholes. I don't know what this is about, but you picked the wrong guy to fuck with."

None answered him, only dull moans coming from open mouths, and as the first one came at him, the others right behind, Jeremy prepared to fight for his life.

* * *

Jeremy raised his right fist in front of him, and when the first attacker came at him, he punched the man in the face. The man was in his early twenties and his body was in relatively good shape so the man took the blow easily.

The head turned with the punch and then slowly, the face turned back. Now the lips had blood on them, the after effect of Jeremy's punch. Teeth had sliced into the man's cheek and now the crimson liquid dripped out of his mouth like he was a drooling baby.

Jeremy stared at the man and then punched him again, this time in the stomach. With the exception of the man bending forward a little, the blow did nothing.

"Oh, great," Jeremy said as the man came at him again. Though Jeremy tried to stop him, the man easily overpowered him and Jeremy found himself on the pavement with the man sitting on his chest.

All around him, he saw more people coming closer and in seconds they would be on him, too.

He felt a panic grow inside him he had never felt before. A small voice told him in his mind this might very well be the day he will die.

The man on his chest growled, saliva and blood dropping off his chin to splash onto Jeremy's shirt. Then the man's jaw unhinged, and as he opened it as wide as he could and prepared to bite Jeremy's flesh, his head suddenly disappeared in a glorious spray of blood and brain matter mixed with skull fragments.

A fine spray of blood floated on the wind to soon disperse and Jeremy blinked up at the headless man. Blood was shooting straight up, and if it wasn't for the wind, the scarlet drops would have landed all over him.

The arms of the man began to spasm and the body twitched like it was being electrocuted. Then it toppled off him to land heavily on the ground.

Jeremy was still in shock. He had never seen a human being's head simply explode and it was something he was having a hard time wrapping his own head around.

"Come on, son, get outta there if you want to live!" a voice called out from across the street.

Jeremy turned his head to the side and saw Mr. Kingston.

The man had a large caliber revolver in his hand and he was waving for Jeremy to get up and come to him.

"Come on, son, if they get you that's it, you're done for."

Something sparked in Jeremy and he realized the man spoke the truth. Rolling to his feet, he avoided other grasping hands and dashed across the road. Behind him, the people began to follow.

Mr. Kingston, or Rob to his friends, was a church going man. He went to Mass every Sunday rain or shine, sick or healthy. He never cursed and would get upset if others did so around him and he was the best shot at the Marblehead Gun Club. Some said he could shoot the wings off a fly at a hundred yards, though that was a slight exaggeration. Maybe fifty, but no, not a hundred.

"Mr. Kingston, what the fuck is going on here?"

Mr. Kingston frowned deeply. "Now that's enough of that foul-mouth talk, son. Every time you swear an angel loses its wings in Heaven. If you want to stay with me, you better keep the language clean, you got it?"

Jeremy stared at the older man like he was absolutely nuts. He'd heard stories of how Mr. Kingston was, some saying he was the live image of Ned Flanders from *The Simpsons*, but he wouldn't have believed it if the man hadn't just told him what he'd heard.

"Uh, listen, Mr. Kingston, I think we should go. Just what exactly is going on around here?"

Mr. Kingston pointed to the walking people coming for them. At the rate the people were moving, they had about a minute to either fight or run for it.

"What's happened is it's the rapture, son. The end of the world, and it looks like all my prayin' and church goin' was for naught. After all, if I was as pious as I thought I was I shouldn't be here with men like you."

"Uh, sorry?" Jeremy said, not really getting what the man was talking about.

Mr. Kingston frowned again and gestured to the people heading for them with the barrel of his revolver.

"Zombies, son, the living dead. Real live walking around zombies. What, have you been under a rock for the past day?"

Jeremy thought back to his oblivious drug and alcohol induced sleep and realized what the old man said wasn't far from the truth.

"I guess, yeah, sort of."

A woman with curling irons in her hair and wearing a house-coat, tried to come at Jeremy from his blind side and Mr. Kingston shot her in the face. Her head snapped back and she dropped to the street, the back of her head now missing. Crimson-black blood seeped out of the open hole in her skull to steam in the sun.

"Holy S... uh, crap!" Jeremy corrected himself, not wanting to anger the only man in the area who, A; had a weapon, and B; could hopefully save him from being killed.

"Come on; let's get back to my place. I've got the place secured good. It's like a fortress."

Jeremy only nodded, not knowing what else to do. His parents were out of the country and he was all alone. Mr. Kingston's invitation sounded very good.

Another attacker lunged for them and Mr. Kingston turned and shot the dead man in the chest. A large, fist-sized hole appeared where the man's heart was, but the guy never slowed. He did pause as his body absorbed the blast, but immediately righted himself and was on the attack again. Jeremy could now see right through the man's chest. And all he saw were more people with the same look on their faces.

Mr. Kingston grabbed Jeremy's arm and pulled him with him.

"Come on, son, the longer we're out here the better the chance of gettin' killed."

Jeremy didn't reply, and he had to pull his eyes away from the man with the large hole in his chest. How was the guy still walking around without a heart?

It was impossible.

Following the older man across the sidewalk and across two manicured lawns, they arrived at a quaint, two-story home with a brick façade and flowers lining the walkway. Mr. Kingston stepped on the flowers, crushing the pedals to mush as he cut across the lawn to reach his front door. Pulling out his keys, the man calmly slid one into the door lock, like he'd just come home from church.

"Welcome to my home, son, and remember, mind the cussin' or you're back out on your butt."

Jeremy nodded, mumbled a quick, "Yes, sir," and entered the home. Mr. Kingston stepped in behind him, and the second he closed the door, there came a thump, followed by another one. The attackers were on the porch and were now pounding on the door to get in. Mr. Kingston turned the deadbolt as well as the three other locks on the door. Then he picked up a large two-by-four and stuck it in two brackets on either side of the door. With the added security it would take an army to get through that door.

That was what Jeremy was afraid of.

Mr. Kingston turned away and placed his revolver on a side table, then began to shrug out of his jacket as calmly as if he'd just come back from a walk.

"Go 'head and make yourself at home. I reckon' we're gonna be here a while."

Jeremy nodded and took a few tentative steps into the house, immediately eyeing the windows which were all boarded up with heavy plywood. The bright light, which he thought was from the sun, was from halogen lamps spread out across the floor in different corners on the living room and hallway.

With the men and women pounding on the door and windows to get in, Mr. Kingston walked past Jeremy and into the kitchen. He came back a second later holding two cold cans of beer. Handing one to Jeremy, he cracked his own and took a sip.

"Oh, and seems we're gonna be roomies for a while, you might as well call me Rob."

Jeremy stared at the man's smiling face and felt his world falling apart. Remembering he was holding a beer in his hand, he cracked it open and drank it in one long gulp.

When he was finished, he felt a slight rush go to his head, but he quickly realized he would need a lot more than one beer before he could even begin to come to terms with what was happening.

* * *

Rob didn't know much more about what was going on than Jeremy did. The television was out as was the internet. Rob had no cell phone and Jeremy had lost his a week ago and hadn't bothered to get a new one.

He found it amusing that in less time than it took to drive across the state, the entire neighborhood had been thrown into the Dark Ages.

So much for technology.

Rob filled him in on the first time he'd run into one of the people outside, what the man had casually called *zombies* like it was the most common term in the world.

He had been at the cemetery visiting his late wife's grave. There had been an altercation coming from a few rows over and at first he hadn't given it much thought. Probably just some mourners so filled with grief they were letting it out in public, he'd thought.

But when he heard a scream, well, then he knew something was wrong.

So he walked over to investigate, his nature always being a helping one, and he saw a man in dirty coveralls on top of a woman in a white dress. A bouquet of flowers lay near the woman's out flung hand and Rob knew she was being attacked immediately. Running up the grassy incline, he grabbed the attacker by his shoulders and pushed him off the woman.

He gasped when he saw the missing ear and a part of the woman's cheek bleeding crimson. Blood seeped from the wounds to soak into the grass and her white dress was quickly turning scarlet.

"Are you all right?" He asked her, but she only shrieked again and took off, her arms flailing in front of her while she screamed for help.

Rob was about to go after her when her attacker sat up. He was surprised at that. Usually when a rapist or a murderer is caught in the act they would run for it, but this man seemed to want to fight.

Well, Rob was willing to give him one. He'd served two tours in Vietnam and knew how to fight, dirty or clean, it was all the same to him.

When the man lunged for him, Rob was ready, and he brought his elbow down on his foe's neck. The man dropped to the grass hard with an 'oomph' coming from his mouth. Rob figured that was the end of it. He had used that blow before and he'd put down more men than he could count.

But not this guy.

After a few seconds passed by, the man rolled over and pushed up on his elbows. Rob stared fascinated and did what anyone would do in his position.

He kicked the man so hard in the face that teeth shot from the open mouth to fall onto the grass. The man's head rocked with the blow, but still he wasn't down. Rob wondered if the guy was on PCP or some other mind altering drug. When he had been in Vietnam, the worst he'd used was some pot, but since he had found God years ago he'd been clean.

The man spit blood and teeth and growled low in his throat. Rob stared at the man's eyes and saw the blankness there.

Whatever substance the man was on, there would be no talking him down easily.

Rob began backing away, not wanting to kill the man despite his deserving it. He stopped when his back came up against a tall tombstone.

The man was on his knees now and then stood up. With a growl of rage, he charged at Rob, moving at a fast walk. Rob waited for his foe to reach him, sidestepping the outstretched hands. Then, grabbing the man's left arm, he swung him headfirst into the tombstone he'd had his back against only a second ago.

The sound of cracked skull filled the glade and the man dropped to the grass. He didn't move and Rob breathed a sigh of relief.

He looked up to see the woman was coming back to him. She wasn't running now, but it wasn't a walk either. More of a slow jog, really, her legs stomping the grass and flowers of the graves without care.

Rob understood that she was probably in shock.

But when she reached him, he saw her face had that same glazed look as her attacker and he realized whatever the man had been on she now was on it, too.

She moaned loudly and came at him, but she was smaller than him and one good punch to the chin snapped her head back and sent her to the grass with a broken neck.

He stood over the two bodies, breathing heavily, not understanding what had just happened. More yells and screams came to him and he looked across the cemetery to see similar cases of violence happening.

Only in these cases the attackees weren't as fortunate as Rob.

Knowing it was time to go, he took off at a run, getting to his car and speeding home. All around him were the same signs of violence, people attacking one another and then the victims rising to turn on others. Police cars and fire trucks were everywhere, but they, too, were overwhelmed. He saw a man take three bullets to the chest and still continue onward until he'd jumped the cop who had been firing at him.

When he reached home, the neighborhood was already in shambles and it was shocking how fast it was all crumbling. He'd raced into his house and had gone straight to the cellar and garage, gathering all the wood and supplies he could find. He then boarded up the house and got ready for the long haul, patiently waiting for the government to get things back together.

Before the TV stations went out, he'd learned the rest from the news stations, about some kind of viral disease that made people crazy.

It was just before the last news station went off the air that they began talking about dead people walking around and attacking the living, and worse, eating them.

But when he had seen Jeremy out on the street alone and knew the young man wasn't infected, he'd taken the risk and had gone outside to fetch him.

And so here they now were, waiting until help arrived.

Jeremy only nodded at the end of the story, finding it hard to believe. But every time he tried to deny the man's words, the pounding on the house told him different.

Instead of asking a question, he gestured to the kitchen.

"Can I have another beer?"

Rob nodded. "Sure, help yourself; I got ten cases in the garage. I like my beer; it's one of my only vices."

Jeremy stood up and crossed the kitchen and from the garage he could hear the steady drone of the generator, the only reason they had power. Outside, it was already growing dark and through the cracks in the wood over the windows he saw the street lamps weren't coming on. The power was out; there was no doubt about it.

When Jeremy returned with a fresh beer, Rob was cleaning his gun.

"What kind is that?" He asked Rob as he sat down and took a sip of the cold beer. It felt good, and with each one he drank, he felt just a little better.

"This is a .357 Magnum. Like the one Clint Eastwood used in Dirty Harry. You ever see that movie?"

Jeremy shook his head. He knew of the guy, but the actor was too old for his tastes. He preferred horror movies.

Rob finished checking the gun, and after loading more bullets, snapped the cylinder closed and showed it to Jeremy.

"The bullets in this gun will not only stop, they will destroy you. You get me?"

Jeremy only nodded. He had never been into guns. Mainly because he had a rather large penis and so had never felt the need to fire a weapon, but that was what he'd heard from a few friends. The bigger the gun and all that, the smaller the you know what. He decided not to mention that to Rob.

More banging on the doors filled the living room with sound and Jeremy cringed in his chair.

Rob chuckled. "You need to get used to that, son. They don't stop, ever. That will continue until either we leave here or I go out there and kill 'em for good."

Jeremy said nothing, but stared at the boards on the windows. Wherever there was a small line of light where two boards were placed next to one another he could see shadows moving back and forth. A chill went down his spine and he wished he could crawl back into his bed and pretend none of this had ever happened.

"So what do we do now? Just sit here and wait for help?" Jeremy asked.

Rob nodded, finished with the gun, and set it down next to his chair.

"I guess so, there's not much else to do. From what the television said, this outbreak is happening everywhere. New York and Chicago are the worst I hear as there are so many people. Whatever started this just crossed the globe in less than a day. They say it's because of the airplanes. You can get sick at noon and by four o' clock you're in another part of the country, spreading the virus as easy as you please."

"What? That's bullsh... ah, crazy," Jeremy said, watching his tongue. He had never really thought about how much he cursed until now when his life was on the line. He'd heard stories about Rob and knew if he ignored his order and continued swearing, the man would toss his butt outside without a second look.

Rob shrugged. "Look, son, we all deal with stress in different ways. I use this," he said while holding the gun up. "You'll have your own way. But sooner or later you'll come to your senses and accept what's happened."

"Oh, yeah, and what if I don't?"

Rob shrugged again, stood up, and began crossing the living room to get to the kitchen for another beer.

"Then you'll die and end up like those poor souls out on my front lawn." He disappeared into the kitchen, and as Jeremy sat in his chair with his empty beer can in his right hand while listening to the pounding of flesh on wood, he realized the older man was correct.

And that now he needed another beer desperately.

*   *   *

The next week passed slowly for the two men.

Rob had taught him how to play gin, and though Jeremy found it boring, there wasn't much else to do in the home.

Unless he wanted to read Bibles all day and night.

The more he got to know Rob, the more the man was a conundrum. While he abhorred cursing and loved God, he wasn't some kind of wuss. He would shoot any ghoul that threatened his home and had already done so on more than one occasion.

Whenever the crowd got too big outside, he would go to the second floor window in his bedroom and begin picking off the bodies like it was target practice at the gun range.

One time he even let Jeremy try.

"Go 'head, son, but be careful, she's got a kick."

Jeremy took the large gun in his hands, amazed at how heavy it was, and then moved to the bedroom window. Sticking his head out, he swallowed the knot in his throat, leaned out as far as he could without falling out, and lined up a zombie's head in the gun's sight.

When he fired the gun, it rose into the air, but he hit what he wanted. Though he missed the head he was trying for, the ghouls were so close together there was truly no way to miss.

The head next to the ghoul he had aimed for exploded, splashing the other zombies with blood and brain matter.

None of them noticed their brother's demise, but continued banging on the doors and windows of the house.

"Wow, that's awesome!" Jeremy exclaimed as he held the weapon in his hands. His wrist was a little sore from the kickback, but it was worth it. "Can I shoot another one?"

"Sure, son, go 'head, just be careful."

Jeremy nodded, and with more energy than he had felt in a long time, he moved back to the open window and lined up another one.

He recognized the face actually. It was Mrs. Monahan from three houses over. One time he'd been out drinking with his buddies when he was fourteen and she had seen him behind the liquor store with a bottle of Jack Daniels. She'd wasted no time in going to his parents and informing them of his antics, who had promptly grounded him for two weeks straight.

Of course he had ignored them, and when he wanted to go out, he'd just waited for them to go to bed and then slip out his bedroom window.

Well, now he had a chance at payback in a big way.

The woman's hair was a bright white and her eyes had on so much blue mascara she resembled a circus clown. Jeremy used one of those blue eyes for a target, and as he slowly let out his breath like Rob had taught him, he squeezed the trigger, not pulling it.

The gunshot sounded loud, even over the noise of the banging ghouls, and Mrs. Monahan's face disappeared in an amazing circular explosion. The top of her scalp popped straight up into the air and landed on another ghoul, a man, two feet away. The man didn't notice he now wore a new hairdo and continued pounding with the others, blood dripping down his face and ears.

"Oh, wow, man, that's so cool!"

Rob reached out for his gun.

"Okay, son, that's enough for now, let's have it back."

With reluctance, Jeremy did as he was told.

"Can I have a gun, too?"

"Sure, I don't see why not. I don't have anymore here, though. You know, Massachusetts gun laws and all that, but maybe if we leave here we can see about finding you one."

"Okay, that'll be great."

Rob moved to the window.

"Okay, why don't you let me take out a few more of the troublesome ones and then I'll meet you downstairs," Rob told him.

Jeremy nodded, and left the room, walking down the stairs, while behind him, the Magnum trumpeted death with each shot.

* * *

It was six days later when the generator gave out on them, plunging the house into darkness. It had been a little past nine at night and Jeremy and Rob had been playing gin again.

"What the...?" Rob had said as the room was plunged into darkness.

"Oh, shit, are we in trouble?" Jeremy had asked; the fear in his voice apparent.

Rob frowned at the young man's language, but he let it pass for now. The windows of the house were shrouded in shadows, only a few slips of moonlight sliding through the cracks. Constant shadows crossed those lines, more ominous now that there was no light in the house.

"Now, just relax, son, I think the generator must be out of juice. Stay here and I'll go put some more gas in it."

Jeremy nodded, but realizing Rob couldn't see him, he mumbled an, "Okay."

Rob reached around in the shadows, and a second later a flashlight beam stabbed through the darkness.

Standing up, Rob patted Jeremy on the shoulder and headed to the attached garage where the generator was setup.

"I'll be right back, now no peeking at my cards," the man joked.

"How? There's no damn light?" Jeremy stated as the man disappeared, the light of the flashlight bobbing and weaving as the older man made his way through the house.

Rob made it to the garage and strolled over to the generator. The first thing he detected was burnt oil and he frowned deeply at this. With the flashlight in his left hand, he bent over and began inspecting the generator.

The garage doors were moving softly in its frame, the dozens of ghouls pounding on it. No doubt because they could hear the generator chugging away.

Checking the fuel level and then the oil, he winced at the odor of the oil once again. On a closer inspection, it smelled more like burnt rubber.

When he was as satisfied as he could be that the generator seemed to be full of gas and oil, he tried to start it again. He pulled and pulled for almost ten minutes straight but it wouldn't turn over.

Finally giving up and wincing and heaving from the strain, sweat now under his arms and back, he had to admit the generator had given up and died on him. Well what did he expect? Instead of going to a Home Depot and getting a good one, he had gone to a chain branch that had carried the generator, white bread and detergent, plus a couple pairs of slacks, all at the same place. That should have told him what he was buying right there and then.

They had sold him a lemon and now he was paying for it, perhaps with his life.

Grabbing a few more batteries off a shelf in the garage, he found another small flashlight and returned to Jeremy.

"You want the bad news, son, or the bad news," Rob said as he moved through the house, stopping by the front door. He checked it again, though he knew it was secure, but it made him feel better. Pounding filtered in, flesh and bone banging on the thick wood door and he wondered how many chips and scratches the ghouls were making on his home as they slapped their rotting hands against the siding.

"Just tell me, will ya?" Jeremy asked, his patience level low.

"The genny's up and died on me, that's what, son. From now on we don't have power. Hope you don't mind if your beer's warm."

"Are you serious? So where does that leave us?"

Rob moved back and sat down in his chair again. He'd found some candles and matches while he'd been moving around the dark room and he lit two of them, turning off the flashlight as he set them on the end table next to him.

"That leaves us in the same predicament, son, just now we're gonna be in the dark at night. That's all. We're still safe in here and we'll stay that way until help arrives."

He picked up his cards and inspected them in the dim candle light.

"So, who's deal is it?"

Jeremy stared at the older man for almost ten seconds, not understanding how Rob could be so calm. Rob smiled and gestured for Jeremy to pick up his cards. With nothing else to say and nothing else to do but sit tight, he did just that.

And now, with the candles flickering each time one of them moved, they played cards while the ghouls continued to pound on the doors and windows like wild animals starving for the food they knew was waiting within.

* * *

Karen Mills stared out the second floor window of her house in Nahant, still finding it hard to believe her new reality was truly happening.

Just a day ago she'd been worried about using the coupons for her groceries before they expired and now she was wondering if she would be alive by the dawn of the next day. She checked her watch, seeing she had a few more hours to go.

Twenty-five miles south of her, she was able to see the bright fires that were the city of Boston. The conflagration must be massive if she could see the fires as far north as she was.

Looking to the street again, she saw more than two dozen bodies moving about as they entered and left her home. Her front door had been forced in hours ago and now she was trapped in her bedroom with nowhere to go.

Outside in the street, the wreckage of two police cars and an overturned fire engine lay like dinosaur bones from an excavation. The people who had been driving them were long gone, only the dull brown stains of what was once bright-red blood remaining. She'd heard the men scream as they were torn apart, but all she could do was hide in her home with her hands over her ears

After all, what could she do? She wasn't strong enough to fight off those people and she was scared out of her wits for Heaven's sake.

She had always lived a sheltered life, and now, when she should be using her independence to save herself, she found she had none.

There was a heavy pounding on the bedroom door and her eyes flicked to it for the hundredth time tonight.

She knew who was behind that door.

It was Eric, her husband.

But he wasn't really her husband anymore. When the front door had been caved in it was he who had tried to protect her, but he'd only ended up getting himself bitten.

All those hours ago they had been hiding together and she'd felt safe with him near her. He had always protected her, and told her what to do, and she had loved that about him. She'd never felt the need to go to work or worry about how the mortgage and other bills would be paid.

He had done everything for her, and now, as she looked back on her life with her husband, she realized he had done far too much for her.

In his own way, he had controlled her, preventing her from flourishing as a responsible human being, and now she was as helpless as a five-year-old girl.

It had been dumb luck that she had ended up in the bedroom and Eric in the hallway. It had happened hours ago. Eric had felt sick after being bitten and as the day passed he had become paler than she had ever seen him. So that night he had taken a nap, which she felt was very odd as they were under siege by people that were obviously crazy and were killers to boot.

But as always she had done what he told her and had let him rest. Then he'd woken hours later, or so she had thought, but when she had seen his eyes for the first time, she realized he had changed somehow.

And if she was still unsure as to his state of mind, she knew she was correct when he attacked her and she managed to climb over the bed to escape him.

Her husband was now like them, like the people outside.

She had dashed for the bedroom door and just managed to open it when she felt his hot breath caress her neck. Ducking, she'd thrown open the door, cracking Eric in the nose in the process. Blood had poured from his fractured nose and he growled in anger, or so it seemed to her.

She darted down the small hallway until reaching the bathroom and had then barricaded herself inside to wait out the storm. Sooner or later help would arrive, it had to.

But less than ten minutes later, Eric had forced the thin bathroom door in and she found herself trapped in the bathtub.

It was unlike her, but something inside her came alive, and though she had panicked, she had acted, too. When Eric came for her, she pulled the shower curtain down and the plastic drapes had covered Eric like a shroud. While he thrashed around trying to free himself, she dashed back to the bedroom, this time slamming the door and barricading it with the bed.

Moments later, Eric's body crashed against the door, but the door was solid wood and he couldn't get inside.

She had stayed there, hearing the ghouls moving about below her feet on the first floor. It was only a matter of time before they found the small stairwell that led to the second floor and joined her husband in battering the bedroom door.

She knew when that happened they would get in and she would die.

She knew this because she had seen people on her street earlier that morning, and had seen them overrun by a crowd of what could only be called zombies, as ridiculous as that sounded. More than half the crowd had life-threatening wounds and some had large chunks of their flesh missing, while others had bullet holes so big in their torsos she could have pushed her fist through, not that she would have wanted to.

There was a bottle of water on her nightstand and a full case in her closet. Eric didn't believe in her buying water when she could get it from the tap for free so she had to hide it from him. So, too, did she hide the candy bars she kept hidden in the drawer of her nightstand. They were there for when she got a sugar craving in the middle of the night. Eric didn't like her eating at night and would yell at her, telling her, "The kitchen was closed."

So she wouldn't starve, at least not yet, the candy and bottled water enough to live on for at least a week, maybe more if she was careful. But she doubted that would be a problem, figuring Eric would break the door down long before them.

But whatever was happening outside was happening to her, too, and there was nothing she could do about it. She accepted her fate, knowing it was only a matter of time before they got to her and either changed her like them or ate her as she had seen them do, the mob resembling a pack of wild animals more than humans.

The only question was, how long would that be?

* * *

While Karen sat alone, gazing out her bedroom window, two towns away, the living room windows collapsed in a mess of shattered glass and wood, shocking Rob and Jeremy from a shaky slumber.

Both of them had fallen asleep in the living room, neither wanting to go into the back of the house or upstairs to the bedrooms. Rob was the first to react to the imploding windows and he jumped to his feet, swaying back and forth as he tried to make himself wake up just a little faster. Jeremy was slower to react and he stared around himself, not understanding where he was for a few seconds.

The room was dark, only the wan moonlight filtering in past the bodies as they began climbing into the house.

Rob, with his Magnum still in his hand, the man never setting it down when he had drifted off, brought up the weapon and aimed it at the first shadowy figure. There was a deafening roar when the gun went off and a flash of light, like lightning, filled the interior of the room. A ghoul's chest and back exploded, drenching its brethren in gore. The body fell back and the ones behind it struggled to get past the obstacle, but soon their legs had pushed the corpse out of the way and more began surging into the room.

"What the fu...?" Jeremy spit, then stopped himself at the last instant. In his mind, he finished his epitaph and then stared at the shadowy forms swarming into the room.

"Don't just sit there, son, get up and fight or we're dead!" Rob screamed, shooting another ghoul in the head. The head didn't just explode, it simply disappeared, the round continuing on to impale another zombie behind the now missing head. The body balanced for a brief second and then toppled over, now just one more obstacle for the others.

Jeremy looked around and couldn't find anything to use as a weapon. Then to Rob's shock, he ran off towards the kitchen.

Rob had time for the briefest of glimpses of the young man's back, wondering where he was going. Was he running away? Would he actually leave Rob to fend for himself after Rob had saved his life days before?

Then Rob had no time for thoughts as the bodies came for him.

Staying calm despite the frantic situation, he calmly began firing round after round at the closest ghouls. When he cycled dry, he kicked the next ghoul in the face, opened the cylinder to the weapon, shook out the empty casings, and began sliding in new ones as his hand reached into his pocket. All the while he was backing up, giving ground as the ghouls swarmed inside his home. There were almost a dozen already inside the room with as many lying dead on the floor, staining his carpet a mottled red.

Snapping the cylinder closed, he cocked the gun and shot a ghoul as it reached for him, the zombie only inches away from his face. He could smell the blood on the dead man and then the ghoul was flying backward, the impact of the high caliber round tossing him away like he had been slapped by a giant hand. Five more shots and five more ghouls down, and it was when Rob was going to reload that he knew he wasn't going to make it in time. He snapped open the cylinder, trying anyway, and then glanced up to see foul teeth coming for him.

He was about to try and brace himself for the assault when something heavy blurred by the corner of his vision and the ghouls went down with a meaty thwack.

Half the zombie's head was caved in and brains seeped from the jagged head wound. Rob turned to his left to see Jeremy standing next to him, breathing heavily as he waved a large rolling pin in the air like a club. The pin had been his wife's and he realized she was saving his ass from beyond the grave. He was glad he hadn't decided to get rid of it when he'd been cleaning the house a few months back.

Jeremy didn't speak, there was no time, and as the next ghoul, an old woman in a sweater and pants suit, came at him, he swung the pin like a bat, knocking her teeth out and collapsing one of her milky-white eyes.

Rob shook himself from his stupor and finished reloading the Magnum. Snapping the cylinder closed again, he began firing at each body that came for him. When he was out yet again, Jeremy covered him while he repeated the process. Soon he'd killed every ghoul entering the house and was then standing at the windows, keeping them at bay.

"Get the hammer and nails out of the back closet! Now!" Rob ordered Jeremy. The younger man obeyed, dashing to the rear of the house. His digging noises were unheard by Rob as the ghouls moaning and growling overrode any sound he might make. Rob continued firing, having to step on the fallen bodies of the men and women he'd just killed.

Jeremy appeared with a container of nails and a heavy hammer. As he reached Rob, a pale face stuck its visage through the window and Jeremy screamed, then swiped at the head with the hammer. Metal met bone and the head was smacked away, the body going to the ground outside where it twitched like a robot with its wires crossed.

"Here, get that board over here and start nailing it to the window frame!" Rob snarled, shooting a ghoul in the face. The bullet went into the left eye and exploded out the rear of its head, the body twisting from the gunshot. Blood geysered from the open wound like head wounds do and he found his shirt was now covered in gore.

Jeremy did what he was told, and after kicking a young female ghoul in the face to get her away from the opening, he began sinking nails into the wood, re-boarding the window. After the first few nails, the wood was secure enough for him to go to the next window, and in no time that was secured, too. When Rob felt it was safe to put the gun down, he took the hammer from Jeremy and with the skill of a carpenter began sinking nails one after another.

"Get that coffee table behind you, I want to use that, too," Rob told him.

Jeremy did as he was told and in seconds the coffee table was across the window. There were a few small gaps here and there, but the ghouls couldn't force their way inside again. They didn't seem to understand how to get around the barricade, but just pounded continually with their hands and fists. If they had an ounce of intelligence they could have ganged up together and easily forced their way inside, but none did this and so Rob sighed in relief when the windows were covered once again.

"What the hell just happened?" Jeremy asked as he stared at the few bloody hands sticking through the gaps in the wood. He wanted to take a pair of large scissors and just cut those hands off, but he knew how stupid that would be.

"Just what it looks like, Jeremy, the evil things forced their way inside. But we boarded it up good, they won't be getting in anytime soon, and when the sun comes up, I'll make extra sure it's good and safe." He turned to look at the younger man. "That was some quick thinkin' on your part, son. Good job with the rolling pin."

"Thanks," Jeremy replied, not feeling the need for more of an answer.

Rob moved to the chair he'd been sleeping in and dropped down with a sigh. He lit a candle so he could save the batteries in the flashlight and gestured for Jeremy to sit down across from him. Not knowing what else to do, Jeremy complied and as he stared at the older man, Rob picked up the playing cards and began to shuffle them.

"Well, son, I don't know about you, but I think I'm done sleeping for the night. We can clean this mess and get rid of these bodies when it's light out." He grinned slyly. "So, how 'bout another game of gin?"

Jeremy nodded slowly, not really having an answer. And with the ghouls struggling to get back inside and decimated bodies lying all around the living room floor, blood soaking into the carpet, Rob began to deal the cards while the undead moaned and wailed like lost souls trying to escape from the very pits of Hell.

* * *

A little more than a week had passed trapped inside her bedroom like a prisoner, when Eric managed to break into the room, followed by more than a score of undead followers.

Karen had been sitting on the floor in the corner of the bedroom, curled up tightly in a small ball, her arms wrapped around her legs. The steady pounding on the door, coupled with the moans of the undead outside, were enough to drive her mad and she had taken to shoving pieces of Kleenex into her ears to try and dull the noise.

She had been nodding off when it happened.

Weak from hunger, the candy bars and water now finally finished, her head lolled on her shoulders when she felt a heavy thud through her butt, which was connected to the floor. She glanced up to see the bedroom door was shaking very badly, much more than it had in the past few days. Plucking the tissues from her ears, she stared at the door as if it was about to sprout a mouth and begin talking to her. The heavy door was strong, but not so formidable an obstacle to withstand the repeated fists and bodies being thrown against it.

She could do nothing, so she stared, watching the door jump in its frame. With each passing second, the door seemed to jump a little more in its frame, and the hinges seemed to loosen, the screws beginning to be pulled from the wood.

For twenty minutes the door shook, the onslaught slowly weakening it.

And then it happened as she knew it would.

With a crashing of wood, the door was knocked in; a pile of bodies riding the falling door like it was a surfboard. Karen jumped to her feet and did the only thing she could. She dashed for the open window and climbed out onto the roof.

The instant she did, she scrabbled for support. The roof was far too slanted to let a body crawl on it without some other support system such as a rope or a ladder.

Behind her she felt a cold hand clamp on her right ankle and she screamed, alerting every ghoul below her that she was now on the roof.

The undead went wild, clawing at the side of the house and tearing the vinyl siding off as they attempted to reach her. But they couldn't climb the house and for that, at least, she was thankful.

She managed to turn around to peer over her shoulder, and when she did, she saw Eric's pale-white face gazing back at her. His mouth was slanted to the side and his tongue hung out like he was a slack-jawed idiot. But she saw the hunger in his eyes and knew she didn't want to go into his waiting embrace.

He pulled her to him and she screamed, then, with her free left foot, she kicked out, the sole of her sneaker catching him right in the nose, adding to the damage she had done with the bedroom door days before. Cartilage collapsed and a few fragments slid into Eric's brain, but he was still active, only now one eye was slanted to the left and his nose looked like someone had pounded it flat with a hammer. Blood gushed out of the shattered nose to splash on the windowsill, and when Karen's foot connected with his face, he let her go, stunned momentarily by the blow. She immediately crawled away, careful to somehow maintain her tenuous grip on the shingles. They hurt her hands and it was like she was climbing on sandpaper.

Behind her, the open window was disgorging bodies, but no sooner would a ghoul climb out onto the roof then it would tumble to the ground below, taking out up to three zombies with the impact of their bodies. With a whimper in her throat, she climbed higher, but she knew she couldn't stay like this forever. Her legs were throbbing and it was a constant strain on her back to keep herself from sliding down the roof. There was a small vent for the attic sticking out of the roof and she slowly, cautiously, moved towards it. Just when she thought she wasn't going to make it and she began sliding downward to the crowd of ghouls, she reached out like she was a drowning woman going for that tossed life preserver and her left hand grasped the vent. The thin metal bent from her weight, but it held. She scurried up a little more and when she was as good as she could get, she sighed, knowing she'd managed to let herself live for yet another hour.

She was able to see her bedroom window from her vantage point and she could see Eric staring at her, his once blue eyes now white. He hadn't climbed out onto the roof, as if he knew he would only fall to the ground. His chest heaved and his lips and chin were scarlet red as he stared at her, his milky-white orbs seeming to pierce her soul.

She stared back for more than five minutes and finally she had to look away. Eric never ceased his deathly stare, his gaze locked on her like a wild animal who had spotted its prey.

With nothing else to do, Karen began crying, wondering just how long it would be before she was finally killed and if she should just let go and get it over with.

With the ghouls moaning below her, their wails of sorrow and hunger filling her with dread, she added her own symphony of self-pity to the mix.

The song of the dead filling her mind with sadness.

* * *

Jeremy strolled to the first floor bathroom, preparing to do what people do every day. Plopping down on the porcelain bowl he got busy while his eyes played over the bathroom.

Though he had already been in the small room countless times, he hadn't really studied the room, just did his business and left.

This time, with nothing to do, and the daylight spilling in through the small window against the far wall, just over the shower, he really looked at the room. There were feminine toiletries here and there and there were two toothbrushes on the sink. That was odd as Rob had said his wife was dead, for a while now if he was correct.

He noticed a magazine hiding under a bunch of others and he pushed the Redbook and Good Housekeeping aside and was surprised when he came up with a Playboy in his hands. The issue was a few years old, but it was still amusing to find it in here where Rob probably needed it most.

He was already planning on bringing it to the kitchen where Rob was now and tease the old man a little when he heard what sounded like a muffled explosion coming from far away. A slight tremor ran through the house, like when a really large truck drives by.

Finishing up quickly, his heart already pumping faster thanks to the adrenalin in his system, he pulled up his pants and flushed the toilet.

Only it didn't flush.

Frowning, he took off the back cover of the tank and saw there was no water. Dropping it back with a clang, he tried the faucet, but all he got was a few drips followed by air.

"Great, the water's out," he mumbled to himself.

Deciding he could worry about it later, he ran out of the bathroom and into the kitchen. Rob was already up from his kitchen chair, and when he saw Jeremy, he waved him to follow.

"Come on upstairs, we can get a better view from up there," he told Jeremy as he clomped up the stairs in his heavy work boots.

The two men moved up the stairs and in seconds were in Rob's bedroom again, the half-made bed and dirty laundry exactly where they'd been the last time Jeremy had been in the room.

Rob moved to the window facing south and picked up a pair of binoculars from a nearby table drawer. Placing them to his eyes, he began searching the neighborhood.

It didn't take him long to find what he was looking for and as Jeremy stood behind him, the younger man could see what Rob had spotted even without the binoculars.

About a half mile in the distance, give or take, there was a large, black and gray pillar of smoke meandering into the sky. The smoke looked like a living thing as it twisted into the air, the wind slapping it like a mother to an errant child.

"That's not good," Rob said as he lowered the binoculars.

"Ya think?" Jeremy said. "What do you think it is?"

Rob shrugged. "Who know? Gas main, tanker truck, could be a dozen other things." He raised the binoculars to his eyes again, zooming in as close as they would allow.

"Whatever happened, it's bad. The smoke's getting bigger, and since we got up here the amount of smoke seems to have already doubled in size."

"So what's that mean?" Jeremy asked as he stared at the undead on the lawn below. They were banging on the house, still trying to get in. Some were stepping on their fallen brethren, flattening the corpses to mush. Some were nothing but puddles of blood and bones, wrapped in filthy gore-covered rags.

"It means, son, that the fire's spreading." Rob pointed to Boston in the distance. The city wasn't visible, but the pillars of smoke were. "Boston's no better."

Jeremy made a disgusted sound, like a raspberry. "So what? We're all the way over here, let it all burn, they can put up a parking garage when it dies out. I'm going back downstairs," he said and left the room without another glance outside.

Rob stared at the smoke as it billowed into the clouds like grey columns and hoped Jeremy was right, because if he wasn't, then real soon the two of them were going to have yet more problems to deal with.

* * *

Two days later Jeremy frowned as he stared at the kitchen cabinets. They were all thrown open and he didn't like what he saw. Rob entered the kitchen and saw what the younger man was doing.

"You don't look pleased," Rob said.

"I'm not, Rob. Look at this. There's nothing left to eat."

Rob nodded. "Yes, I know, and I was going to talk to you about that later."

Jeremy's eyebrows went up a little. "Oh?"

Rob nodded. "Come up stairs with me, will you please?"

Jeremy nodded, and with one last look at the empty cabinets, he followed Rob back up to his bedroom on the second floor.

Rob handed Jeremy the binoculars and pointed out the window. Below, the undead continued to wail, clawing at one another to reach the two men in the upstairs window.

"Have a look, son, and tell me what you see," Rob told him.

Jeremy placed the binoculars to his eyes and searched the horizon, or what he could see of it. For the past two days since the first initial explosion, the fires had been burning out of control. And worse, just as Rob had predicted, the conflagration was spreading. Where the smoke had been relegated to one spot days before, now the entire southern landscape was nothing but a rolling ball of fire. Jeremy could taste the ash on his tongue and feel it tickle the back of his throat, but he'd been ignoring it for the past two days, knowing there was nothing to be done about it. What did he care if a bunch of rich assholes lost their homes?

"So, what do you see?" Rob asked.

"A bunch of sh...uh, stuff, going up in flames, why?"

"Well, I would think it's obvious, even to a nitwit like you, Jeremy."

Jeremy glanced away from the horizon to sneak a peek at Rob. The man was smirking slightly so Jeremy let the jibe pass.

"Go on, I'm listening," Jeremy said.

"Well, son, with that fire growing closer, I think we have a few days at best before it'll be so bad we'll end up becoming surrounded. It's like those wildfires in California. Once they get started there's nothing to stop them, and with no emergency services..." he shrugged, knowing Jeremy got his meaning.

"So, what, you want to leave here? Where are we gonna go?"

Rob rubbed his chin and nodded. "We're almost out of food and now with this fire, well, yeah, I think we should leave. I've been thinking about that long and hard and maybe we can try for the police station or something similar. There has to be others like us, we just need to find them. Surely the police or the military have set up some kind of outpost or camps."

"And what, you want to just go for a drive and go looking? With them out there?" Jeremy pointed to the undead.

"I don't think we have a choice, do you?"

Jeremy glanced down at the zombies on the lawn and then back out to the horizon. The smoke was so thick he didn't need the binoculars to see how bad it was getting.

Setting the binoculars on the nearby table, he pursed his lips, knowing Rob was right. They had no choice. If they stayed where they were, they would either starve or die from the smoke or the fire.

Not to mention there were more ghouls with each passing day, their fists pounding on the house like it was a giant drum.

With a slight smirk, Jeremy nodded in agreement.

"So, when do we leave?"

* * *

The undead milled around the house, still trying to get inside. Flies were everywhere, feeding on the inanimate corpses of their fallen brethren. Dozens of corpses lined the denuded lawn and sidewalk of Rob's house, proof of his marksmanship. The other ghouls paid their slaughtered brethren no mind, but continued to batter the house's windows and doors.

On the west side of the home, a ghoul got lucky, and when its shattered hands pounded on the wood for the thousandth time, the wood cracked, the bloody hand sinking into the opening. In seconds the ghoul began tearing at the wood, jagged splinters slicing into its cold flesh. But the zombie felt no pain and continued onward.

In seconds, the window was free of the wood nailed to the frame, and the ghouls began swarming inside. The window was low to the ground and they fell into the opening, landing heavily inside the home. One at a time they entered, until more than a dozen were bouncing off the walls and knocking knick-knacks and shelves to the floor, their feet stomping the items into a hundred shards of debris.

The moans filled the home and they began searching for the two humans they knew were hiding somewhere inside.

More spilled into the window, some two at a time, their arms becoming sliced by the exposed nails still sticking out of the edges of the frame.

Soon the house was full of zombies and yet the two humans were nowhere to be found. Many went upstairs, falling onto Rob's bed, while others went to the bathroom. But still the two humans were absent.

More than a dozen ghouls pushed their way into the kitchen and still there was no sign of the meat they so sorely desired. One ghoul, a little more inquisitive than the others, noticed that the oven had been pulled away from the wall. Thinking the prey was hiding back there, the ghoul leaned over to see if he was correct.

What he found was a broken gas line, the flexible hose bent upward so that the end was pointed directly at the thermostat on the kitchen wall.

The temperature dial was set to eighty degrees, and as the small red line slowly climbed, the gas filled the house.

When the thermostat sensed the temperature had reached the desired mark, a small spark appeared in the back of the thermostat, just where the small glass bubble of mercury was located. The spark ignited the natural gas in the room and an instantaneous fireball blossomed, consuming every ghoul in the kitchen as it rolled through the house like a living being.

There were more than fifty zombies in the house with more still forcing their way through the window when the house ignited, blowing up and out and destroying every ghoul within fifty yards, either by flames or by flying debris that sliced heads off bodies and cut limbs off corpses like they were made of wet paper mache.

The thunderous blast ripped through the neighborhood, blowing out the windows of every house on the street, the flames already catching on the wind as the cinders landed on other homes, and in their yards, the dry leaves in the bushes easy kindling for the cinders. Soon the entire neighborhood was ablaze, the flames licking to the sky, large columns of black smoke rising into the air, a fitting bookend to the pillars of smoke still moving closer from the south.

As the initial blast subsided, blackened corpses littered the street, some being blown clear across the road to land on cars and in shrubbery. Headless bodies and scattered limbs decorated the sidewalk and road, looking like some bully had gone mad with a bunch of life-size, plastic dolls, plucking the limbs off to toss them about. The sickly sweet smell of cooking meat filled the area as the flesh of the ghouls bubbled and boiled off their bones. More than one was blind, their eyes roasted in their heads like small hard-boiled eggs.

As for the two humans that had resided inside the home, there was no sign.

*   *   *

Three minutes ago, just before the explosion.

While dozens of ghouls swarmed inside the house, more than a score stayed on the front lawn and in the driveway, searching for other ways into the barricaded home.

The crowd of undead cocked their heads at the same time when the garage door began to open like the large mouth of some giant beast.

A few, impatient to see what was inside the opening portal, dropped to their knees, preparing to crawl inside. It was dark inside the garage and their milky white eyes couldn't see past the edge of the door.

One ghoul was smack dab in the middle of the driveway, and it was on all fours as it prepared to crawl into the dim interior, when all of a sudden, two headlights pierced the gloom and blinded the ghoul like a deer caught out on a country road with an eighteen wheeler barreling down on it.

The ghoul stared at the headlights, its dead brain not able to quickly process what was happening.

And then its face was flattened and pulverized by the front grille of the small, four-door Honda Civic shooting out of the garage like a small battering ram.

The ghoul was pushed to the driveway to roll three times before the Honda reached the body and drove over it. The head was caught in the front right tire well and was literally ripped off the shoulders of the prone body. With the headless body twitching in the sun, the head was slowly rubbed raw until only the white of bone showed through in places. When enough flesh had been flayed from the face, the head popped out of the tire well to bounce across the street like an errant ball.

All around the Civic, bodies began to pound on the hood and glass. Inside the car, the two men stared in horror at the faces of the dead.

"Go, Rob, go!" Jeremy screamed as he stared at the face of a woman with half her left cheek gone, the exposed muscle and tendons glistening in the morning sun.

"I can't, they're all around the car! There's too many of them!" he screamed loudly, his eyes darting back and forth. His knuckles were white on the steering wheel as he struggled to roll through the undead crowd, but the small, compact car just didn't have the weight to push its way through.

Jeremy figured this out quickly and yelled at Rob.

"Why the hell couldn't you drive an SUV like everyone else in the damn state?"

"Watch your mouth, son, or I'll wash it out with soap," Rob warned as he snapped his head away from a man's face on the glass as the ghoul pounded on the window. The ghoul's face was sliding on the glass, leaving trails of red ichor and pus. The nose was running, and if Rob didn't know better, he would have guessed the zombie had a bad cold. But the eyes told him the truth, that the man was dead.

As dead as the rest of them, and that he and Jeremy would be joining them if they didn't move fast. Already the car was rocking on its shocks as the ghouls threatened to roll the car over.

Rob picked up his Magnum from the seat and aimed it at Jeremy's passenger window.

"Open that window; I need to shoot some of them before they flip us over!"

Jeremy's eyes went wide.

"What? Are you crazy? Open your own damn window!"

"I can't, son, I need to have at least a few feet so I can line up a shot. You need to scoot over here so they can't get you when the window opens!"

"That's crazy, I'm not doing it," Jeremy snapped as he stared at the ghouls.

"Jeremy we don't have a choice. We can't go back, now go!"

Jeremy did as he was told and reached out and pressed the electric switch to lower the window. The instant he did, pale hands shot inside and he screamed, kicking them away from him. Rob pushed Jeremy down and fired three quick shots, sending the rounds directly into gaping faces. The bullets were like small hammers that flattened heads and blew out skulls.

Then the three minutes were up since they had left the house and there was a massive explosion that threatened to break every window in the car. The only reason the glass held was because bodies of the undead which surrounded the car protected it from the initial blast when the house went up in a blazing fireball.

"Holy shit! What the fuck just happened?" Jeremy screamed as the world became fire all around him.

Rob hadn't told him about setting the gas main to blow, there hadn't been time, and now the younger man knew.

"I set the house to blow up, so I could take out as many of these devils as I could," Rob said matter-of-factly.

"Are you crazy? What if we needed to get back in there?" Jeremy yelled. Rob fired again and a face disappeared, spraying the inside of the front windshield with blood splatter.

"There's no going back, son. There's only forward."

The blast had blown many of the zombies off the car and Rob felt the shaking lessen. Dropping the Magnum to the seat, he floored the gas pedal, the car surging forward. There were large bumps, like he was going over speed bumps, but then the ground leveled and he was moving.

Jeremy screamed and Rob turned to his right to see him battling with a ghoul who had charged the car, half its body now inside the vehicle with them as its feet dragged along on the ground. A shoe was lost to tumble away as the ghoul's legs kicked fruitlessly.

"Get that thing out of the car, son. Now!" Rob spat as he avoided a large knot of bodies in the road. Pieces of flaming wreckage were raining down around them like shrapnel and he had to spin the wheel or risk striking what was once his living room couch, but was now a flaming ball of fire. His refrigerator landed ten feet to his right and empty bottles of mustard and ketchup tumbled into the street. He floored the gas while Jeremy continued doing battle with the ghoul.

The snarling face kept trying to take a bite out of Jeremy and every time the young man tried to push the zombie out of the car, the teeth would clamp down, luckily only on empty air.

The Civic hit an old woman with a sweater in her arm, the sweater now bloody and filled with bits of gore.

He struck her head and the top half of her body bent over like she'd been smacked from behind. Her face struck the hood of the car and she was in the shape of an L, her feet now dragging on the ground. Instead of flying off the grille, Rob hadn't been going fast enough, and she had folded onto the hood. Her arms were to her sides and she struggled to escape the moving battering ram.

She was blocking his view, so he decided to take passivity and stepped on the brakes for a moment. The cessation of inertia caused the woman to slide off the hood to roll onto the pavement, her arms and legs chaffing from the rough asphalt. Rob stepped on the gas again and drove over her body, his two left tires getting her in the stomach. Though the car was small it was driving over a weak spot in a human body and the ghoul was bifurcated like a stuffed sausage.

Rob had time for one glance in his rearview mirror and he saw the woman was now dragging herself after the car, trailing intestines behind her like a clump of red and glistening ropes.

Jeremy had managed to get the ghoul partly out of the car and now it was mostly the head still inside. Ducking below the snapping jaws, he pressed the switch to the window and the glass began to rise.

The ghoul's neck was directly in the track, and as the glass closed, it began to slice into the pallid skin. After more than two weeks of being dead, the muscle and tissue wasn't as tough as it once was and the sharp glass began to cut into the neck like a dull blade.

Jeremy could hear the electric motor in the door whining over the noise around him as it tried to complete its function. The ghoul's face was a snarling mask of anger as it tried to escape the mechanical headlock.

The window seemed to hesitate for a second and Jeremy could almost feel that the motor was going to give up; not able to take the strain required of it. But then the motor pushed past the point of no return and the top of the window closed, severing the head messily from the ghoul's body.

The headless corpse dropped away from the car to roll along the pavement, the Civic leaving it behind, but inside the car things were still moving at a fast pace.

The head, now severed from its body, spit blood out of the neck to splatter on the dashboard as it dropped into Jeremy's lap. But the head was still quite animate and Jeremy screamed as teeth opened to clamp down on his junk.

Shrieking in terror, he grabbed the head like a football and began juggling it. The entire time the teeth were snapping, the eyes were rolling and Jeremy was screaming. Rob was still busy driving and he managed a glance at Jeremy, almost chuckling at the younger man's predicament.

"Toss it in the backseat, son. We can get rid of it later," Rob stated calmly, like Jeremy was wondering what to do with an empty soda bottle instead of an animate head.

Jeremy tossed the head from hand to hand and with an 'alley-oop', sent the head into the back seat. It bounced off the headrest and then dropped to the floorboards. Jeremy took a peek and saw the head rolling back and forth gently with the rhythm of the car. He sighed, relieved to be free of the head and he glanced to Rob.

"The head was still alive, Rob, did you see that?"

"Yes, son, I know. It's the brain you've got to take out. When they first began attacking people I took a few shots at arms and legs, not wanting to kill anyone. Back then I didn't know what I was dealing with. But later, I realized they were dead or close to it and I took a shot and blasted one in the head. The sucker went down and stayed down, not like the other times. That when I knew the only way to take them out for good is a shot to the ole' brain-pan." He tapped his forehead.

Jeremy stared at Rob for ten full seconds. Rob was still avoiding bodies, dozens and dozens on the road, all attracted to the explosion.

"Do you want to explain to me why you just blew up your house?" Jeremy inquired.

"I told you, we can't go back, not with that fire getting closer. So I figured if we can't have my house then they sure as heck won't get it either." He frowned slightly. "It was my house, son, I can do with it what I want."

"Yeah, but..."

"But nothing; just leave it alone. It's over, it's done. Yakkin' about it ain't gonna change a thing."

He pointed with his left hand to the road in front of them. The ghouls were spaced out and he was driving in and around them like a sixteen-year-old avoiding red cones at his driving exam.

"The question is where are we gonna go now."

Jeremy shrugged. "Don't look at me."

Rob did and then promptly looked away, concentrating on driving. He had slowed his speed to around twenty and was gently knocking bodies that tried to get at the car. They would bounce off the bumper or quarter panels and fall to the street. But they weren't hurt and once they were standing again, they would begin walking towards the taillights of the Civic, not having anywhere else to go.

Rob drove through the next two towns, seeing more of the same devastation and walking corpses.

Inside the car, Jeremy gazed around himself. He knew where he was, but not knowing where they should go. Then he saw a green sign for the interstate.

"The exit to Route 95 is a few streets over, maybe we should try for the highway," Jeremy suggested.

Rob glanced at him and nodded.

"Okay, that's a good a place to go as any other," he replied.

Rob felt better having a destination, even if it was a loose one, and as he stepped on the gas and began driving with more determination, a scream floated on the wind, penetrating the closed windows of the Civic.

"You hear that?" Rob asked.

"Yeah, but I thought I might have been imagining it."

"Nope, I heard it, too."

"Yeah, but where did it come from?" Jeremy asked as he cracked his window to hear better. The window was covered in gore and he didn't want to touch anything. For that matter, so was he. His pants were sticky and he felt cold, the blood seeping into every crevice of his pants and flesh beneath.

The scream came again and Rob's head jolted to the side. His eyes danced in his head as he tried to find out where the scream was emanating from.

The Civic reached the end of the street and then Rob let out a cry of surprise and triumph as he pointed to the left.

"There! Over there on that roof!"

Jeremy looked where Rob was pointing, and sure enough, there was a woman trapped on the roof of a house with dozens of ghouls on the grass below her. She was at the edge where the gutter was located and she looked to be balancing precariously. And if that wasn't bad enough, more ghouls were climbing out of the open window on the second floor as they tried to reach her.

And as Jeremy watched, it looked like a few more ambidextrous of the undead were about to do just that.

Rob spun the wheel in the direction of the house and shot forward, Jeremy's head banging against the headrest.

"What're you doing? There's more than two dozen of them over there!"

"Yeah, but we've got to save that woman or she's dead."

Jeremy said nothing, and as the Civic surged forward, he held on to any place in the car that wasn't covered in gore.

* * *

Five minutes ago.

Karen was at the end of her limits as she struggled to remain on the roof, knowing to slide off would be her death. Her calves and thighs were an aching mass of muscle as she strained to keep herself seated. She was so tired she could barely keep her eyes open and it was hard to believe she had been out on the roof for almost three days. Her mouth was so dry she didn't think she could talk if she wanted to and her stomach was so empty it felt like she'd ingested rocks, the pain was so bad.

Come to think of it, if she had a rock in her hand she would probably eat it, she was that hungry.

Seven feet away from her, as far as she could get, the open bedroom window was filled with ghouls. Each one tried to reach her with outstretched hands, but didn't seem to understand why she was out of their reach. A few had tried to climb out and get her, but as soon as they were fully on the roof, they tumbled to the ground below, usually crushing their brethren when they fell. The sickening crunch of bones when the plummeting bodies connected stayed with her always. Her husband was in the window, but for some reason he never climbed out on the roof. She didn't give this much thought, but instead closed her eyes and leaned her arms against her upraised knees. She had found this was the best way to remain still and not slide off. A few times she had drifted off to sleep, so tired even the undead wails weren't enough to keep her awake, and each time she did, her muscles relaxed and she would begin to slide off the roof.

With a jarring jolt she would pop awake and stop herself, then scoot back up to where she had been before drifting off.

But now she was falling asleep again and this time she was so exhausted she never felt herself moving as she began to fall to the left. Before she could snap awake this time, she was rolling down the steep roof and it was only luck that caused her to wake up before tumbling off the edge. Her right arm stretched out, and it lodged in the gutter of the house, stopping her from falling. She screamed long and loud and felt her shoulder pop from the force of the blow, but it had stopped her from falling to the ground below, so she was thankful.

She couldn't move however, and knew the instant she tried, she would fall off the roof, the ghouls below moaning in anticipation. She turned and glanced up to the open bedroom window and her eyes went wide when the first zombie climbed out, its dead eyes turning to glare at her.

Like the ones before it, the instant the ghoul had both feet on the roof it lost its balance and tumbled head over heels. Only now Karen was in the way. She screamed again as the ghoul plowed into her, its dead hands trying to grasp her. But the body rolled over her, and the stench of decay filled her sinuses as she fought off the urge to dry heave. The ghouls rolled off the roof like an acorn from a tree and plunked down on two dead women who were too slow to move out of the way. Bones crunched like dried twigs and the three zombies flailed about, their limbs intertwined.

Karen glanced back to the open window to see yet another ghoul coming out. This one fell sideways and it literally cartwheeled off the roof, head and hands helping the body miss Karen by a mile.

But then her husband came out, and for whatever reason, Eric was more careful. He slid out, and like he was sledding, began sliding head first directly at her.

She screamed as she stared at those undead eyes and the mouth now wide with killer teeth.

It was just as he was about to reach her that her instincts took over and she took her arm out of the gutter, her body rolling the rest of the way off the roof.

But she wasn't finished yet, and as she fell off, her hands wrapped around the gutter, fingers turning white instantly from the strain of holding her up. Her arms were shaking, exhaustion taking its toll on her and she knew she wouldn't be able to hold on for long. Her arms were now outstretched and her legs were dangling like she was hanging from a high wire by only her fingers.

Eric slid past her and continued off the roof, his right hand grabbing a piece of her shirt as he went by. The material ripped and he tumbled into the air to land head first in the churned up mud that was once his pride and joy lawn.

His neck cracked like a toothpick and his body dropped over, the zombies stepping on his corpse like he was nothing but a slight mound of dirt.

As for Karen, she held on and screamed one final time, knowing deep in her heart she had seconds before she would let go and fall to her death.

She imagined the teeth sinking into her flesh and she cried tears of sadness and fear. She began to shake as she thought of the ghouls tearing into her torso and ripping her pulsing organs out like tinker toys being played with at a child's birthday party.

She wondered how long before she would pass out from the pain and fall into oblivion.

And then she realized she wouldn't have to wonder for long as she shrieked one last time and felt her fingers begin to slip.

* * *

The Honda Civic barreled across the street, knocking ghouls aside like tenpins. Inside the car, Jeremy held on while body after body was brought down by the little car.

"She's gonna fall!" Jeremy yelled as he stared at the woman hanging from the gutter of the house. Below her dangling feet, the zombies were agitated, each struggling to climb over one another on their sole mission to reach the woman.

Jeremy watched a ghoul slide off the roof to plunge into the crowd of undead and he knew the woman couldn't hang on like that forever.

Rob put the car in low gear and continued onward.

"Have you thought about what exactly we're gonna do when we reach her?" Jeremy asked.

Rob shook his head. "We'll figure that out when we get there," he replied curtly and promptly took down an old woman who still carried knitting needles in her hands. The body was plowed over and under, the car jumping slightly in the air. Behind the car, when it was past, the churned up body of the ghoul remained. There was a large red welt on her beat-up face, thanks to her head bouncing off the undercarriage and the hot muffler.

Rob pressed the horn on the car and the shrill beep filled the area. Most of the ghouls turned to the new disturbance while others paid it no mind, their dead eyes only for Karen.

On the house, Karen could feel her fingers ready to go. Though she strained with everything she had, she knew it was too little. She was exhausted. Lack of food and water for days had made her nothing but a shell of her former self. She found it ironic how she had worked so hard over the years to lose weight and now she had to have dropped ten pounds in the past week's ordeal.

Her mouth was open and she uttered one last shriek, barely more than a whisper as her fingers slid free of the gutter. She felt herself falling for one brief second and then there was a jarring impact that was definitely not the grass or bodies of the zombies.

It took her a second to realize she had dropped onto the roof of a car, and though her legs hurt from the impact, it was better than where she would have ended up.

"Hold on!" a muffled voice called from inside the car. It was male and the only reason she could hear it over the cacophony the undead made was because the man had cracked the driver's side window a little so his voice would travel further.

She did her best to do what she was told, realizing instantly she just might live to see the next five minutes, when the car jerked under her. There was the loud retort of a gun blast and a ghoul to her right was blown off its feet, more than half its chest disappearing in a pink spray of blood and gore.

Then she was balancing, her hands trying to hold her upright, but yet always pulling them back when undead hands tried to grab her.

There was only one tense minute when two ghouls got her by the right arm. She felt the cold palms on her flesh, and when she tried to pull her hand back, she found it was stuck, like she had jammed it into a vice.

She turned to gaze into the pallid, stretched face of what was once her neighbor. Skip had been in his late thirties and was a yuppie through and through. He still had a sweater tied around his shoulders and the small alligator emblem on his shirt above the left breast pocket was worn like a badge of honor.

His once white teeth were now stained with blood and his manicured fingernails were blackened and bruised from where he'd been digging at the side of her house. He snarled like a wild animal as he tried to pull her from her perch. Deciding she was through playing the victim, she spun on her butt and kicked Skip in the face with the sole of her right sneaker. Cartilage was crushed and bone was forced into the brain of the once familiar ghoul. The zombie began to jerk and the bone fragments interfered with its movements. Then the car was out of the crowd and driving over the sidewalk.

Karen held on for her life as the small car smacked bodies out of the way. Growling faces were swept past until they were more than a quarter mile down the street. The Civic slowed to a stop and both doors to the vehicle were thrown open. An older man and a younger one, the latter looking like he had just graduated from high school, stared at her with wide eyes.

"Well, don't just sit there," the older man said. "Get inside before more of them reach us."

As if to punctuate his words, six ghouls appeared from behind shrubbery and through open front doors of nearby homes.

Karen nodded, and though still in shock, climbed off the roof with the older man's help and let herself be ushered into the car. Climbing in the back seat, the two men hopped in and the car took off, leaving the approaching zombies behind.

Karen leaned back in the seat, exhausted and spent, and no sooner did she let out a breath of relief then she felt something worrying at her left sneaker.

Gazing down casually, her mind not able to identify what could be chewing on her sneaker, she let out a screech when she saw a decapitated head on the floor, the mouth open and chewing on the tip of her sneaker like a toddler with his first teeth coming in.

"Oh my God, what the hell is that?" Karen screamed as she tried to kick the head away from her.

But the teeth were clamped tight, and when she kicked her foot in the air, the head jumped about and seemed to float around the inside of the vehicle like the bouncing ball on a sing-along DVD. The teeth held fast, like a dog with a play bone.

"Oh, gees, I forgot about that," Jeremy said as he watched the head jumping back and forth. He acted like the head was nothing more than a discarded paper bag from a fast food restaurant.

Rob had to concentrate on driving, so he couldn't help him.

"Here, hold still and I'll get it off you," Jeremy told Karen.

Though freaked out, she managed to stop struggling for a few seconds. The teeth of the severed head were pressing on the leather tip of her sneaker and she could feel the pressure, but she seemed to be safe. As she held her leg up, blood seeped from the jagged neck wound of the head.

Jeremy reached out and grasped the head by each of its ears. "You ready?"

"Just get it off me, please," she said in a frightened, soft voice.

Jeremy braced himself and yanked back, the teeth sliding on the leather, leaving jagged marks like someone had scraped a fork across her sneaker. Then the head was off, a piece of the sole trapped in its jaws. The eyes darted back and forth and the mouth spit out the rubber, the foul taste not what it was after.

Carefully holding the head by its hair, Jeremy rolled his window down and dropped the head out the window.

The decapitated head rolled and bounced down the street like a dropped tennis ball and came up in the gutter. Facing outward, now battered and bruised, the white eyes looked back and forth and the mouth moved up and down, like the head was singing a tune only it knew the words to. The eyes watched the Civic disappear around a corner and then it was alone.

Inside the car, Karen was breathing easier. With the head gone and the car moving at a good clip, she was finally able to drop her guard, if only slightly.

"Do you have anything to drink, please? I've been trapped on my roof for days and I'm so thirsty."

"Sure, hold on," Jeremy said and began digging around in a small backpack on the floorboard by his feet. The top of the pack had blood splatter on it and he ignored the sticky sensation, opening the flap and taking out a bottle of water. Handing it to her, she smiled in thanks, and after downing half in a few gulps, she wiped her mouth with her sleeve and finished it.

"Thanks, thanks a lot," she said. "And not just for the water. If you two hadn't come along, I don't even want to think... Well, you know."

Jeremy nodded as he gazed at her. He was looking over his left shoulder, his body slanted to the side.

"Glad we could help, but it was Rob here who heard you calling for help."

"Rob, huh? I'm Karen, by the way," she said.

"Hey, Karen, I'm Jeremy, and as I just said, this old codger is Rob."

"Watch it, son, or you'll find yourself walkin'," Rob said in jest. His voice was hard, but there was a small smirk on his lips.

"Do either of you know what's going on? What's causing all this? Was it a terrorist threat? Biological attack maybe?"

Jeremy shrugged. "Don't know how it happened, but believe it or not, the dead are walking."

Karen made a face. "What? That's crazy. The dead don't walk, it's a physical impossibility. I mean, once you die and your heart stops pumping, all your blood goes to whatever part of you is the closest to the ground, which are usually your legs. It's called vicidity and it's a medical fact."

Jeremy flashed her a recriminating gaze as he chuckled.

"Oh, really. Then how do you explain that?"

He pointed to the right side of the car at a lone man walking slowly down the sidewalk. The man walked with slumped shoulders, and as they slowly passed him, Karen and Jeremy could see the man's mottled gray flesh and torn pockmarked arms and face. Where the man's abdomen was, there was now a mess of hanging entrails, the ropes swinging back and forth with each step the ghoul took. As the Civic passed him, the zombie turned to watch them, the arms rising in front of him as he tried to speed up and catch the car. But the Civic was past in an instant, leaving the lone ghoul behind.

Karen stared at the ghoul, and when they were beyond the pathetic creature, she turned back to Jeremy who was looking at her with an air of superiority.

"Well?" he asked.

"I...I... I don't know what to say to that."

"Yeah, I thought so." Jeremy reached over and turned on the radio. "Let's see if there's anything on. A few times over the past weeks me and Rob would go to the car and see if there was anything on one of the radio stations. It was pretty quiet, mostly static, but sometimes we got a signal." While he was talking, he was playing with the tuner. Rob glanced at him and then continued focusing on driving. They had been slowly working their way to Route 95, but the going was tough and finally Rob had given up, deciding to head deeper into the town. Bodies and vehicles were everywhere, parked and crashed at all angles. The hardest part was when Rob had to drive over the prone corpses in the road. After laying there for more than three weeks, the bodies were bloated and filled with maggots. When the tires would run over them, the insides would shoot out and up, spraying the undercarriage and tire wells of the Civic with a fetid, viscous fluid that had them all gagging and breathing through their mouths. The sound the tires made was not unlike driving through a large pool of mud, the suction sticking to the tires as they squelched their way through.

Flies were everywhere, buzzing and feeding, like large storm clouds had come to earth for a pleasant respite.

It was a nightmare scene made all the more horrendous because all three knew it was absolutely real. This was no movie set for a new horror movie or a documentary of what might happen if all the people in the world died.

This was reality, bittersweet as it was.

"Ah, I think I got something," Jeremy said and turned up the volume. "Yeah, I think…"

"Okay, son, be quiet and listen, then," Rob snapped softly, wanting to hear what the announcer was saying.

"…We're back on the air, but I can't say for how long. The generator was down for a while, but one of the interns knows his way around an engine, thank God. So, to recap from the last announcement, there appears to be an event happening on a national scale. All across the continent, the dead appear to be rising. I know it sounds ridiculous, but that is what is happening from all reports we have received thus far. Though no one seems to know how the outbreak first began, what is known is that the first victims were attacked almost three weeks ago and when they succumbed to their wounds, they in turn somehow came back to life. But alive wouldn't be the correct term. Let's say reanimated, and they then attacked other victims. The hospitals appear to be the worst hit as the wounded were brought there immediately and upon succumbing to death they then reanimated and attacked the very same doctors and nurses who'd been trying to save their lives only moments ago." There was a shuffling of what had to be papers and the announcer cleared his throat.

"The first known cases happened on the east coast, but quickly spread across the nation thanks to air travel and other expedient forms of travel. The President and joint chiefs are even now in a closed conference with our nations most intelligent minds as they seek to identify what has caused this calamity and correct it. As to the location of that conference, the news is sketchy. Some say they are in NORAD, at Cheyenne Mountain, and others say they are in an undisclosed location where the staff has the top most level of security clearance. But what is known is that at this time, the military is shattered and social services such as fire and police are all but extinct. If you are safe, we here at WGON recommend you stay where you are and wait for help, and if you are not secure, you can try for one of the rescue stations that have been set up for all citizens, though at this time the information is sketchy as to which ones are operational." There was a slight hesitation and the announcer continued. "We go now to Trisha Ross who is lucky enough to have one of the leading professors of U-MASS with her. Trisha, take it away."

Rob leaned over and turned off the radio.

"Hey, I was listening to that," Jeremy said like a spoiled child.

"Yeah, so was I, and I heard all I needed to."

"And that is?" Karen asked from the back seat.

"That the people in charge know less about what's happening than we do."

"But what about the rescue stations they set up. We could go there?" Karen suggested.

Rob shook his head as he drove around a crowd of ghouls. A few hands slapped the windows of the Civic, but then the car was through them and moving on.

"No, ma'am, I think that would be a mistake. All it would take is one person who was infected to get inside the camp and it would be chaos. Just imagine all those people crammed in together and then one of them changes. It would be death to all of them. And where would you run? They must have some kind of perimeter fences. They would be trapped with the dead inside and out." He shook his head. "I've been doing just fine on my own since this began. I think I'll just stay that way till it's over."

"Amen, Rob," Jeremy said, his face serious.

Rob glanced at Jeremy and began to chuckle at the younger man.

"Thanks for the support, son."

"Don't mention it," Jeremy replied with a grin.

"Okay, then if we don't go to a rescue station, where do we go?" Karen asked.

Rob turned a corner and headed down a long road with a thin yellow line in the middle.

"I've been doing just that, little lady and I think we're here," he replied as he came out onto a large parking lot.

Jeremy's eyes went wide as he saw the large complex in front of him.

As common as an automobile, the large shopping mall stood tall, two floors high with more than two hundred stores and boutiques.

"I thought we were gonna get to Route 95 and leave the city?" Jeremy said as he studied the empty parking spaces where hundreds of cars and trucks should be. At the moment, there were less than thirty; all spaced around the lot like a giant hand had dropped a handful of dominoes from a massive palm.

"Yeah, me too, but then I thought this might be a better place to hole up. I mean, think about it. There are stores filled with food, clothing and drinks. There's a bunch of restaurants with freezers full of stuff. I mean that's probably bad, but there's still gonna be canned food galore," Rob said with a grin.

The Civic drove up to the main doors of the shopping mall and Jeremy read the large sign over the doors, though he knew the name by heart.

Northshore Mall was spelled out with large, black letters three feet high and two wide. Inside the mall were a Tiffany's, a Sam Goody's, a Borders bookstore, and enough clothing stores to clothe a small country for weeks at a time.

Plus, the food court had donuts, ice-cream and pretzels, a Burger King, and the two oriental restaurants that each served almost identical food, but were in constant battle for your taste buds and money.

The Civic slowed to a stop with a squeal of brakes at the main doors. At the moment, the area was clear, though at the far end of the parking lot, shambling forms could be seen moving closer.

Whatever they were going to do, they needed to do it quickly.

Jeremy shifted in his seat so he was looking straight into Rob's eyes.

"Let me get this straight, Rob. For all purposes there's a zombie apocalypse happening and your idea is to hole up in a shopping mall. Is that right?"

Rob nodded. "You bet. Great idea, huh? I can't believe I thought of it. It just came to me while we were driving to the highway."

Jeremy waved his hands in front of his face to get Rob to stop talking.

"No, wait a second, Rob. This actually isn't such a new idea; believe me when I tell you this."

"Why? I didn't see you suggesting it, did I? It's a good idea, Jeremy. We can stay here until help arrives, and even if it doesn't, we should be okay for a long time."

Jeremy stared at Rob with an incredulous look on his face.

"You're really serious, aren't you? I mean, you really think you're the first to come up with this idea." He leaned back and looked to Karen. "What's next, a helicopter on the roof?"

Rob was becoming aggravated by Jeremy's tone and knew he was being mocked, though for the life of him he had no idea why. It was Karen who asked the question Jeremy was itching to speak.

"Rob, you don't watch a lot of horror movies do you, especially monster movies," she said softly.

Rob shook his head proudly.

"Nope, never. Hate the stuff. TCM movies are about it for me, why?"

Karen smiled wanly, understanding perfectly. "No reason, Rob, it's fine." She turned to Jeremy who was staring at Rob with quiet fascination.

"Jeremy, I have a question for you now."

"Shoot," he answered.

"Okay," she said, "what I want to know is if someone comes up with a great idea thirty years after another person has already thought of it, but the second person never knew about the first person's idea or has never in any way been influenced by that first idea; does that make the second person any less brilliant than the first?"

Jeremy's forehead creased in concentration as he thought about what she'd said and in the end he came to a realization.

"No, I guess it wouldn't matter. Why?"

"See? You just answered your own question to Rob. His idea is as good as anything else, isn't it?"

"Just what in blazes are you two talking about?" Rob asked, slightly annoyed. He knew he wasn't privy to some information that evidently Jeremy and Karen had and it was becoming very aggravating.

Jeremy shook his head and waved his hand to dismiss the question. Then he took another look outside the car and opened the passenger door.

"Never mind, Rob, forget it. Actually, Karen's right. I think the mall is a great idea." Rob's visage cleared like the sky after a summer rainstorm.

"Oh, good, that's good, glad you agree with me." He opened his door and stepped onto the pavement, his eyes watching the slowly approaching bodies. By the way they walked, it was clear the people weren't healthy and it was pretty much a definite they were dead or worse...if there could be a worse.

Karen stepped out of the car as well and the three stood together, their eyes on the glass doors of the shopping mall. Rob had his Magnum in his right hand and he led the other two to the doors.

"Hey, Rob, just do me a favor, will ya?" Jeremy asked.

"Sure, son, what is it?"

"Just keep your eyes peeled for any motorcycle gangs."

Rob stared at Jeremy, but didn't understand his words and Karen slapped Jeremy on the shoulder.

"Will you quit teasing him? He's got a gun for Christ's sake."

Chuckling softly, Jeremy nodded and then waved a hand to Rob.

"Sorry, Rob, forget I said anything."

"Hmmph, that'll be real easy, son. Now come on, if you're done messing with me, we should get inside before company arrives."

Jeremy glanced over his shoulder to see the bodies were closer. They were like boiling water. The second you looked away the water went from flat to a rapid boil. So, too, did the ghouls seem to cover more distance when you weren't watching them, yet if you did, they plodded along like old men and women with arthritis.

Jeremy pulled his eyes away from the ghouls and proceeded to follow Karen who had begun walking behind Rob. He idly noticed she had an attractive backside though she was almost twice his age.

No, she was more Rob's age than his, so even if he tried something he knew she would shoot him down. That was okay, he wasn't really into milfs anyway. He was more into college co-eds.

So with an extra step to his gait, he sped up to catch the other two. Hoping the shopping mall would be the safety they each so desired and needed.

* * *

By the time Jeremy had caught up to Rob and Karen, he could already tell things weren't going as Rob had planned. The man's arms were by his sides, the Magnum aimed at the pavement as he stared through the glass doors of the main entrance to the mall.

There was an odd sound coming to Jeremy's ears now that he was closer, like when someone bangs on a drum or perhaps plays with a large elastic, twanging the band like a guitar string.

It was when he was directly behind Rob that he realized what the older man was staring at with such a dejected posture.

"Oh, you have got to be kidding me," Jeremy said to himself as he stared over Rob's shoulder to the inside of the mall

"It's unbelievable, isn't it," Karen said as she, too, gazed through the glass doors.

Or she tried to anyway, as the glass was covered in a slick, crusting splatter of dried blood and viscera.

The reason for the doors being so filthy was made apparent every four or five seconds.

Inside the mall, on the opposite sides of the glass doors, stood more than a score of walking corpses each looking worse than the one before it. More than half held miscellaneous body parts and were using them like clubs, banging them against the glass. A few used severed heads like rocks and threw them at the glass, but the softer skulls just bounced off the thick safety glass to roll back to the ghoul's feet. They would pick up the heads and then toss them again, acting like retarded monkeys as they tried to mimic the living people they once were.

With each slap of a body part on the glass, another black, red or brown smudge would appear. Jeremy could see almost all the zombies were once senior citizens, a few still using their walkers, only now they used them as clubs. Some of the female ghouls still wore shawls over their shoulders, their once sweet and wrinkled visages now corrupted by death.

As the three survivors stared at the ghouls pounding on the glass, wanting to get out and attack them, it was painfully obvious the shopping mall was not a safe place. Jeremy was sometimes able to peer past the shifting forms and further into the mall, thanks to the overhead skylights. There were more ghouls shambling about, mimicking what they used to be as they roamed from store to store. In reality, there wasn't much difference now as he looked past the main mob of the undead. The ghouls wandered to and fro, more than one still carrying a bag from a store in their hands, usually because the plastic had become entangled around their wrists or upper arms. A few ghouls wore the uniforms from the food court or had name tags on their chests. One wore an outfit like a referee and Jeremy guessed the staff working at the Footlocker was dead as well.

"Maybe I'm wrong, guys, but I think the mall is closed for the foreseeable future," Jeremy said.

"No kidding?" Karen said, the annoyance on her face apparent.

"That's just great, a great idea down the toilet," Rob mumbled. But then he caught something out of the corner of his eye, the reflection bouncing off the glass like a mirror.

Rob took a step backward from the glass doors and spun around so he was facing Jeremy.

Jeremy figured he had said one wisecrack too many and was about to get yelled at by Rob when, before Jeremy could do or say anything, Rob raised the Magnum to Jeremy's head and prepared to squeeze the trigger.

Jeremy had time for one quick: "I'm sorry," before the loud blast filled his ears. He closed his eyes and waited for the impact of the round that would blow his head clean off his shoulders, knowing it would be upon in him in less time than it would take to let out his last gasp.

* * *

But instead of feeling a massive blow to his head and feeling his brains exit the back of his head, he felt a rush of air as the bullet flew by his left ear.

At first he didn't know what to do, but he quickly opened his eyes upon hearing Karen let out a scream.

Then another blast filled the air and he stared at Rob who was looking over his shoulder to the parking lot. Spinning around, Jeremy realized Rob hadn't been shooting at him, but at the decrepit ghoul with its stomach torn open. After more than a week of being dead, the ghoul's open wound was filled with writhing maggots and flies, each feasting on the rotten meat. The larvae dropped from the body to twist in the sun and then attempt to crawl away, not understanding where their meal and home had gone to.

And then Jeremy had no time for staring as another zombie came at him from his left. There were almost a dozen ghouls approaching the three survivors and Jeremy realized they had taken too long at the shopping mall's doors. Shrubbery lined the walls of the mall and bodies now shambled forth after making their way around the building. The blasts of the Magnum only alerted more that were out of eyesight, but not out of earshot, and they all began converging on the three humans.

Thinking fast, not wanting to end up as lunch for a ghoul, Jeremy dashed across the sidewalk and picked up a sign that was held up by a cement block. The sign read **No Smoking** and the cement base had to weigh at least twenty pounds.

Karen screamed again and backed away from pale hands as a woman in a housecoat tried to grab her. Running to her aid, Jeremy used the sign as a club and pushed the dead woman away from Karen, the impact of the cement from the sign more than enough to crack half her ribs and send her spinning away. But she was back almost immediately and Jeremy realized he needed to take more drastic measures. Off to his side, Rob was shooting the ghouls as they came closer, picking them off one by one. After he expelled his ammo, he reloaded with precision, emptying the spent brass onto the sidewalk.

Jeremy had to turn away to deal with the dead woman. A few of her ribs were now protruding from her chest, making her look like a pincushion. Jeremy ignored the macabre site and whacked her in the side of her chest with the sign, causing the woman to fall to the sidewalk.

Not hesitating, knowing he needed to do this quickly, as there were two more ghouls fast approaching, he lifted the sign into the air as high as he could, and when it was at the peak of its height, he slammed it down onto the dead woman's face, splattering her brains and skull like a watermelon at a Gallagher show.

Little red slugs of meat splashed onto the cement and Jeremy felt his insides heave from the sight. When he lifted the cement base off the smashed countenance of the ghoul, there was a sucking sound that had him tasting bile.

But he forced it down, knowing there was no time for such sensitivities.

Karen had found a two-by-four amongst debris discarded near the side of the doors. There was a broken saw horse lying nearby and he guessed she must have managed to work one of the boards free. There was a large nail on the end of the board, almost as if she had placed it there, and when a ghoul came at her, she whacked the board at the dead man's head.

The long nail sank into the skull, piercing bone like it was a sponge, but the man kept coming. And to top it off, the nail had become lodged into the man's head and she couldn't get it free!

"Guys, I could use some help please!" She called in a shaky voice. She was trying to be brave, but she felt her bladder wanting to let go and her stomach felt like it had a thousand butterflies in it. She kept a firm grip on the board, splinters slicing her palms, but as long as she held it the dead man couldn't get close to her. His arms were raised as he tried to grab her, his fingers only an eighth of an inch from her nose, and she could smell the stench of death coming off him. As she watched, maggots squirmed under his skin while they fed on the massive meal of meat.

"Duck!" Rob screamed. "Now!"

Karen heard the order and saw Rob turn to face her. Doing what he told her, she dropped to the sidewalk while still holding the board. The ghoul bent over, too.

"Let go of the board, Karen, and get out of the way!" Rob barked angrily.

She let go of the board and rolled away, but just as she knew it would, the ghoul came for her. She yelped in fear, knowing the man would get her this time.

But then the gun blast ripped through the area and the man's head exploded into a hundred shards of scarlet bone and brain matter. She was peppered with red bone shrapnel and she screeched, rolling away even more.

Her right hand came down in something squishy, like spaghetti, and when she turned to see what she had pressed her palm in, she saw the flattened, jellied remains of the woman's head Jeremy had flattened with the sign post.

Slowly, she removed her hands and tendrils of slime appeared, connecting her palm to the mess of brains and gore.

Her stomach rolled inside her and she found she couldn't hold it in. With a hot gush of vomit, she added her own fluids to the visceral mix, the water she had consumed only a short time ago now washing the blood and gore off the sidewalk.

Then she was lifted to her feet when Rob picked her up and dragged her away.

"Come on, Karen, there's no time for that now. Later, if we're still alive," he said as he shot two scrambling ghouls that crawled over the sidewalk like new born babies. Their legs had been pulverized, crushed by a car or truck days before, but they were still mobile and wanted to feed desperately.

"Jeremy, get over here!" Rob snapped, the younger man swinging the sign one last time and then shuffling towards the other two.

He was breathing heavily from his exertions and there was a tight pain in his chest. The cement block was heavy and using it was like lifting weights.

"We need to get to the car before there's too many to fight," he told Jeremy as he shot another in the chest. The ghoul was thrown backwards to collapse onto another, but soon it was rolling onto its side and trying to stand once again. There was a massive hole in its chest, the ribcage poking through as well as internal organs which fell out of the wound like a paper bag stuffed too much by a lazy bag boy from the local supermarket.

Not wanting the ghoul to come at him again, Rob fired point blank into the ghoul's face, destroying the snarling visage in an instant.

A dead woman came up on him from behind and he spun around and fired at her. But he rushed the shot and missed her by a few inches, the bullet passing her by.

But the bullet needed to go somewhere and the glass doors of the shopping mall were directly in the round's path. In a cacophony of crashing, the bullet penetrated the glass, causing it to shatter as the old ghouls pounded on it without end.

Like a wedding dress sale, the old ghouls flooded through the shattered doors, walkers and canes shoving one another aside. In truth, with the exception of the mortal wounds on their bodies, the geriatric zombies really didn't look that much different from when they had been alive. Their skin was still withered and wrinkled, more than one having a pallid yellow glow from not getting enough sun. They still walked with hunched steps, some so bent over they were able to study all the cracks in the cement walkway.

"Oh, now come on," Rob spit when he saw the glass doors collapse under dozens of bodies.

"Why'd ya do that?" Jeremy yelled as he slammed a ghoul to the cement and promptly splattered its brains across the walk.

"I didn't do it on purpose!" Rob yelled back, shooting two more ghouls in the head before running out of ammo.

"I'm out! Cover me while I reload or we're all done for!"

Jeremy nodded, and with Karen by his side, the two joined Rob. Karen retrieved the two-by-four which was a bloody mess. The nail had a large piece of red flesh dangling from it, and when she swung the wood, small droplets of scarlet would fling across the area. Jeremy noticed bits of hair in the flesh and assumed it was a part of a scalp. Then he was swinging his makeshift battering ram as more ghouls came at them. His arms were killing him and with each swing, the sign with the cement block was growing heavier and heavier. He knew after a few more swings he wouldn't be able to lift it anymore.

Once again, Rob shook out the spent casings and quickly reloaded from his voluminous pockets. When he was finished, he snapped the cylinder closed in the nick of time, firing at a ghoul who was about to take a bite out of Jeremy.

Behind them, the dead octogenarians shambled forward, like the three survivors were social workers who had their social security checks and didn't want to give them back.

"We've got to get to the car before there's too many to fight. Come on, follow me and be careful!" Rob yelled as he kicked an ancient woman away from him. He kicked her in the stomach, the blow so hard she doubled over. Her dentures shot out of her mouth like they'd been self-propelled and she fell to the sidewalk, breaking a hip when she landed.

Rob ignored her, knowing they needed to move fast. Any delay could be their last.

As a team, they slowly moved to the Civic, battling the undead with each step they took. Teeth clamped down on Jeremy's arm, and it was only the material of his jacket that saved him from becoming wounded. He pulled his arm away from the foul mouth and used the top of the sign like a ram. Like a giant blade, the sign slid into the open mouth of the ghoul, slicing deep. The head was barely severed, the top half only remaining connected by the scalp in the rear of the cranium. Then the ghoul shifted position and the top half was snapped back, exposing the sliced brain which glistened in the sun.

The zombie toppled over like a felled tree, the brain popping out, but there were more to take its place.

Not slowing, his stomach dancing inside him, Jeremy swallowed the knot in his throat and continued onward. Next to him, Karen was fearless, her jaw set tight. Her eyes were hard and Jeremy saw a passion to live, one he wouldn't have shared before joining Rob and finding out the world was now ruled by the living dead.

But though he had been a slacker in his past life, this new world had given him a chance to shine, to become more than he once was. And he'd be damned if he was going to throw that chance away.

With renewed vigor, he began swinging the sign at the undead bodies, knocking them aside like tenpins. The cacophony of noise filled the parking lot near the three survivors, the noise drawing every ghoul in a half mile radius straight towards them. Of course, those undead souls would take time to arrive and Rob planned on being long gone before they appeared.

Down to his last round, Rob jammed the muzzle of the gun into a ghoul's mouth. The hot barrel sizzled on the black, gore encrusted tongue; the scent of cooking pork filling the area, overriding the redolence of death as the muffled blast seemed to obliterate the head like an M-80 shoved into the ass of a frog.

Jeremy was the first to reach the Civic and he threw the sign at a ghoul blocking his path. The cement base careened into the zombie's torso, the dead man bending at the waist from the impact. The man's back was slammed against the front fender of the Civic, pelvis now crushed, and as Jeremy reached the passenger door, the ghoul reached out with arms that still moved, the lower half of its body now limp thanks to a severed spine.

Jeremy kicked the dead man in the face and opened the door, the panel bouncing off the ghoul's forehead, leaving a bloody smear on the door of the Civic. Jeremy never noticed this, too engrossed in staying alive.

Karen was next, and when the door was opened for her, she literally dived into the car, Rob right behind her. The ghouls swarmed in, and if the Civic hadn't been there, the three survivors would have been torn apart in seconds as the undead feasted on their fragile human bodies.

But the car was there and the three climbed inside, Jeremy the last to enter. As he closed the door, three sets of hands plunged into the interior and he slammed the door so hard fingers were severed at the top joints, the twitching digits dropping into the car like segmented worms. One landed inside his shirt and he began to jump up and down, fighting to find the finger. As the undead pounded on the metal and glass of the Civic, Jeremy danced a jig on his seat as he desperately tried to find the finger.

"Got it!" he yelled as he pulled the index finger from out of his shirt. There was a gold ring still on the lower half and Jeremy dropped the finger to the floorboard, thoroughly grossed out knowing the finger had been touching his skin.

The car was rocking from side to side as the three survivors held on.

"What are they doing?" Karen asked with fear in her voice, her eyes wide with terror as she stared at the blank stares of the dead.

"I don't know, but they want us, that's for sure," Rob answered. His voice was strong, but anyone who knew him well would have detected a slight uncertainty there also. The man wasn't afraid of anything, but even this crowd of ghouls would make a hardened war veteran cringe.

It was hard to focus, the staccato of fists on the outside of the vehicle making it sound like there was massive hail coming down outside, pounding the car with ice.

Rob was trying to reload, but it was difficult with all the shaking.

"Rob, shouldn't we get going?" Jeremy asked.

"In a second, son. I'm not moving until I know my gun is loaded again," Rob said as he finished sliding in new bullets and slapped the cylinder closed.

Only seconds had passed since they had climbed inside the car, but it felt like hours.

"'Sides, they can't get in here, they're just stupid animals now," Rob added as he got situated behind the steering wheel.

So he was the most shocked out of the three of them when a ghoul managed to pick up the sign Jeremy had used as a weapon, and with another zombie helping, prepared to smash it into the rear window.

Only their flailing strength saved the people inside the car from being pelted with glass, the cement base only cracking the window.

"Jesus Christ, Rob, get us the hell out of here!" Jeremy screamed as he turned at the sound of cracking glass.

"Watch that mouth, son, I warned you about that," Rob said, but he did as he was told, starting the engine and shifting the transmission into drive.

But as he tried to move forward, the car wouldn't move. It was like the emergency brake was still on.

"What's wrong? Why don't you go? Step on the gas!" Karen yelled from the rear seat. Her head continually flicked back and forth to the undead faces glaring at her and she really, really wanted to leave.

"I am Karen, I swear, but the car won't budge!" Rob yelled as he pressed the pedal harder. The undead were everywhere, like a carpet of flesh consuming the small vehicle. They were like a swarm of locusts with only one purpose in mind, and that was to get at the humans within the car.

The motor surged under the hood, but the car barely moved.

"Is something blocking the wheels?" Jeremy asked. "'Cause I think we need to go, Rob!"

Rob's face was filled with angst as he shifted into low gear and tried again. Nothing, only the engine revving.

"Try going backwards," Karen suggested, her voice high with terror.

Rob nodded. "Yeah, okay, good idea."

He let the engine lower its rpm and then shifted into reverse. He was sweating now though he was trying to maintain a façade of being calm. Inside his chest, his heart was pumping fast as to what might happen to them if the car wouldn't move.

Stepping on the gas, the Civic began to back up, slowly at first, but soon he was moving faster. He couldn't see where he was going, bodies were everywhere, covering the glass, and before he realized it he was jumping the curb lining the sidewalk and heading straight for the shattered glass doors of the shopping mall.

The doors were relatively empty now, the geriatric ghouls now outside, and the small Civic plowed through the remaining glass and metal frames, the rear window of the car cracking and turning into a kaleidoscope of crystals. One good punch on that window and the entire sheet would fall in; allowing the undead access to the three survivors huddled within.

But the Civic kept moving, and before Rob realized it, he was inside the shopping mall. All around him were the opulence of modern society, mixed in with a healthy dose of death.

Bodies, rotting and maggot filled, were everywhere, draped over benches and hanging out of clothing stores. Karen and Jeremy stared at the stores as the Civic drove backwards down its wide aisle.

Both had been to this mall countless times, and though it seemed familiar, it was vastly alien now.

Red and maroon, with a few healthy coats of black, were the color of the day, plenty of entrails, severed limbs, and corpses were scattered about like tinker toys in a child's bedroom.

The tires screeched on the stone tiles and Rob struggled to maintain his direction, but he was panicked, and before he could stop himself, the car crashed into a stone pylon in the middle of the wide hallway and the car was jolted to a heart wrenching stop. The rear window shattered as the three people inside were tossed about like rag dolls and the rear bumper of the Civic wrapped around the pylon like two lovers in a close embrace, the trunk compressing like an accordion.

For a few heartbeats that stretched into minutes, none of them moved, too shaken up from the crash, but slowly, eyes were opened and heads moved about as each tried to remember where they were and what had happened.

While they struggled to regain their faculties, the dead were approaching, drawn to the crash like Pavlov's dogs to the dinner bell.

"Oh, my head, what the hell happened?" Jeremy mumbled, his vision swimming about him like he'd drunk way, way too much the night before.

Rob groaned heavily and slowly sat up. As the driver, he was the best prepared for the crash though he didn't know it.

It wasn't until an undead face slapped against his window that Rob snapped awake, staring at the dead eyes as the nose and mouth dragged themselves across the glass, leaving a slime trail filled with maggots.

"Sweet lord in Heaven, where's my gun?" he gasped as he stared at the ghoul. The zombie had once been a store clerk, the off-white shirt now covered in dried blood. The ragged gash on the clerk's neck attested to how he had died and the blood-covered teeth attested to how he had risen again and fed on some other poor victim.

Rob's eyes couldn't help but lock onto the gold cross the dead clerk wore around his neck. As the zombie moved back and forth like in a snake dance, the cross swayed like a tiny pendulum, catching the ambient light inside the mall.

Jeremy was awake and had heard Rob's query about his gun and it was he that found it on the floor near his feet. Picking it up, he handed the massive revolver to Rob.

"Thanks, son, I have a feeling we're gonna need it in a second. See, that's why I wanted it loaded before we tried to leave."

Jeremy only grunted, his head hurting like a steel drum was stretched across his scalp and a dozen men were banging on it. Karen came to and screamed when dead hands reached through the shattered rear window and grabbed her.

She tried to fight them off, but there were too many, and as she kicked and screamed, her legs flailing, Rob and Jeremy watched as she was dragged out of the car. Reaching out, Jeremy tried to hold her, his hands wrapping around her left ankle, but she was pulled from his grasp, his fingers sliding along her leg and her sneaker popping off like a cork from a wine bottle.

Staring at the sneaker in his hand, Karen's screams filled the shopping mall.

Rob took one look at the sneaker and reached for the door handle.

"Well, don't just stand there, son, let's get her before they tear her apart!"

That snapped Jeremy out of his stupor, and with Rob opening his door and shooting the dead clerk in the face, Jeremy took that as a trumpet call to arms.

With the sound of the Magnum echoing in the mall, and Karen's screams for help adding to the tempo, Jeremy opened his door, pushing a ghoul out of the way, and charged out to save Karen, though he couldn't help but wonder when it all went to Hell just who was gonna save him.

*   *   *

Karen Mills knew she was about to die, and that dying was going to be very, very hard.

She couldn't remember ever really being frightened in her life now that it came down to the end.

71

When she had been a little girl, her father had always been there for her, and even when he wasn't, his calming influence was there in spirit. Her mother had been a strong woman, as well, not afraid to give her point of view to her husband, especially at a time when women's rights weren't at an all time high just yet.

Her school life had been reasonably calm, with good friends and no enemies to think of.

When she had married Eric, he had taken over the role of her father, protecting her, feeding her, and giving her a warm place to live with a roof over her head and money in her pocket.

Yes, as she thought about her life, she realized it had been a good one, and though she was petrified with terror at the monstrosities surrounding her, she was sad it was almost over.

The redolence of rotten fish came to her nose and she fought the effort to gag. Pale hands were dragging her out of the car's shattered window and one hand had wrapped itself around her hair, pulling the roots to the point of breaking, and taking a large chunk of her scalp with it.

She could hear Rob and Jeremy calling her name, but it was as if it was from far away, like they were at the opposite end of a vast canyon.

Growls and moans filled her senses and she stared up at death with such sadness, and she knew she would have cried if she'd had the time. But she knew she didn't, and as the first mouth of fetid decay leaned down to bite into her soft flesh, she could only pray her suffering would be quick and that at the end there wouldn't be enough of her to come back and walk around again.

She didn't want that, Lord no.

Her eyes were locked onto the set of jaws coming for her, and to say she was surprised when the mouth seemed to stop in mid-bite to then hover over her was somewhat odd. In this new world, the dead eating the living was as natural as a cat eating a mouse, so then if this was so, then why was this dead man not finishing the job and tearing her skin from her bones?

All this flashed through her mind in less than a second and in another second she received her answer when the zombie's head parted directly down the middle.

It was like a sliced apple, the two halves falling away from one another, like a sculpture molded in two pieces. Blood geysered from the neck stump, and as the two halves flopped to each side, the eyes moved for another second, as if they were asking why their vision was now sideways.

Then Karen saw the reason for this strange occurrence.

Behind the sliced and diced ghoul, another zombie stood, but this one was holding a large sword, like a katana.

The face was female, she knew that, but anything else was lost on her. The body was covered from head to toe in gore, pieces of flesh and gobs of meat hanging from the torso. Her eyes just got the glimpses of stained rope or twine, which appeared to be how the meat was attached.

Karen could only lie on the tile floor behind the Civic and watch fascinated as the zombie woman began carving through the ghouls like they were chattel.

The way the female ghoul moved belayed what should be slow, treacle-like movements.

Where the ghouls were slow, almost methodical in their plodding gait, the female ghoul was like a dervish, slashing and hacking arms off torsos and severing heads from shoulders. Karen looked behind her and saw a pile of bodies, some almost cut in half, littering the mall floor where they were none only moments ago. This was the result of the female ghoul's actions, no doubt.

In less time than it would take to ask what was happening, more than ten ghouls were taken down by dismemberment, and when all the bodies in the vicinity that posed a threat were removed, the female ghoul turned and began walking toward Karen's prone form.

Karen felt a scream crawling up her throat, but when she saw the dark green orbs of the female ghoul, she stopped, not letting that scream leave her mouth.

Where the other zombies had pale white eyes which were blank of intelligence, the female ghoul's were like fire, burning brightly with humanity.

The female ghoul reached out with her free hand and wiggled her fingers for Karen to take and did something no ghoul had done since the first outbreak had reached her home.

The ghoul spoke.

"Come on, hon, get off the floor. There's more of them coming."

Karen lifted a shaky hand and was pulled to her feet. She didn't speak, too shocked with what was happening, and still too filled with the terror of expecting death to have come for her.

It was when she gazed past the female ghoul's right shoulder to see Rob lining up his Magnum to take off the dead woman's head that Karen realized this woman wasn't a zombie at all and most definitely wasn't dead.

All the pieces came together.

The string tying rotten flesh to her body, the very human eyes, and that she could speak and move like a real, live person. But Rob was squeezing the trigger to the gun and Karen knew there was no time to stop him.

Still holding the woman's blood covered hand, Karen yanked her closer, removing her head from the space it occupied only a moment ago.

The heavy caliber round of the Magnum split the air and missed the woman's head by inches.

The sound echoed off the walls and the woman spun, pulling free of Karen's grip as she brought up her sword, ready to defend herself.

Rob was already getting ready to fire again.

"No, Rob, wait, she's one of us, she's not dead!" Karen screamed. She could see more zombies coming for them from the now shattered glass doors and they had mere seconds before they were overrun again.

"What're you talking about? Get out of the way before she bites you!" Rob snapped at her as he prepared to fire again.

But it was Jeremy who got in the way, blocking Rob's shot.

"No, Rob, stop a second, will ya? Just look at her. She's got a sword for Christ's sake."

Rob's eyes creased and his jaw went taut and Jeremy realized he shouldn't have taken Jesus Christ's name in vain.

"Uhm, I mean for Heaven's sake, Heaven's sake, now stop, please."

Rob paused for a moment and took a better look at the woman in front of him. It only took him an instant to realize Karen and Jeremy were right, she wasn't dead.

Questions came to his mouth, but he held them in check, his head turning at the sound of slapping feet and moaning. The ghouls were pouring into the shopping mall through the now open doors and it would be seconds before the survivors were surrounded once more.

Then the woman spoke again, the voice sounding oddly melodious as it was coming from a face lathered in blood and gore.

"Come with me if you want to live, I've got a place on the second floor."

Without waiting for a reply, she spun on her heels and began jogging off down the hallway. A few ghouls got in her path, but she hacked them down, limbs dropping off like cordwood and blood seeping from exposed wounds like sap.

"Well, what do we do?" Jeremy asked with impatience, his eyes darting to the approaching ghouls. He wanted to run away, but not without Rob. It wasn't so much a sense of loyalty, but the simple fact that Rob had the only gun.

"We follow her," Karen said matter of factly. "What else are we gonna do?" Then, she too, spun on the heels of her one sneaker and sock and took off down the hallway, dodging any shambling bodies that tried to grab her. She was far too swift and the few undead were spread out, like lazy morning walkers who had arrived early at the shopping mall's opening to get some exercise.

Rob watched Karen jog away and he turned to look at Jeremy, then at the closing ghouls.

"Come on, son, it's not like we have a lot of options right now."

"Yeah, tell me about it." Then he took off behind Karen. He skidded past a slow moving dead woman who looked to be in her late eighties and then he was catching up to Karen who had slowed when two zombies blocked her path. Jeremy picked up a nearby trash barrel and tossed it at the right ghoul, knocking the dead man to the floor.

Taking her hand, Jeremy led them past the other one and down the long hall, the swordswoman was still in sight, but just barely. Jeremy wasn't worried about losing her though. The way she was going led to a small cul-de-sac where you either took the elevators or the escalators to the second floor. So she was either going into one of the first floor stores or she was going to the second floor.

Rob watched Jeremy and Karen dash away and then he sighed, spit a wad of phlegm onto the floor, and after shooting the closest zombie to come for him, he too, dashed down the hallway. He avoided the few ghouls who blocked his path, not wanting to waste any ammunition if he didn't have to. He wasn't as fast as the others, but he knew the mall also and had an idea where they were going.

Avoiding the outstretched, pale hands, he pushed on, wondering what exactly he had gotten them all into by driving into the mall and destroying their only means of transportation.

As he ran, and the undead followed him, their wails tickling the back of his neck, he was beginning to think maybe his bright idea about going to the shopping mall maybe wasn't so bright after all.

* * *

By the time Rob reached the others in the cul-de-sac, the woman covered in gore was climbing up a rope hanging from the second floor railing, her sword slung over her shoulder.

Off to his right, he studied the escalators. Both the up and down sides were filled with a mish-mash of furniture, trash barrels and clothing, not to mention a few odds and ends, some still appearing to be moving.

With the blockade of wreckage filling the metal stairway, the ghouls were helpless to get through, the testament the dozen or so corpses lying below on the floor. They had been the unlucky ones who had tried to climb the wreckage, only to tumble to the ground below, smashing skulls, breaking limbs, and flattening faces.

When the climbing woman had reached the glass railing at the top, she waved the others to follow. Rob noticed she didn't speak; the hand gesture more than enough supposedly.

Jeremy was next, and as youth will attest, he shimmied up the rope like a monkey, only slowing near the top, his shoulders and arms not used to the climb. There were knots tied into the rope every foot or so, and if it wasn't for them, even Jeremy would have had trouble.

Karen was next, and the instant she began to climb, Rob knew her ascent wasn't going to go smoothly. Before she was eight feet off the ground, she began panting, her face turning red with the exertion.

"Come on, Karen, you can do it," Rob said as he shifted his gaze behind him.

More than two dozen ghouls were approaching, more on the way behind the first wave. With the glass doors now shattered, every zombie in the area had free reign to enter the shopping mall.

"I can't, I'm not strong enough," she gasped as she hung by one of the knots in the rope.

"Yes you can, now put your feet on the next knot and keep climbing!" Rob snapped, hoping to motivate with tough love.

But Karen wasn't listening; her eyes closed and sweat beading her brow.

Turning all the way around, Rob realized he had seconds before he was overrun by the oncoming ghouls, Deciding it was either start blasting or die, he began climbing the rope, Karen screeching as it bucked in her hands like a living snake.

"What're you doing? I'm gonna fall!" Karen screamed.

"No, you're not, now get up that rope or so help me, I'm gonna shoot you in the butt."

That seemed to penetrate her fear-struck mind and she opened her eyes and gazed down at him.

"You wouldn't dare," she said indignantly.

With a hard face, he replied: "Just try me."

He was directly below her now, but he was still in range of the ghouls and he knew he needed to climb higher.

Karen still hadn't moved and Rob decided she needed yet more motivation.

Pulling the gun from his waist band, he poked her in the left butt cheek with the muzzle.

That got her moving, and with a squeak like a young girl getting goosed, she began climbing again, though not very quickly.

Rob followed and cringed when he felt a rotting palm caress his leg, but then he was higher, and though the ghouls tried to follow, they didn't have the motor skills to climb the rope.

When Karen was at the top, Jeremy was there to lean over and help her the rest of the way. Both tumbled to the second floor in a heap of limbs, Karen heaving like a beached fish struggling for oxygen. Rob didn't want to admit it to himself, but as he reached the last few feet to the top, he felt his own arms wavering and shaking. But he persevered and made it to the top, wondering why no one was there to help him.

It was the woman who came to his aid, reaching a bloodied arm towards him. Rob wasn't about to be choosy, so he grasped the outstretched hand and let her pull him over the railing. As he was helped, he noticed how she managed to carry his weight rather easily and he wondered what was under all the clothes and gore covering her body.

Truth was, with her face slathered in gristle and blood, her visage was all but unidentifiable. Only her bright eyes shone through, like two candles in the night.

"Thank you," Rob said as he turned and leaned back over the railing to see the undead swarming like killer sharks in the ocean deep. They reached up with upturned faces and hands to the balcony, wanting the humans they knew were up there.

"No problem," she replied, and without waiting to see if they were following her, she said, "Come on, my place is down this way." And then she was moving off.

Rob coughed loudly, clearing his chest while he helped Jeremy and Karen to their feet.

"Where's she going?" Jeremy asked.

"Don't know, but we might as well follow," he replied and headed off in the same direction.

Karen was still breathing heavily and Jeremy cast her a concerned glance.

"You okay?"

"Yes, dear, thank you for your help. I'm just not in that good of shape, is all. Getting old, I guess."

"Aww, come on now, Karen, you're not that old, are you?"

She chuckled. "No, honey, not that old. I'm forty three if you must know, but right now I feel fifty three."

He smiled at that. "Aww, I don't know, you don't look a day over forty."

She smiled wanly and shook her head. "You don't have a lot of experience with women, do you, Jeremy."

He shrugged. "Well, uhm, no, I guess not."

She patted his arm. "It shows, but that's okay, honey, when all this is over you'll get plenty of practice.

"Hey! Are you guys comin' or what?" Rob called from across the balcony. His voice wasn't as loud as it should have been, the undead moans filling the air to stifle all but the loudest sounds.

Jeremy waved to him to tell him that, yes, they were coming, and then in an unusual act of courtesy for himself, he held out a bent arm for Karen to take.

"My lady, shall we go see what's going on?"

She giggled like she was eighteen again, her hand over her mouth.

"Why, thank you, young man, maybe there's hope for you after all."

Jeremy only grinned a reply.

And so the two set off, arm in arm after Rob and the mystery woman who was covered in gore from head to toe, while the undead moaned their frustration at losing their meal.

* * *

For a few seconds Rob thought he'd lost the strange woman, that is until he heard a short whistle coming from his right. He turned sharply to see the woman standing in what was once a furniture store, but was now set up to look like a bedroom, dining room, and living room.

Deciding the whistle was an invitation, he strolled towards her as his eyes tried to take in everything at once.

He saw the metal grating for the store was up, the keys hanging from the two silver padlocks, and as he moved closer, he saw there was more than one bed nearby.

And one of the beds was occupied though from where he stood all he could see was from the waist down. The body was still, and either said person was dead or was just sleeping. For his sake, and that of his friends, he hoped it was the latter.

The woman was wiping the blood from her face, plucking the meat from the strings as Rob moved closer to her. She was standing on a blue tarp and there were buckets of water nearby. From the way she moved, Rob had a feeling the woman had done this before, as she moved without hesitation, placing the meat into a bucket while wiping her arms and face clean with towels and washcloths. He saw the meat had been held on with string, but at the end of the string were fishhooks, the barbed tips easily snagging the gristle and tissue she covered herself in.

And then, before Rob's eyes, she began undressing, sliding out of the one piece overalls she'd been wearing. Rob got an eye full of tender flesh colored a rich brown, and he immediately turned to the side, deciding a decorative lamp on his left was much more interesting.

He heard the woman chuckle and he felt himself blushing, but he refused to turn back.

"What's wrong, pal, never seen a woman naked before?" She asked snidely.

"I was married for longer than you've been on this earth, young lady, so yes, I have. I'm just being polite."

She snickered softly. "Why? I'm not ashamed of my body, look all you want. God put us on this earth naked, and the way I see it, it's perfectly natural. All those hang-ups about sex and nakedness, well, that's the old world."

Rob nodded and snuck a peek to see what she was doing. She wasn't even looking at him as she toweled herself off; he quickly looked away again.

"Perhaps, but I still feel it's impolite to stare at a lady who's un-clothed."

She laughed now, long and hard. "A lady! Shit, never thought I'd be called that again by anyone."

Rob frowned at her coarse language, but kept his opinions to himself on vulgarity. At the moment, he was this woman's guest and he didn't want to anger her.

Jeremy and Karen could be heard talking from out in the hallway, and when they were passing the open entrance to the furniture store, Rob called out to them.

"Okay, hon, I'm finished and I'm covered now," the woman said and Rob turned to see her in a faded-blue robe.

Jeremy reached Rob and his eyebrows went up at the sight of the dark-skinned woman in her early twenties. He saw the bloody clothes on the ground and his eyes went up as his imagination took over, and he glanced at Rob with a lecherous sneer.

Rob saw his expression and he shook his head.

"Forget it, son, nothing was happening here but a woman washing up. Get your mind out of the gutter."

"What? I didn't say anything."

"You didn't have to," Rob quipped back and turned around to see the woman now that she was clothed.

She was an attractive specimen of the female form with long legs and smooth skin. Her eyelids were slightly slanted, giving her the subtle impression she had some Asian blood in her. Her lips were thin and her nose petite. Her hair was a dark black and was shoulder length, the ebony tresses straightened either by nature or by hair products.

Her eyes were a dark green-brown, depending on the light, and filled with a fire that said she was no mere woman, but a fighter who would defend herself to the last breath.

Jeremy found his blood pulsing faster as he eyed this woman, and especially when he noticed the front of her robe was hanging open slightly, allowing him a clear view of a partially clad breast. The woman looked down to see what he was looking at so intently, but when she found her robe open, she did nothing to cover up. Jeremy felt his pants becoming slightly tighter and he shifted position.

Karen was the first to break the ice, walking across the room to the woman.

"Hello again, I'm Karen Mills, thanks for saving me downstairs. If you hadn't been there, well I..."

"Sure, hon, it's cool, happy to help." She flashed an annoyed stare at Rob as she spoke her next words. "Just wish you guys had found a better way to get in here other than to wreck my doors."

"Your doors? Since when is this your place?" Rob asked, wanting to defend himself.

The woman dropped the towel in her hand, but picked up the sword she'd carried downstairs and had used to such damaging effect.

"Since I took this entire floor back from the dead folk who were in it, that's when. And I was slowly taking back the first floor, too. That is, until you hotshots decided to see if you could drive a car through the middle of my shopping mall."

"Now just wait a second there, young lady," Rob said, but Karen stepped between him and the woman. She didn't know Rob at all, having only met him earlier, but after being with him for the short time she had, she'd gotten a good feel for the kind of man he was and knew she needed to step in or this argument would get worse before it got better.

"Please, Rob, she saved my life, after all, don't."

Rob closed his mouth and looked into Karen's eyes. Seeing the pleading there, he melted. He'd always been chivalrous with women.

"Fine, whatever," he said and turned and walked away to the main hallway in front of the store. He grumbled to himself and Jeremy was considering going to talk to him, but then the woman turned to him, her robe sliding open a little more, exposing a perfectly shaped breast.

"And what's your name, baby?"

"Uh, Jeremy, Jeremy Tyler."

"Well, I'm Valerie Williams, but call me Val for short." She reached out and took Jeremy's hand in hers, squeezing it gently. When she removed it she slid her fingers across his palm seductively. Jeremy paused for a second, wondering if he had just imagined it, but then Rob stepped back in and the thought was lost.

"Are you sure we're safe up here? I saw that the escalators were blocked, but what about the stairs at the other end of the mall?"

Val waved a hand in dismissal of his question.

"Don't worry about it, sugar, the stairs have more shit on them than a dump after Christmas trash day. They won't be gettin' up here."

"Oh, yeah, and what if they do? How are you gonna know?" Rob asked.

She shrugged casually and moved to pick up her bloody clothes, carrying them off to the side and dumping them in a large plastic bucket with a snap top. Jeremy thought that was a good idea, as the smell was ripe already.

"I'm gonna know, mister all talk and grumpy, because I piled glass jars and metal cans on the top. If they ever get that far, they'll knock 'em over and the shit will make so much noise I'll know somethin's up."

Rob frowned slightly, but he couldn't disagree with the logic. The undead were clumsy, and if they tried to climb over the pile of junk, the cans would make quite a ruckus.

"Well, I guess that should be safe enough."

Val made a disgusted noise with her tongue and lips. "So glad you approve, I ever so want you to be happy with what I've done here. If there's anything else I can do for you, please let me know." She said this with an insincere smile, like a waitress who'd been dealing with a table of rude customers, but had to be polite or else.

Rob didn't seem to pick up on it and Karen smiled, getting Val's meaning easily. She quickly turned away from Rob so he wouldn't see her expression.

"Oh, okay, well thanks, I will," Rob said, feeling placated.

Karen began giggling then and Rob glanced at her, not understanding why she was laughing.

Jeremy began chuckling too and soon Val joined in as Rob stared at the three of them, not understanding that he was the butt of the joke. Placing his hands on his hips, he frowned deeply.

"I just don't know what's wrong with you people," he said and turned and walked away, deeper into the store. He needed to get away from them, and even though he didn't understand why they were laughing, he wasn't a fool either.

He knew something was off about their good humor and he suspected he was the cause of it.

With the three talking together, and the laughter dying down slightly now that he had left their presence, Rob moved away, and as he passed by the section with the extra bed, he paused at the small form wrapped in blankets as his olfactory senses detected the distinct redolence of decay.

The form didn't appear to be alive as there was no movement, the chest seeming to be still, and as he stared at the lump more intently, it was easy to see it was the shape of a thin body.

Stepping closer, his hand on his gun, he slowly reached out to the edge of the blanket covering the supine form and pulled it back, gasping in surprise.

And then he reached for his Magnum.

*   *   *

Valerie Williams was still chuckling as she talked with Jeremy and Karen. They seemed nice enough and she was glad she had saved Karen from being killed. Rob seemed like an old fart, but even he was okay in her eyes, and Jeremy was a cutie only a few years younger than she was.

Her peripheral vision noticed Rob moving in the direction of the second bed and her heart began to race, knowing what he would find.

Without telling the other two where she was going, she stopped talking in mid-sentence and dashed across the carpet, her sword already raised to chest level.

Just as she reached Rob, she saw the man reaching for his gun. She didn't know what kind of gun it was, but it looked like it could blow a hole through a person big enough to put a fist through.

Rob had one hand on the blanket, pulled back to expose the frail form underneath, and just before he could aim the gun, Val rushed him, knocking his arm to the side just as he squeezed the trigger.

The gun blast filled the store and Karen and Jeremy jumped, as both had relaxed slightly, believing they were safe for the time being.

A neat black hole appeared inches from the gaunt skull lying on the pillow, the rest of the body a decent match, and Rob shouted in pain as the sword jarred his arm.

He'd been lucky and Val had used the backside of the blade, because if she had used the razor sharp edge, Rob would be nursing a bloody stump right about now. Feathers from the destroyed pillow floated in the air, like soft snow on a December morning.

"Get away from my mother, you bastard!" Val screamed as she jumped in front of Rob.

"But she's one of them! How can you leave her like this! She's dead!" Rob snapped back.

"I don't care. She's all I have left. If it wasn't for her I'd be all alone. Now get back, or so help me, I'll cut your fool head clean off your shoulders!"

Rob hesitated for a fraction longer than Val would have liked, but in the end he lowered the gun. In reality, there was no danger. Both the arms and legs of the frail body on the bed were secured with rope, or more like scarves taken from one of the boutiques.

Rob glared down at the undead eyes as they glared at him, the mouth opening and closing slowly. It was then that Rob notice the small bite on the ghoul's left arm, no larger than a quarter. After that it was simple to piece together what had happened.

"When was she bit?" Rob asked as he studied the frail ghoul. The once ebony skin was now covered in blotches of gray, the skin tightened and the limbs stiff from rigor mortis.

"Just a few days ago." Val's voice softened a little. "She did it to herself you know. She had cancer and said she didn't want to suffer. It's not like we could have brought her to a hospital now, right? She stuck her hand close and let one of them bite her. I've been debating what to do with her, but for Christ's sake, she's my mom!"

Karen and Jeremy moved up to the foot of the bed and both stared at the old, dead woman in awe. This was the first time any of them had seen one up close. That is, up close when the ghoul wasn't trying to bite their face off.

Jeremy moved closer and reached out a hand only to yank it back when yellow teeth snapped at him.

"Careful, handsome, she's a biter. Learned that when I was tying her up."

"Oh, Val, I'm so sorry for you. I lost my husband, too. He tried to get me, but I managed to escape him by climbing out on my roof. That's when these two found me," Karen said softly.

Val nodded. "The roof, huh? Good thinking."

"Look, Val, you can't keep her like this, especially if we're gonna sleep here, too."

Val's eyebrows went up a notch.

"Oh, yeah? And who said anything about that? This whole floor is empty. You don't like it here then go somewhere else. The J.C Penney's got a lot of couches and beds, try there."

Rob shook his head. "I don't think that's such a great idea. This place isn't that secure. We should all stay together."

"Yeah, I agree with Rob," Jeremy said as he snuck a furtive peak at Val's breasts. In her haste to reach Rob, her robe had opened more and Jeremy felt himself growing excited. He shifted position and tried to think of baseball, or algebra, or anything to distract him from Val's exceptional body.

"Oh, I get it. I save your asses and now you all are gonna come in here and take over, is that it?"

"No, Val," Karen said. "That's not it at all."

Her face filled with anger as she pointed to each of them accusingly with the tip of the sword.

"Let's get something straight right now, people. This is my place and if you stay here you follow my rules. Don't like them then get the fuck out."

Rob frowned deeply at her choice of words and Val picked up on it.

"You got somethin' to say, old man?"

"Well, yeah, for one, your gutter mouth is very annoying, and two, I'm the one with the gun." He held the Magnum up as if to illustrate his point.

In the blink of an eye, Val had flicked the sword towards Rob and slapped the hand holding the Magnum. He cried out, dropping the gun, and before anyone could do a thing, Val swooped in and scooped up the gun, spinning on her heels with it in her possession.

"Well, now I got the gun, so you do what I say, got it?"

Rubbing his hand and realizing he was at a disadvantage, Rob nodded, as did Karen and Jeremy.

"Good, now for the first item on the agenda, get the hell away from my mother, and Jeremy, cover her up again, will you, she gets cold."

She spun and walked away without waiting for him to answer and Jeremy frowned as he looked at the others.

"Of course she gets cold, she's dead."

"Just do it, Jeremy, please," Karen asked.

Jeremy did as he was asked, careful to keep his hand away from the snapping yellow teeth. The old woman hissed at him, but other than that was silent. It was eerie, as all the others would moan and groan as if they were trying to speak.

"So what do we do now?" Jeremy asked once the ghoul was covered again.

"We do what she tells us...for now, anyway," Rob said, and with one last glance at the old, dead woman, he spun around and walked away, still rubbing the red welt on the back of his hand.

"If you folks are hungry, I got food here," Val called from the front of the store. "Lot's of it."

That had Jeremy looking up with pleasure, realizing he hadn't eaten since morning, just before he and Rob had driven out of the garage before the house blew up.

"That sounds like a great idea. I'm starving," Jeremy said as he headed of to get some food. Karen stood alone now, hovering over the old woman. She was famished too and wanted to eat badly, but the withered woman in front of her caused her to stare. The eyes of the old woman opened wider and one tear rolled down the wrinkled and pale cheek.

Karen blinked, wondering if she'd just imagined what she'd just seen, and then hissing came to her ears and Karen felt a chill go down her spine. Then, wrapping herself in her arms, she too, followed Jeremy, though she didn't feel that much like eating anymore.

* * *

They ate in silence, no one wanting to be the first to speak.

Val had put a damper on their good spirits by taking Rob's Magnum. The gun sat next to her on an empty chair as the four survivors dined on canned food and stale bread.

Rob had been the last to join them, the man still nursing his pride, but eventually the smell of the opened cans of food attracted him to the table and now he sat as far from Val as he could while he chewed silently on a rubbery piece of meat from a can of beef stew.

Karen concentrated on her can of Chunky soup, eating it with a fork. She marveled inwardly how the food was just like the commercial, it was true, and she could eat the soup with a fork!

As for Jeremy, he felt himself drawn to Val, and though the dark-skinned woman sat with her sword on her left and the gun on her right, he didn't feel the least bit threatened. To him, she was like an Amazonian woman, fierce of heart and full of fire. As he chewed on his franks and beans, his imagination went wild with thoughts of sexual adventures with her. And not for the first time he was glad he was sitting down, his lower half hidden from the view of the others.

The undead moans coming from the first floor weren't as bad this deep inside the store. The dining room set had been laid out so that Val was facing the front of the store, as if the woman didn't trust her back to the opening.

None of the others gave it much thought, but Val and her mom had been alone for more than two weeks and such things had become second nature to her.

When they were finished eating, Val offered to let them wash up.

"You have running water here?" Rob asked. He was still sore at her, but even he couldn't stop his curiosity.

"No, not really, I managed to figure out a system that would let me collect water. If only I'd thought to save water when it still ran from the tap, but I never gave it a moments thought, ya know? I mean, who would have thought things would have gotten so bad so fast?"

"Tell me about it," Jeremy added, agreeing.

"Come on, the bathroom's this way," Val said as she stood up from the table and led the three new arrivals to the rear of the store.

Once they had reached the bathroom, Val led them in and pointed to the buckets of water on the floor.

"I've been lucky. It's been raining off and on for the past week, so I managed to collect a lot of water."

They all went to the sinks and filled them with water from the buckets and washed up while asking questions, Val seeming happy to answer them. Rob felt an ache in his gut as he looked at his Magnum sticking out of her waistband, and he was sorely tempted to try and take it back, but then he saw the razor-sharp sword in Val's hand and decided maybe now wasn't the best time.

"Raining? Why's that important?" Jeremy asked as he finished washing. It barely helped. Now that his arms and face were clean, he was more aware how the rest of him felt. He was sweaty and felt clammy from all his exertions of the day.

"Come on, I'll show you. We gotta go up on the roof, though," Val said and exited the bathroom with the others behind her. Jeremy took an extra second to pee, but was soon catching up to the others as he followed Val's voice while she filled the others in on how she had survived

Walking down the long hallway, the balcony railing on their left, Rob glanced down to the first floor. The dead were wandering aimlessly, like the typical consumer would do on a Sunday afternoon. A few spotted him and the others and soon heads were raised as the zombies wailed for the food above them.

"Man, that's creepy," Jeremy said, and then waved his hand in front of his face. "And the smell, whew!"

"You get used to it after a while," Val told him. "At least I did. Not like I have a choice. 'Sides, I burn scented candles sometimes when the smell is too much for me."

When they passed a Footlocker, Val pointed to the sneakers lining the shelves and then to Karen.

"Hey, hon, why don't you get yourself a new pair of sneakers or somethin'."

Karen glanced down to her shoeless foot and bloody sock and realized she'd been so preoccupied, she had totally forgotten about it.

"That's a good idea," she said. "Will you guys wait for me?"

"Wait? Hell, I could use a new pair myself," Jeremy said as the two went into the shoe store.

"How 'bout you, Rob, need a new pair of boots?"

The man frowned, still feeling that the two people were looting the footwear.

"No, I'm fine with what I have on. They've been broken in, so I like them."

Jeremy shrugged. "Suit yourself." Then he was gone, Karen and him talking together as they hunted for new footwear.

Val stood silently next to Rob, but not too close. Rob cast her a furtive glance, but turned away when she seemed to look in his direction. He had nothing to say to her, at least not as long as she held his gun.

In a few minutes, just when Rob was about to call out to Jeremy and Karen to hurry up, the two stepped back into the hallway, both sporting brand new sneakers. Jeremy had a pair of Nike high-tops that would have run him over a hundred dollars, while Karen had picked the moderately priced white sneakers with no special name brand, old habits dying hard.

With the two enjoying their new sneakers, Val turned and escorted them the rest of the way to the roof.

Soon they had reached the stairwell for the roof and all were walking up the stone steps, their footsteps echoing off the concrete walls.

Upon stepping out onto the mall roof, Rob was surprised to see hundreds of buckets, bowls and dishes, plus dozens of plastic Tupperware containers.

"What's all this stuff?" Jeremy asked as he moved to the first bowl and nudged it with his new sneaker.

"I put these out here to catch water when it rains, and see that over there?"

She pointed to a large, blue tarp which was angled on a slight incline. Below the tarp, which was attached to metal poles with cement bases once used for volleyball nets, were more containers.

"That tarp catches the morning dew and then it rolls into the buckets. So far it's worked well, though now that you guys are here I don't know how much we'll have."

"What about the CVS on the first floor? They have bottled water and juice there right?" Rob asked as he studied the setup. He had to admit it was ingenious.

"Sure there are," Val said. "But there's a whole mess of them dead guys in there. They won't come out. I've been weeding them out little by little, but the ones in there just don't want to leave. Most of them were employees and I guess they remember enough of when they were alive to think they still work there."

"You've been killing them?" Karen asked.

"Yup, sure have. Remember when you first saw me, back when I split that dead guy in two?"

Karen nodded.

"Okay, well remember all that meat and blood I had all over me?"

"Yeah, I wanted to ask you about that, but there hasn't been any time," Rob stated.

"So ask," she replied.

Rob didn't as he had already stated he was interested.

Val realized he wasn't going to ask and she decided to continue, wanting to share how smart she was.

"Fine, I'll tell you then. I found out a little more than a week ago that the dead folk don't seem to know I'm not one of them when I'm covered in their blood and junk."

"How'd you find that out?" Jeremy inquired, curious.

"By accident actually. I was taking out a bunch on the second floor so me and my mother would be safe and I gutted one from waist to neck. Well, I slipped in the guy's blood and when I fell to the floor, I was covered in his intestines and shit."

"Eww, that sounds awful," Karen said while she made a disgusted face.

"Hell, yeah it was, but what happened next was what was really wild. You see, there were about a half dozen nearby and when I fell I thought I was a goner, but as they moved towards me, they stopped, sniffed like animals and then moved away."

"So what did you do then?" Jeremy asked.

"I got up and finished the dead guy off, taking his head off his shoulders, then I stood there with my sword in hand. I found this in a back storeroom of one of the shops, and as I didn't have a gun, I figured it would do the job." She smiled proudly. "Think I've gotten pretty good with it, too."

Rob wasn't impressed.

"So, go on, what happened next," Rob prodded her.

"So I realized they didn't see me anymore, it was like I was invisible. So after I got over my initial shock at not having to fight them all, I went to work, taking out each one. Then, after they were all down, I dragged their dead asses to the back of the building to the loading dock." She frowned deeply then. "That reminds me, if you're trapped downstairs and need to get away, don't go in there. It's ranker than a thousand road kills piled into a dumpster. The flies alone will swallow you whole. I jammed a few rags under the doors so none of the little buggers can get out."

Rob merely nodded at her words.

Moaning floated to the rooftop and all heads turned at the sound.

It was coming from down below.

Rob was the first to investigate and he strolled across the rooftop, zigzagging through the buckets and bowls. By the time he reached the edge of the roof, he'd walked almost twice the distance, having skirted dozens of obstacles.

Down below, he could see the dead moving about. By coincidence, he could see he was overlooking the same entrance where he and the others had first arrived. He couldn't see the glass doors, now shattered, but he could see the sign post Jeremy had used along with the prone corpses and crushed body parts he and the others had left in their wake.

Hundreds of ghouls were moving in and out of the opened, destroyed doors, some having come for more than a quarter mile, Rob's gunshots alerting them to his presence.

"Jesus, will you look at them all?" Jeremy breathed as he joined Rob to stare down below.

"Don't use the Lord's name in vain, son, and yeah, I see 'em all."

Val joined them along with Karen, and they gazed down at the crowd of sunken-faced, pale and bloody bodies.

"Christ, look at them all, there's more than twice what was here this morning." She turned to Rob. "You brought them here. Now I'll never clean this place out."

Rob pulled his gaze away from the crowd and looked at Val.

"Well, maybe that's a good thing. Heck, maybe we did you a favor."

"A favor? How? I was happy in here. I have food, water and I was safe. Well, as safe as you can get since this shit went down."

Rob shook his head while Jeremy and Karen continued staring at the undead.

"Were you really? Seems to me you were a prisoner in here and just didn't realize it," Rob told her.

Val waved her hand, dismissing the statement.

"Doesn't matter what you think. Look, I'm going back downstairs to check on my mom. If you folks want to change out of those dirty clothes, just pick a store and take what you want. The owners are all dead anyway." Then she turned and strolled away, leaving the three survivors alone on the roof.

"That woman is a fool," Rob said to Karen and Jeremy as he watched Val cross the roof and disappear through the open roof door.

"Why? 'Cause she doesn't want to do what you want to do?" Karen asked. "From where I stand, I think she's a strong, independent woman who's managed to take care of herself. And us too." She turned to Rob so she was facing him, placing a hand on his arm. "Maybe you should give her a chance before you condemn her."

Rob frowned, looked down at the corpses on the sidewalk and then back to Karen.

"Yeah, but she took my gun, Karen. I need that if we're gonna survive."

Karen smiled softly, thinking Rob looked like a little boy who'd had his favorite toy taken away from him when he was bad.

"Tell you what, when I go back inside, I'll have a talk with her about that. Maybe I can get her to give it back to you, okay?"

Rob didn't like having Karen fight his battles for him, but unless he wanted to try and attack Val and take his gun back, he was truly out of ideas. Nodding, he lowered his shoulders in defeat and said. "Fine, thank you, Karen, I would appreciate it."

"No problem, Rob, I owe you." She turned to Jeremy and rubbed his arm, too. "Both of you, actually. I don't want to think where I'd be right now if you two hadn't come along.

Jeremy pulled his eyes away from the undead below and turned slightly so he was making eye contact with Karen.

"That's easy, Karen, I know exactly where you'd be right now."

"Oh?" She asked.

"Yeah." He pointed to the zombies milling about like Sunday shoppers. "You'd be one of them."

Karen nodded slowly, his words sinking in. "Oh, yeah, I guess you're right."

Jeremy turned back and gazed down at the undead, Rob and Karen joining him. The three survivors stood on the roof, one next to the other, looking down at their shattered world and wondered if that same world would ever be able to pull itself back together again.

*   *   *

The rest of the day moved in silent anxiousness as the three new survivors struggled to get used to their new surroundings.

All were now wearing brand new clothes, pilfered from one of the dozen or so clothing boutiques on the second floor.

Rob was wearing a plaid shirt and denim jeans while Jeremy had chosen a pair of Dockers with a black shirt of his favorite rock band. Karen had gone for simplicity with a blue blouse and a pair of white slacks, elastic at the waist for more comfort. Underwear was also fresh and they all relished the feeling of cleanliness, even though their bodies were still slightly dirty from the exploits from earlier in the day.

Val was sitting with her mother for most of the night and only joined the others around nine, right before Rob and the others were planning on turning in for the night. The ordeal getting them to the inside of the mall had been long and stressful and they were all looking forward to a relatively safe and good night sleep. Karen especially was looking forward to sleeping on something soft. After days on her roof, having to remain sitting upright, she longed to stretch out and let sleep fold her into its gentle embrace.

She was the first to leave, not able to remain awake any longer.

With a slight wave, she headed off to find a couch with her name on it.

That left Rob, Jeremy, and Val, the two latter talking quietly together while Rob acted like the third wheel, so after more than ten minutes of no one talking to him, he decided he might as well turn in, too.

With a quick goodnight to the young couple, he wandered away to find a place to sleep, still itching to get his Magnum back. He felt naked without it and hoped he could talk Val into giving it to him in the morning.

That just left Val and Jeremy who talked for more than an hour about life, movies and music. The two were only a few years apart and got along great and it was only when Jeremy continually yawned that Val got the hint.

"You're tired, hon, why don't you go crash and we can talk more in the morning."

"Yeah," Jeremy said, stifling yet another yawn. "That would be great. Sorry, but it's been a long day."

"No problem, it's cool, 'sides, I want to go check on my mom."

Jeremy made a slight grimace and Val caught it, though Jeremy tried to hide it.

"What? You wanna say somethin'?"

"No, no, I'm okay, it's just..."

"What, go on, spit it out, I'm a big girl."

"Well, it's just... your mom, you know, she's dead. I mean, I get why you don't want to say goodbye to her and all, but then again it's kinda creepy, you know, 'cause she's dead."

Val sighed heavily. "Yeah, I know, hon. But I just can't do it. Not yet. I will, I know I have to, but before you got here it was just me and her, you know? I could still talk to her and I didn't feel so alone." She nodded. "I'll do it soon, I promise, but just give me a little longer to get my courage up, all right?"

Jeremy stood and stretched, yawning again. "Sure, it's cool. You do what you want. As long as she's tied up, I guess I can live with it." He smirked. "Just don't blame me if I want to sleep in the other side of the store." He began walking away. "'Night."

"'Night, hon, sleep well."

"Yeah, you too," Jeremy replied back and then disappeared around a large oak cabinet and matching hope chest.

Val sat alone for a few minutes, only the wails of the dead coming from outside on the first floor. Then she got up, walked over to the front of the store and lowered the metal grating, locking the padlocks. The key was hanging to the side in easy reach, and she always closed the grating at night, not wanting to take any chances.

Then she walked away, her sword over her shoulder as she went to tuck her mother in for the evening.

* * *

Jeremy was dreaming.

In his dream, he was tumbling down a sidewalk in his old neighborhood. His feet made slapping sounds as he walked, and when he glanced down, he saw he was barefoot. His toenails were long and curved, making him look like he hadn't trimmed them in years. They also made a sound each time his foot slapped the cement.

Click, click, click, came to his ears.

Only the noise was muffled, as if it was coming from far away.

As he walked, he noticed others around him, all seeming to move about aimlessly.

He tried to remember why he was out today, where he was going, but each time he tried to focus his mind, only a dim cloud would appear. With nowhere to go and nothing on his mind, he kept walking, others passing him with barely a glance.

He glimpsed an old couple to his right who were having some trouble walking. When he slowed and paid them more attention, he saw the old man's right leg was hanging on by a few tenuous bits of slimy tendrils. Blood dribbled onto the sidewalk and gobbets of flesh and meat slipped from the gaping wound, but still the old man carried on, his cane and his wife somehow keeping him going.

He seemed to hop like he was playing hopscotch as he moved along. Jeremy watched for another few seconds and then turned his attention forward again.

Even in his dream, his real self knew this was odd. To see such a sight and to not find it shocking was definitely strange.

In the distance, a woman with black hair, a pierced lip, and nose ring was moving towards him carrying what looked like a coil of rope in her hands, and when he was close enough to see her better, he saw she had a jagged wound in her abdomen and what he thought was rope was her intestines, glistening dark red in the morning sun.

As she moved closer to him still, her hold on the slippery coils was lost and they tumbled to the sidewalk to splash red. She never stopped walking, and while she moved, behind her the cords were spread out, like she was leaving a rope trail to find her way back from whence she had come.

Jeremy passed her finally, and she never glanced at him, though Jeremy gave her a good looking at. Her cheeks were sunken in and her eyes were dull, white orbs, the pupils faded to nothing. Her skin was pale white with splotches of brown and green where rot was taking hold. When she was even with him, he saw a few white maggots squirming in her ear, one or two falling out to writhe on the warm cement.

Then he was past her and moving along.

All around him people were in the same state of decay and damage. Mothers dragged dead children along behind them while their breasts hung from their bodies like sagging water balloons. Men shambled about, some still carrying briefcases, but their attention focused on something other than work.

Dark stains were everywhere, the blowflies and maggots squirming in the viscous liquid, feeding on the drying plasma.

Jeremy stopped walking, turned, and then climbed onto the hood of a nearby car parked haphazardly on the sidewalk, the rear tires still in the street.

He stared at the road beyond and the people around him as he watched them moving about.

It was then he realized everyone was the walking dead.

There were no living humans anywhere.

It appeared that in the end it would be the dead who inherited the earth.

But if everyone was dead, then that would mean that he was...

No, that would be impossible.

Climbing down to the street, he turned and moved to the mirror on the driver's side door of the car. Without preamble he ripped it off the panel and brought it up to his face.

When he saw his reflection, his mouth opened and a hoarse cry escaped cracked lips. Dropping the mirror to the ground, it shattered into a million pieces, each one now a reflection the horror he had become.

He stumbled away then, too lost in the terror that was now his life.

Turning a bend in the road, he saw a transit bus lying on its side. Moving closer to it, he stopped at the rear window, the blood splatter glistening in the sun from the inside like crystals.

He stared at his reflection again and this time studied his features better.

Where once his clean shaven face and dark blue eyes would have looked back at him, instead he saw a mask of death and decay. His black hair was falling out, only a few tufts still remaining, and his face was a pale white, his eyes matching the color, the pupils faded to nothing. He opened his mouth wide and where his white teeth and tongue would have been there was now a black orifice with a slug-like thing that flicked back and forth as he tried to talk. His teeth were stained brown and yellow, brown spots looking like dried blood in-between the molars.

He tried to cry out in his pain, but nothing came out except a guttural growl, a moaning lost with the wind.

He slumped to the street and hung his head low, wishing he could cry, but decayed tear ducts not letting him. He didn't know how long he sat there, but as the sun reached its zenith, a crowd appeared from the end of the street and slowly made its way towards him. When they had reached him, the first one in line held out a rotten hand missing three fingers for him to take.

"Come with us, Jeremy, we'll make things better than they were before. You're welcome with us."

Jeremy gazed up at the dead faces and then looked to the leader. Then he reached out and took the proffered hand. When he was standing, multiple pale hands slapped his shoulders and rubbed his arms, grunts of acceptance coming from parched lips.

He was led down the street as more of the dead gathered around them.

And as Jeremy moved along with them, he suddenly felt his still heart beat once with hope, that maybe things wouldn't be so bad, and in fact, maybe they would actually be better.

He stirred on the bed he was using for the night, still feeling the gentle caress of the zombies as they led him to a brighter future, but then he opened his eyes and came to his senses, realizing he was in a furniture store in a shopping mall filled with the undead.

But if he had been only dreaming, then why did he feel a warm hand on his chest? Oh wait, that same hand was moving lower to his underwear, his pants lying on the floor at the foot of the bed.

His body went taut as he tried to understand what was happening and then he heard a seductive voice in his ear.

"Relax, hon, I just thought you could use some attention. Lord knows I could."

He rolled over onto his back and in the dark gloom of the store he saw the ebony face of Val looking back at him.

"Val?" He asked in a groggy voice.

"Shhh, don't talk too loud, the others are nearby; they don't need to know what we're about to do."

"And that is?" Jeremy asked, still baffled and a little foggy from his dream.

"This," she stated and leaned in and kissed him softly, her tongue slipping between his front teeth to wiggle his tongue. The feeling was electric, and like a lightning strike, the blood shot through his body straight to his now growing erection.

While Jeremy may have been a slacker in most things in life, he'd already been between the sheets with a woman more than once and wasn't about to let this once in a lifetime opportunity get away, so while she kissed him passionately, he wrapped his arms around her and brought her closer.

In the darkness of the store, she was only a dim shape, but his hands filled in the blanks for what his eyes couldn't see. She was warm and soft and when he reached between her legs he found the softness therein, and slid one finger inside of her. She gasped with pleasure, ignoring her warning of a second ago, and kissed him harder, her tongue dancing inside his mouth.

He was rock hard now and she reached down herself and wrapped one hand around him, stroking him gently.

He was already feeling like he was going to explode and so he removed her hand, though he did it casually enough she didn't give it much thought.

Then he pushed her to the bed and began kneading her breasts, taking each nipple between his teeth and gently biting them just enough to illicit another gasp from her.

"Oh, be nice, you," she breathed as she slapped him playfully on the cheek.

He didn't reply, nor did he need to, and as he sucked on each dark nipple, he slid out of his underwear, Val doing the same with her own nightclothes.

Soon he was inside her, stroking in a steady rhythm while her head was buried in a pillow so she wouldn't make any noise.

Jeremy could barely see her face, but her eyes picked up the ambient light and reflected it back to him, and he found it even more arousing. The idea of not seeing his lover, to not see her face, was more intoxicating than he could ever have imagined.

He felt himself coming to the breaking point and Val sensed this too and buried her face into his chest, her hot breath warming his skin as he pumped for all he was worth.

His eyes were closed now, lost in a world of pleasure. His entire body was concentrated at the end of his member as he slowly felt himself climaxing.

Then, when he could stand no more, he knew it was time, and he prepared to pull out, not wanting to get her pregnant when she whispered huskily into his ear.

"No, baby, stay in me, cum in me. I can't get pregnant."

That filled him with even more pleasure to finish the way nature intended, the way he always wanted to, but would have to fight the natural urge to stay in and yet pull out every time.

Grunting three more times in excitement, he felt his world explode and small flashes of light filled his eyes as he erupted inside of her. She moaned in pleasure and bit down on his right nipple, the pain causing him to gasp himself, the pain and pleasure mixing to make this one of the best orgasms of his life.

Then he was spent and he dropped on top of her, the two melding into one person as each enjoyed the after glow of sex.

"Wow, Val, that was intense," he said into the nape of her neck.

"Yeah, it was, baby, you're damn good for your age."

Then she gently pushed him off and she rolled off the bed, sitting up and reaching down to retrieve her clothing. Jeremy stretched out as he watched her in the shadows, not quite understanding what she was doing.

"What up?"

"Nothin's up, hon, that was great and I thank you for it. But now it's over and I'm going back to my bed. Plus, I want to go check on my Momma."

Jeremy felt perplexed. "Really? You're just gonna leave like that?"

She shrugged, but in the gloom it was barely perceived by him.

"And why wouldn't I?" Then she paused, thinking. "Oh, wait a sec', you don't think this meant anything, did you? Look, hon, it was great, really, but I'm not looking for a relationship. I just needed to get my groove on. You okay with that?"

Jeremy hesitated for a second, taking it all in. Slowly it sank in that he'd just been used for sex, like men did to women thousands of times daily when they met them at bars or even in marriages.

"Uh, yeah, I guess so, it's just..."

"It's just nothin'. Look, we can do this again, too, sometime if you want, just don't make a thing of it, okay?" She stood up and leaned over and kissed him on the lips, a peck really. "Thanks for a fun night. I'll see you in the morning."

Before Jeremy could reply, she was padding away to be lost in the darkness.

Jeremy stared at the ceiling, listening to the moaning undead coming from outside the store, and he shook his head, a little shocked at what had just happened.

"Holy shit, I think I just got taken advantage of." There was silence then as he breathed in and out, then he smiled in the dark. "Cool," he said with a wide grin, and after stretching, rolled over and went back to sleep.

This time, with the exertions just committed, he slept dreamless, his slumber devoid of nightmares.

* * *

On the morning of the fourth day in the shopping mall, as the four survivors were sitting around the table they used regularly for their meals, Rob raised something he had been hesitant to bring up.

"Look, guys, it's been almost a full four days and we're already low on water and food. We need to go downstairs and get what's in that CVS."

"Maybe we don't have to go there. The food court is on the first floor, too, and it's at the other end of the mall," Jeremy suggested and turned to look across the table to Val. She wasn't looking at him and he wished she would. She had treated that first night of sex as if it had never happened, and truth be told, Jeremy wanted it to happen again. But every time he tried to get something going she would shut him down. "Hey, Val, can we get to the food court? There's got to be a lot of food there."

Val shook her head, her ebony tresses flowing about her head. Jeremy thought she looked beautiful, the sex from that first night more than enough to cause him to fall head over heels for her.

"No way, if you think I said the CVS was bad, then you don't want to go to the food court. It seems to be one of the places they hang out. Maybe it's all the meat in the walk-ins, which should be real ripe by now, but they always seem to wander back there, well, there, the CVS and the Build-a-Bear store on the south corner.

"Build-a-Bear? Why would they go there?" Karen asked.

Val shrugged. "Got me, but they seem to hang out there, too."

"Maybe they're makin' zombie bears and undead dolls. Hell, it could be the new thing," Jeremy joked as he chomped down one of their last snack bars.

"This isn't funny, Jeremy, and I wish you'd take this more seriously," Rob said in a stern voice. "If we don't get food and fluids, we'll die a very painful death."

Jeremy swallowed the last of his bar and tossed the wrapper to a small waste can a few feet away. The wrapper missed and he smiled wanly.

"I'll pick it up when I get up, I promise," he said to anyone who cared. Then he looked back to Rob. "Okay, Rob, if food's an issue, why don't we just get outta here? Why stay at all? There's lots of places out there in the big old world with food."

Rob shook his head. "That's not an option right now, son. Have you gone out on the roof lately?"

"No, why?"

"Well, I did last night before we all went to bed and there's got to be hundreds of them out there. And we don't have anyway to get through 'em." He shook his head sadly. "No, son, I'm afraid we're stuck here until help comes and gets us out."

Karen looked to Val, who looked back, and then Karen cast a glance to Jeremy who looked to Rob, who in turn looked at each of them. As they stared at one another, minds were working, debating his words and it was Val who finally spoke up, solidifying what they were all thinking.

"Dammit if the old fart isn't right, guys. We really don't have a choice. I told you before I've wanted to take a crack at that store again, but didn't have the numbers. With you people with me, I just might be able to pull it off. There's enough soda, juice and bottled water to last us a good long while. Not to mention all the canned goods, chips and cup o' noodles." She flashed Rob a wide smile, her teeth perfect.

"I'm with ya, old man, but if we do this, we need to do it my way or we don't do it at all."

Rob nodded, not liking being called old man, but not about to start trouble now that Val was on his side for a change.

"Fair enough, and do I get my gun back when we do?"

Val smiled slightly. "We'll see how it goes on that one. Just because you've been here for a few days still doesn't mean I trust you."

Rob took his right hand off the table and made it into a fist.

Damn, he almost had his weapon back. If things didn't change fast, he was going to have no choice but try something drastic. So far he'd gone along with it because they had seemed safe up here on the second floor. But if they were going down into a den of the ghouls, then he would need his weapon back or he would be going on a suicide run. And though he may love God, he wasn't in a rush to meet him anytime soon.

"Fine, Val, we'll do it your way, but me getting my gun back isn't over."

She grinned. "Maybe, Rob, maybe." She leaned forward on the table, as if she was going to tell them a secret. "Okay, guys, now here's how we're gonna do it, but I'm sorry to say you might not like it all that much, but it's the only way."

And then she spelled out exactly how they would infiltrate the zombies and raid the CVS.

* * *

The four survivors stood at the balcony at the far end of the shopping mall that overlooked the CVS.

From the opposite side of the mall came the sounds of music, a hard rock band with crashing drums, deep bass and riveting guitar solos.

Below the balcony, the first floor hallway was devoid of movement.

"Are you sure this is gonna work?" Jeremy asked while wearing a look of disgust.

"It's worked before, hon," Val told him, "and it'll work this time. Now let's get going. The music only distracts them for a little while and the batteries won't last forever with the cd cranked so loud."

She dropped the rope off the balcony, securing the end to a metal grating of a Starbucks. Inside the coffee shop there was only empty shelving. What had remained after everyone had abandoned the store was quickly eaten by Val and her mother more than a week ago. There wasn't much for food or drink left on the second floor, only clothing and shoe stores, plus two book stores. And though Val loved to read, she couldn't eat books.

"Good luck," Karen said somewhat cheerfully. She was holding her hand over her nose, trying to keep out the smell of the others. It had been agreed she would stay behind and be a lookout, as she had a great view of the lower hallway in both directions. Plus, she wasn't as agile as the others and had already shown she had trouble climbing the rope.

So she would remain behind. And as she looked at her three friends, she was very glad that was so. At least she was able to remain clean, and wasn't covered in blood and gore.

Val, Rob, and Jeremy stood in front of her, each covered from head to toe in a glistening pudding of blood, tissue and body parts.

Val had managed to convince Rob and Jeremy that wearing the meat covering was the only way to get inside the CVS and attempt to steal the food and supplies they needed without being attacked and killed.

So Val had used a noose and had hooked a ghoul around the neck from the second floor balcony, and with the help of the others, had hauled the ghoul up to the second floor, and once over the railing, the four of them had promptly killed the dead man again. Val had used her sword while Rob kicked the ghoul in the chest, knocking the man back to the floor when he had attempted to rise. With one clean slice, Val had chopped off the man's head, the head rolling for a few feet before coming to a stop. Even severed, the mouth and eyes worked, though no sound issued from the severed voice box. Disgusted, Karen had tossed a sheet over the head and wrapped it up. Setting it to the side of the hall, they would dispose of it later.

Then, to all three survivors shock, Val had gutted the man like a fish, pulling out the entrails and organs like she was cleaning a flounder.

"Here," she had told Rob. "Put these on your jackets and stick some of them out of your pants. Use those fish hooks and the twine over there to tie some wherever you can't make it stick."

Rob had been hesitant at first, but when Jeremy had begun doing as he was instructed, he'd decided he wasn't about to show weakness in the eyes of the two women watching him. If Jeremy, basically still a boy compared to Rob, could do it, so could he.

So they had draped themselves in human body parts and lathered the black and red-brown blood in their hair and on their necks, rubbing it on their arms like it was lotion. When they were done, with maggots crawling here and there, they looked like any zombie occupying the mall, except for their wide eyes filled with color and life.

"Oh my Lord, I can't believe how bad this smells," Rob said as he finished lathering his hands.

"You think it's bad now, wait until a few hours have gone by," Val told him as she finished cutting meat and liver and began hooking it to her jumpsuit. She was wearing the one she had worn upon first meeting the survivors, and it was rank to the point of wanting to turn stomachs.

Karen took an extra step back and waved her hand in front of her face, but it did no good.

Val stood tall, and finished slapping blood and guts on her. Gobbets of meat dropped onto the floor and slid off her torso, flies gathering around them by the hundreds.

Karen took another step back and admired the three pretend zombies.

"You know, I've got to give Val credit, Rob, you guys really do look like them."

"Smell like them, too," Jeremy added. "So can we get this done or what?"

"Yes, hon, you're right, let's go while the gettin's good. And remember, no one talk. They hear you talk and they'll know you're not one of them."

Without waiting to see if Rob and Jeremy were behind her, she grabbed the rope and slid over the side, then climbed down, her sword hanging from a strap over her back.

"After you, old man," Jeremy grinned.

"Don't call me that, you hear me? I don't like it," Rob snarled angrily.

Jeremy held up his blood coated hands. "Okay, okay, lighten up, sheesh."

Rob said nothing in reply, but went to the rope and slid over, then lowered himself to the ground. He had a large cleaver hanging from a leather strap, something found in a cutlery store. They had mostly small knives and utensils, but the cleaver would work in a pinch. Now he just needed to get his Magnum back, which was stuck in the waist band of Val's pants.

Jeremy was last over the railing, and just before he slid over, Karen called to him.

"Good luck," she said, "and be careful."

He flashed a sly smile at her as he began to climb down.

"Always, Karen, careful is my middle name, ya know." Then he was gone from sight.

Karen went to the railing, avoiding the gutted corpse on the floor and wrapped her arms around her body for comfort as she watched Jeremy touch down on the floor, then the three of them moved into the CVS.

Now all she could do was wait and hope they returned in one piece.

* * *

Val was in the lead as the three gore covered humans entered the CVS. Debris was everywhere, looking like a hurricane had passed through the store. Packages of food and medicine littered every inch of the floor and it was all they could do to stop themselves from tripping.

The illumination was almost zero, thanks to the power being out, and it was only the subtle light spilling in from the hallway that allowed them to see anything at all. The light from the hallway was thanks to the skylights built into the mall ceilings to allow natural light and to save on electricity.

Val slowed as they approached the first group of zombies. There were five standing together, three of which held packages in their hands. In the dim light, they almost looked like customers who were searching for just the right brand of cough medicine or perhaps allergy pills.

From the other aisles, more scuffling and movement could be heard, signifying that there were many more ghouls inside the store with them. Val turned to look at Rob and Jeremy and raised her index finger to her lips, telling them to both be silent.

Then she moved to the next aisle and began raiding the shelf of bottles of soda and juice.

Both Jeremy and Rob had baskets taken from the front of the store and they began taking cookies and crackers from the shelves. It wasn't long before their small baskets were filled and they carried them back to the front of the store, then returned with new, empty baskets.

But Val wasn't just looking for food on this supply run, oh no, she wanted a little payback, and when she spotted a lone ghoul standing in the far corner of the store, she decided she would start with him.

As she moved closer, the ghoul glanced up at her. The dead man still wore his once white pharmacist's jacket and his wire rimmed glasses still sat on his nose, though slightly askew. Bloody drool slipped from his open mouth and his slack-jawed expression peeked out from behind sunken eyes in protruding sockets, the decay on his flesh was apparent. Though it had been weeks since the dead rose and slaughtered the living, the human body was fragile, and once dead, bacteria quickly set in, rotting the walking cadavers from the inside out.

This dead man was no different, having mottled gray and green flesh, mixed with patches of white. Maggots and blowflies crawled in and out of his ears and up his nose, the ghoul paying them no mind and instead continuing to move the items on the shelf he was standing in front of.

Val crooked her head to the side, curious about this oddity. It was like the ghoul was stocking the shelf, like the dead man had done in his past life, before becoming the walking dead.

Then Val shook the curiosity away, deciding it didn't matter.

Rob and Jeremy were in the next aisle, the two men filling baskets as fast as they could.

Val decided it was now or never, so with three smooth steps, she moved up behind the ghoul, raised her sword over her head, and with a meaty thwack, sliced the ghoul's skull in half.

She felt the blow up her arms and she gritted her teeth to stop from crying out, but the razor-sharp blade did its job well.

The ghoul's head was sliced in twain, the two sides falling away to leave the head looking like a peeled orange with two separate pieces. Blood shot upward and danced for a second and then the dark red fountain slowed. The hands of the dead man became spastic and the items he'd been stocking were knocked to the floor, rattling as they struck other plastic containers. The dead man fell to the ground loudly, taking half a row of aspirin bottles with him, and when Val turned away from her kill, satisfied, she was greeted by five more ghouls who had been attracted to the noise she'd just made.

She stood stock still, letting her disguise do the work for her, but it appeared there was something wrong. One at a time, in single file, the ghouls began moving towards her, eyes locked onto her face.

"Shit, I was afraid this might happen," she muttered under her breath as she raised her sword over her head for another killing blow. Over the past week, some of the ghouls had become wise to her disguise, though for the life of her she had no idea how or why. It appeared some of them were learning, though at the rate of a one-year-old, but still, they were learning nonetheless.

And now she was trapped in an aisle with five of them coming towards her.

Then she remembered the Magnum in her waist band and decided she might as well even the odds a little bit better before having to get in close and personal, so lowering her sword, she prepared to blow the head off the first ghoul in line, but just as she prepared to fire, another zombie came up behind her, taking her off guard.

The ghoul grabbed her arm, knocking the gun to the floor, where it slid a few feet on the plastic bottles before coming to rest near the end of the aisle.

"Shit!" Val screamed, kicking the ghoul who grabbed her away from her as she brought up her sword again, and with a backward swipe, sliced the hand off the ghoul attacking her. Blood shot from the stump to coat the shelves scarlet and Val followed that blow with one to the ghoul's left eye socket.

The sword slid through the eye, puncturing it like a rotten grape, and continued into the brain. She twisted the blade a few times, churning the brain matter to pulp while the sword scraped on the edges of the socket. The ghoul dropped away, its brain sliced to ribbons, the sword stuck in its eye socket.

But she wasn't in time to stop the other zombies who had been coming for her, and as she tried to pull her sword free, she realized it wasn't going to be in time to stop the other ghouls from reaching her.

Gritting her teeth, she redoubled her efforts, though she knew she would be too late.

It looked like she would be joining her mother in death in less time than it would take to let out the breath locked in her chest.

* * *

Rob was filling his fifth basket when he heard Val curse from the other aisle. He turned to look at Jeremy who only shrugged, his eyes wide with panic.

Jeremy only had a hunting knife for defense, Val telling him his disguise would be more than enough for protection.

"Besides," she had told him earlier, "if they figure out you're not one of them, there's gonna be way too many for one knife or club to do any good."

Deciding he needed to investigate, Rob dropped his basket and gestured to Jeremy that he was going to see if Val was all right. Jeremy only nodded, as no more than six feet away a female ghoul was standing, her hands playing with allergy medicine on the shelf. In the dim light, she resembled any old shopper on any given day, who was trying to pick the right brand of medicine to combat her hay fever.

Rob moved through the aisles, careful not to fall on the debris littering the floor. Open soda bottles had soaked into the commercial grade carpeting and his boots squished under the liquid, making his footing more precarious than walking on ice.

As he rounded the end cap of the aisle, he saw the backs of four ghouls and in between their swaying heads, he saw Val's face in the dull gloom.

She looked scared, something Rob hadn't seen her show any of them before, and he could see why. She was trapped between the four ghouls in front of her and it looked like there was three more coming up from behind her.

She was trapped with nowhere to go.

While Rob moved closer, not knowing how he could help, his foot kicked something heavy and metallic. Looking down, he saw the barrel of his Magnum reflecting the dim light and his heart filled with elation.

In one smooth motion, he bent over and picked it up, the grip feeling good in his hand, cringing at the blood he got on the handle thanks to his filthy palm, but he felt infinitely better with the heavy weight in his palm.

Checking to make sure it was loaded; he flicked off the safety and lined up the ghoul closest to Val. It was a tight shot as he had to miss the other swaying heads and hit the one about to reach Val. And to top it off, if he missed, it was very likely he could hit Val, whose head was in the same line of fire.

Deciding there was no choice; he raised the gun and yelled out to Val.

"Get down, now!" Then he fired, the .357 round streaking through the air like lightning and impacting the back of the zombie's skull like the ghoul had been bitch slapped by a giant hand.

Val dropped to her knees and glanced up at the sound of the gunshot. She stared in shock as the face of the ghoul seemed to explode outward, the nose spinning into the air and bouncing off the top of her head before falling away.

The left eye of the zombie flew through the air like a ping pong ball to land on the top shelf to her right. From there it rolled across the shelf until dropping to the floor, where it was promptly stomped on by a stumbling ghoul. The orb squirted a jello-like viscous fluid out from under the ghoul's foot, causing the gelatinous ooze to coat the floor. The sole of the zombie slid in the fluid like it was a banana peel and the zombie went into the air, crashing to the floor on its back with enough force to knock the wind from a living human.

But the ghoul was dead and so merely waddled on its back while trying to right itself, its brethren walking over it as they passed by.

At the sound of the gunshot and Rob's warning, all the zombies spun about, now looking at him with renewed interest.

"Oh, boy, that wasn't so smart, was it," Rob mumbled to himself as he lined up another head in his gun sights. It was as he was about to fire that he realized he was also being surrounded, two more ghouls coming up on him from behind.

He cast a glance over his shoulder and realized he couldn't fire at both groups at the same time and so either way he was going to be attacked; the question was by which group.

In the back of the aisle, he could hear Val cutting a swath through the zombies, her sword flashing in the gloom like caged lightning. The sounds of falling limbs and organs splashing to the floor floated on the air and the stench of death became even stronger when bile splattered everywhere.

Rob decided to fire at the ghouls going for Val, but they had spun at his gunshot, now wanting him, and so lining up a zombie, he shot the next one in the face, the back of its skull flying off to dance in the air.

Behind him, he could hear footsteps and guttural growls and knew he was close to his end, but he decided if he was going to go down, then he would take as many of the dead with him as he could manage.

He shot another in the face, but his aim was off, the bullet striking the zombie in the neck. Dark blood shot from the wound and once again Rob wondered how this could be so. If they were dead, then how could the heart still be pumping? But then matters of biology were lost as he lined up yet another in his sights.

Then he heard the first ghoul coming up behind him and knew he was out of time.

The one in front of him was almost on him and he had no choice but to fire. So with the gun shot filling the store, he turned at the last second to stare at the dead face of a woman, her mascara now running down her face and her lipstick smeared like she was a clown at the local circus.

Rob raised his hands, hoping he could get the gun up in time, but as the dead woman leaned in to bite him, he knew he would be too slow.

In the gloom of the store, another shadow appeared behind the woman, mixed in with the other ghouls approaching him, and it was only when the dead woman halted her progress that Rob realized there was something stopping her from attacking him. In the gloom, Rob could barely see that the ghouls behind the woman were dropping to the floor one at a time like they were robots and someone was turning them off.

Then he saw the ghoul behind the dead woman, and when the zombie smiled, showing white teeth, he got a better look at the eyes and realized it was Jeremy.

He'd been sneaking up on the ghouls and stabbing each one in the back of the neck.

The dead woman slumped to the floor, and as she did, Jeremy was exposed to Rob, his knife held high where it had plunged into her brain stem, severing her brain from her body. As the dead woman slumped to the floor, his blade glistened with blood, and before Jeremy could do or say anything, more ghouls rounded the corner.

"Get over here with me," Rob yelled to him as he fired at the first ghoul in line. The zombie was struck in the shoulder and it spun around in a circle and dropped to the floor, but soon it was dragging itself along like a baby, not taking the time to right itself.

Val came up behind them and held her sword in front of her protectively.

"Thanks, Rob, I owe you one," she said as she eyed the ghouls approaching them.

"Save it until we're out of here in one piece," he replied, shooting another in the face, this one dropping to the floor like a sack of potatoes dropped by a lazy worker.

"Cover me, I want to reload," he said, reaching into his pocket. Val may have taken his gun, but he had kept possession of the extra bullets.

A zombie moved closer and Val swiped at it with her sword, lopping off its hands like they were branches on a dying tree. The ghoul waved its nubs around, not understanding why it couldn't grasp its prey, that is until Val jammed her blade into its mouth and twisted, severing the brain stem from the opposite side.

The ghoul dropped to the floor, sliding off the sword and Val prepared for the next attack.

But there were more coming, and in seconds they would be overwhelmed, despite Rob's marksmanship taking some out.

It was Jeremy who came up with an escape as he studied his surroundings.

"The shelves, we can climb onto the shelves and run to the front of the store!"

"What're you talking about, son? Speak clearly," Rob yelled as he snapped the cylinder closed and fired two quick shots at the first two ghouls, their heads blowing apart like watermelons with dynamite jammed into them.

"The damn shelves, Rob, we can climb on them and run across the top like a bridge, then jump off at the front, come on!" He turned and brushed off the items still on the shelf, using his knees and hands as he climbed the shelf like a ladder. They were strong and held his weight, and in seconds he was on top, standing tall.

"Come on, it's safe up here. They can't get us!"

Rob glanced up and saw Jeremy and realized the man's idea was sound. He pointed up to Val.

"You go next, I'll cover you," he snapped.

"No way, I told you I owe you. 'Sides, you're old and will need me to cover you, now stop talking and go," she snapped as she stabbed a ghoul in the stomach, then twisted the blade to the right and brought it up at an angle.

Entrails spilled out like a waterfall, drenching the shoes of the ghoul, and Val gagged from the stench. It was an overwhelming miasma of death and it took all her will not to vomit, knowing the time it took her to heave would allow the ghouls to reach her.

Rob shot two more in the upper body and then turned and began climbing. It was hard with the gun in his hand and he had no choice but to shove it in his waistband. The muzzle was hot and it burned his skin, but he ignored it.

"Give me a hand, son, I'm not as agile as you," Rob told Jeremy as he reached up to him. Jeremy grabbed Rob's wrists and pulled the older man up, almost falling over the opposite side when he overbalanced.

Val was last, and she slowly backed up, waving the long blade in front of her menacingly. But the undead were fearless and continued to advance.

Crunching bottles sounded from behind her and Val spun to see more advancing on her flank. She was trapped again and there was no time to try and scale the shelves.

Suddenly, another gunshot filled the area and the zombie closet to her was knocked away. Half its head disappearing in a blinding spray of scarlet.

She took the opportunity and jumped onto its back, then lunged upward for the top of the shelf.

Jeremy was there and he caught her left hand, the right still holding the sword.

"Let go of the sword so you can get a better grip!" he yelled to her.

"Not on your life, hon, this sword is a part of me!" she yelled back and her legs kicked under her for purchase.

"Oh, Jesus Christ, I don't believe this," Jeremy yelled back as he tried to pull her up, but she was about his size and he wasn't strong enough.

Val kicked out, her right foot connecting with the chin of a zombie, the ghoul falling away to crash into another shelf, then she struggled to get some purchase on the shelves below her.

Then she felt hands wrap around her legs and there was a slight tug downward.

"Oh shit, they got me. Pull me up, damn it!"

"I'm, trying, you're too heavy!"

Another gunshot sounded and the death grip on her legs loosened. Val swung her legs inward and then she was climbing up the shelves, Jeremy helping her until she'd reached the top.

The ghouls were only a foot below them, but they weren't agile enough to climb up, and the three weary warriors stood still, staring down at the pale, gnarled hands reaching up for them.

"Come on, let's get outta here," Jeremy said as he began jogging across the shelf, careful not to lose his balance.

"That," Rob said, "is a good idea."

Val said nothing, too shook up from her brush with death.

It didn't take them long to reach the edge of the shelf, and with one long jump, Jeremy jumped down to the floor, rolling and coming up in a crouch. Pieces of his meat disguise were knocked off, leaving parts of his arms and legs now exposed with nothing to hide him from the dead. Rob was a little slower climbing down and Val jumped similar to Jeremy. Once they were down on the floor again, they headed out into the hallway and back to Karen who should be waiting for them with the rope, the ghouls still climbing over one another to reach them. But they got in each other's way like a bunch of shoppers at a white sale.

"Wait a second," Val said as they moved to the rope. "I don't hear the music anymore."

Upon reaching the balcony where Karen should be, Jeremy glanced up to see she wasn't there, nor was the rope they needed to escape the first floor.

"Yeah, and Karen's not up there, either," Jeremy said. "Should I call out to her? Maybe she's up there, but not near the railing."

"No, son, you'll only alert every one of them that we're here."

"Little late for that, isn't it?" Jeremy asked as he pointed down the hallway.

Rob and Val followed his gesture and both gasped in shock and awe.

With the music off, all the ghouls in the mall had heard the gunshots and screaming from the three survivors and were now approaching at a steady clip. If they had taken a few minutes longer in the CVS, all three of them would have found themselves totally trapped with dozens of bodies blocking the entrance.

"Oh, shit, that's not good," Val said and held her sword up in front of her. But though a warrior at heart, even she knew the odds were against them.

"On second thought, son, go 'head and call her," Rob said as he quickly emptied out the spent shells and slid in new ones. At least he would be able to take down five of the creatures before he was overwhelmed, and then he would make sure to save one bullet for himself. Oh, no, he wasn't going out like that. Ripped apart to come back and walk around. He would have a clean death and hope the Lord would forgive him for taking his own life. Even He had to give in with extenuating circumstances such as they were.

Just as Rob finished loading the Magnum, a rope dropped over the side, but the ghouls were seconds away. Rob was preparing to fire when Val held her hand up, stopping him.

"No, wait a sec," she hissed in a low voice. "I don't think they know we're not one of them yet, let's see how this goes. Once they move past us, we can climb up."

Rob was hesitant, but there were too many to shoot and not enough time to climb, so he nodded, knowing they had no choice.

Jeremy moved close to Val and mumbled to her under his breath. "Man, Val, I don't like this at all."

"Just be cool, hon, and it'll all be over in a second," she said with slightly more confidence than she felt.

Then the ghouls were surrounding them, some walking past while others slowed to investigate the three of them.

Jeremy stood stock still, not wanting to move and risk being discovered. A female ghoul with dirty blonde hair matted with blood and her left eye hanging out by a few tendrils had found him particularly interesting. She was staring at him, moving her face up and down as she sniffed him like a wild animal. Jeremy tried not to breathe, not knowing what would give him away.

But what he didn't know was that from all his running, jumping and rolling around, most of the meat and gore covering him had come off, and the female ghoul could detect the underlying smell of *life* on him.

She uttered a low moan and Jeremy inhaled her body odor, his stomach heaving inside him. It was like going to a garbage dump filled with the watery waste of a thousand trash runs and sucking in a deep breath so that the odor seemed to suffuse your body.

He felt the bile in his throat and he forced it down, knowing if he threw up now, he was lost. But the ghoul wouldn't stop and her mouth moved next to his groin, sniffing like a dog.

Jeremy gulped deeply and let out a squeak and Rob prepared to shoot the dead woman in the head if she so much as looked like she was going to attack Jeremy. But then a dead man in a postal uniform took an interest in Rob. The dead man was bald and slightly overweight, and Rob couldn't help but wonder how a man who had walked his entire life in the performance of his job could be fat. The man had a large chunk of his throat missing and Rob could hear the air wheezing in and out of the opening, black and red bubbles frothing with each breath the ghoul made. Once more he marveled why the ghoul breathed at all. When you were dead you needed no oxygen, but perhaps when the body revived after death the organs just began working again, whether they were needed or not. It was like the entire internal organs of this ghoul were a large appendix; there, but not needed any longer.

Val had her own troubles, thanks to two old, dead men taking an interest in her. One was still wearing the toupee he had proudly worn in life and the other had a nose so big it looked like an eggplant was glued to his face, the tip dark and purple with blotches of red and black. Both had large gaping wounds on their faces and one was missing all the fingers on his right hand. They were a motley bunch and they had taken a definite shine to Val.

None of them talked, knowing to utter one word would be their doom. At the moment the zombies were just curious, but one spoken word would inform them they were food and not of their kind.

Rob swallowed deeply, turning his face to the side as the postal worker sniffed his head, but luckily there was enough blood and diseased, dead flesh still on him to throw off his scent.

Not so with Jeremy. It didn't take long for the female ghoul to know Jeremy was definitely not right, and before the young man could do anything, the dead woman opened her jaws wide and sank her teeth into Jeremy's arm.

Jeremy had time for one scream and then he felt the pressure on his skin.

With his scream of pain and terror, the other ghouls were jolted to action, Rob shooting the postal worker under the chin, the bullet shooting straight up into his brain and out the top of his skull, blood and brains rising and then dropping to the floor like rain, coating all within a few feet of the decapitated ghoul.

Val pushed the two old men away from her, and with one swipe, slashed both their wrinkled heads from their shoulders in one smooth motion, both heads rolling away like off-balance bowling balls, the toupee landing on the floor like a bloody pelt.

And then the three backed up against one another and all hell broke loose as the ghouls turned and attacked, wanting blood for flesh or vice versa.

In the end it wouldn't matter as dead would still be dead.

* * *

No one spoke as they prepared to be torn apart, but just as the first group of ghouls went in for the attack, a large object dropped down from above and flattened them like a paper cup smashed by a giant hand.

The crash of the heavy, mahogany bureau filled the hallway, wood splinters and blood flying everywhere, and it was Rob who glanced up in time to see an ottoman come tumbling over the railing to flatten two more ghouls into bloody pudding.

As Rob stared at the railing, he saw Karen's sweaty face appear. She was flushed with the exertion of picking up the furniture and heaving it over the side and she waved to them to run for it as she tossed an end table followed by two lamps.

The lamps shattered over a skull each, slicing into scalps and causing tuffs of bloody hair to fall away while the end table hit a ghoul straight on the head, snapping its neck with the weight and causing it to fall over, its head now bent at an unnatural angle. The other ghouls ignored the wounds and continued forward.

"Go! Go now while they're distracted. Get to the stairs!"

Rob didn't reply. But instead grabbed Val and Jeremy by the arms and pushed them through the crowd of ghouls.

"What're you doing?" Val asked as she felt herself being pulled along. She wasn't idle however and her sword was singing a song of death as she hacked and slashed. Rob fired point blank into a ghoul's mouth, blowing out the back of its head and then they were away from the main pack.

The ghouls didn't understand at first what had happened, and were looking for their food, but then one turned around and saw the three refugees moving away.

With a moan and wail, it turned and moved after them, the others following like toddlers huddled together for a walk at day-care.

But Karen wasn't finished, and she continued dropping furniture on them, kitchen chairs, a small table and a microwave cart. Whatever was closest to hand.

The assault of household furniture devastated the undead masses, making them separate as they had to move around the refuse and debris. That gave Rob, Jeremy and Val the chance they needed to escape. Rob and the others were faster, and as they sprinted down the hallway, they knocked ghouls aside, their living bodies far more agile than their undead foes.

"Where're we going?" Val screamed and slowed her movements so Rob had to stop or let her go. Luckily, they were in an area devoid of zombies so they had a few seconds to talk, but not much.

"Karen dropped that stuff on them and saved our butts," Rob explained. "She said to get to the stairs."

"Why? What's there? I blocked them off, remember?" Val asked.

"Don't know, but it has to be better than where we were."

Rob glanced at Jeremy who was holding his arm, cradling it like a wounded bird with a bad wing.

"You okay, son?"

Jeremy shook his head. "Don't know. One of them bit me, Rob. Oh, shit, man, I don't want to turn into one of them," he gasped.

Rob frowned, realizing what that meant and for a second he almost raised the Magnum to do what would have to be done eventually. But then he saw the look in Jeremy's eyes and stopped himself.

"We'll deal with it later, son. That is, if we're alive later. Now, come on, let's get to the stairs, hopefully Karen has a trick up her sleeve."

Zombies were approaching, more than two dozen, and the sounds of footsteps slapping the once-polished floor echoed down the halls like they were a mausoleum, which wasn't far from the truth.

Val was back to her old self again and she took the lead, the two men following her as they made their way to the opposite end of the building and the blocked stairs.

There were more ghouls heading for them and they had seconds before they would end up being in the exact same situation all over again. So far, their only advantage was being quicker than the undead. If they were ever surrounded, it would be all over. There would be no way to fight off so many and the ghouls felt no pain. They would simply swarm around them and smother them, while taking casualties to their numbers.

Upon arriving at the stairs, the three survivors stared at the wreckage of furniture and debris Val had piled onto them.

"Great, so what do we do now? It's not like we can climb over all that stuff," Jeremy said. His arm hurt, but not as bad as he would have thought and he wanted to check out how bad he'd been bit, but there was no time. With his leather jacket on the wound was hidden and it was driving him crazy, though he knew what he'd find and didn't want to see it.

"Oh, shit, here they come," Val said as she turned at the sounds of the undead. They were approaching quickly and in less than a minute there would be far too many to stop.

There was a loud, slapping sound of footsteps coming from the second floor to their right and all three of them glanced up to see Karen hit the railing at top speed and hold her finger in a *wait a second* gesture. Then she disappeared from view.

Rob, Val and Jeremy said nothing as there wasn't much to say.

What could Karen do to save them? Not much. She had no weapons and unless she planned on dropping more furniture on the ghouls, there was nothing else she could do to help.

"You know, in the movie, it wasn't that hard to take back the mall from the zombies. It should be easier than this," Jeremy said as he watched ghouls moving closer.

Rob glanced at Jeremy. "Son, I have no idea what you're talking about, but I do know this. I think going to the CVS was a bad idea,"

"Oh, really, and what gave you that bright idea?" Val snapped.

"Hey, wait a second; don't blame me for it all. Your crazy scheme about wearing zombie guts and blood didn't go over so well, either," he snapped back.

Val turned and was about to say more to him when Jeremy stepped between them both.

"Uh, excuse me, you two, but I've been bit and I'm gonna die, but it probably doesn't matter cause in about a minute we're all about to get torn to pieces. How 'bout a little focus?"

Val closed her mouth and Rob looked down, his hand on the Magnum as he prepared to begin shooting at the ghouls.

"I can save three bullets for us," he said as he watched the first ghouls coming for them. It was a chilling scene and he felt his insides cringe. He wanted to scream in anger and terror, but he kept it inside.

"No way, hon, not me anyway. I'll go down fighting, thank you very much."

"Well then, get ready 'cause here they come!" Rob yelled and shot the closest ghoul in the face. The zombies were coming at them from both sides of the shopping mall. All the ones at the CVS from one side, and the other held every ghoul still pouring in from the open and shattered glass doors Rob had destroyed almost a week ago.

They had twenty seconds before they were encircled and just as Rob prepared to shoot another body, something dropped down and grazed his head and then bounced off his shoulder, causing him slight pain. He glanced down to see what had hit him and his eyes went wide when he saw the brass nozzle of a fire hose, the hose leading up and over the railing. At the railing, Karen's wide eyed and worried face glared back at him.

"Well, don't just stand there, get up here," she beamed, proud of her ingenuity.

"Jeremy, can you make it?" Rob asked him as he pointed to the hose. Jeremy nodded, not saying anything and quickly climbed up. His arm hurt where he'd been bit, but not as bad as he'd thought it would. In fact, it was feeling better with each passing second, which was weird.

"Val, you're next!" Rob called out.

"No way, hon, you go and then you can shoot 'em off me as I climb up!"

Rob couldn't refute the logic in that so he shot two ghouls that were almost on them, slid the Magnum into his waistband, and began climbing up. He felt a sharp pain in his chest as he climbed, but he forced it down, knowing he needed to get to the second floor quickly to help Val.

At the top, Karen and Jeremy were there to help him and he needed it. With a groan from his age, he was toppling over the side and hit the floor hard, wincing when his left elbow hit harder than he would like, causing his funny bone to alert him of its presence. Then he was rolling to his knees and peering over the railing.

Val was slicing and jabbing as she fought and it was easy to see she wasn't going to be able to turn around and climb. The instant she stopped slashing and hacking she was dead. She was like a dervish, taking off arms and hands, slicing heads from their shoulders like a warrior from a bygone age.

Then Rob got an idea and he leaned over the railing, shot two ghouls that were causing her trouble and yelled at Jeremy.

"Pull up that hose and tie it into a loop, and hurry!" he yelled as he shot another in the side of the head. He only had one or two bullets left, he'd lost count and there would be no time to reload.

Jeremy did as he was told and turned the bottom into a loop, favoring his wounded arm. Val realized the hose was gone and she yelled at them; wanting to know what they were doing.

Then Rob took the hose from Jeremy and dropped it back down to her.

"Step into the loop, Val, and we'll pull you up!" Rob called down.

She didn't answer; she had no breath to do so. Rob could only watch her in astonishment as she danced among the undead like an Amazonian warrior.

When she had a brief moment's reprieve, she looked down, saw the loop and stepped into it. The instant she did, Rob pulled it up, the noose going up and under her armpits.

She still kept slashing and Rob gave the hose to Karen and Jeremy.

"Pull, damn it, pull, or she's dead!"

Jeremy and Karen nodded and began pulling, walking backwards as they slowly brought Val up.

Rob leaned over the side, and when a ghoul wrapped his clammy dead hands on her right calf, he lined up the head and put a bullet right through the top of its cranium.

Then Val was free, and with one last slash at flailing fingers, she found herself out of reach of the undead.

Below her they wailed and reached for her, but like a Piñata pulled too high, she was safe from their grasp.

Then she was over the railing and tumbling to the floor, her sword falling next to her in a clatter; the blood dripping from it to pool on the tiles.

"Are you okay?" Karen asked as she moved next to Val. The woman was covered in fresh gore, gobbets of flesh hanging from her hair and upper body to blend with the old stuff.

She nodded, too exhausted to speak just yet.

"Yeah, think so, I'm pretty sure none of this blood is mine."

Rob leaned down and looked into her eyes. "That was some incredible sword play down there, Val, my compliments."

She looked into his eyes and saw no malice there, only adoration for a fellow warrior and she nodded.

"Thanks, Rob, you too. You saved my ass twice down there."

"Glad to do it."

He turned and moved away from her, wanting to see how Jeremy was doing when Val called out to him.

"Hey, Rob, you can keep the gun, in fact, I wish I hadn't taken it from you in the first place."

"Fair enough, apology accepted," he replied with a grin. The two had forged a friendship in battle and nothing more needed to be said.

Val let Karen help her up and she turned and leaned on the railing. The ghouls were massed in force below, some shaking their hands like they were at a rock concert and Val hocked up a load of phlegm and spit. She didn't see where it landed nor did she care.

With the ghouls clamoring for her flesh and the others with her, she turned away to deal with Jeremy. If he'd been bit like he'd said, then he was going to end up like her mother, and while Val had a soft spot for the young man, she didn't love him and knew there would be only one way it would have to go.

So picking up her sword, she raised it, flicked off the excess blood, and moved to Jeremy, knowing if she did it quick before he realized it was coming, he'd be dead before he hit the floor.

It was the least she could do for the young man.

And after that first night they had spent together in bed, she felt she owed him that anyway.

As she moved up behind Jeremy, prepared to take his head from his shoulders in one swipe, the young man had no idea death was only inches away.

* * *

Just a few short minutes before Val was raising her sword to behead Jeremy and put him out of his misery, Rob was inspecting where Jeremy had been bit.

"Go 'head, son, let's have a look and see how bad it is," Rob said as he helped Jeremy out of his leather jacket.

The jacket was a filthy mess of blood and gore and was useless now for anything but trash. When he had his arm out of the jacket and Rob was holding it, the older man tossed it to the floor, disgusted.

Jeremy was rolling up his shirt sleeve to inspect the bite and was shocked to see there was no blood.

Rob was looking, too, and he took hold of Jeremy's wrist.

"Well, I'll be, son, looks like you got off easy."

Jeremy raised his arm higher so he could inspect where the female ghoul's teeth had sunk in and he was pleasantly relieved to see no broken skin, only a few indentations where the ghoul's front teeth had pressed on the leather of his jacket sleeve, but hadn't pierced the material.

"I'm okay," he said in a hushed tone. "Oh my God, Rob, I'm okay, I'm not bit, I'm gonna live!"

Then he heard Val moving behind him and he glanced over his shoulder to see her coming at him, sword raised high, ready to take his head off.

"Whoa, no, stop! I'm okay, I'm okay!" he screamed while raising his hands in front of him, as if that could stop the steel blade.

Rob had taken a step back and he pulled his Magnum, now aiming it at Val, ready to shoot her if she attacked Jeremy.

Jeremy saw this and he shifted his other hand to Rob,

"No, man, don't, it's okay, she doesn't know I'm not bit, don't shoot her!"

"What the hell are you talking about, hon? You said you were bit, I heard you." She had lowered the sword slightly. "Don't make this any harder than it has to be. I'll make it quick, I promise." And then she raised the sword again and began bringing it downward, her shoulder muscles bringing it downward with all the power she could muster.

"No, Val, stop damn it, look, I'm okay, the zombie's teeth didn't get through the sleeve of my jacket!" He shoved his arm out so she could see for herself, and when she saw his smooth skin, no blood or broken skin, she stopped her swing and slowly lowered the sword.

She had been inches from his neck when she stopped the swing.

Jeremy gulped once as the sword was removed from the vicinity of his neck.

"Holy shit, hon, you are one lucky bastard, you know that?"

Jeremy grinned wanly.

"Yeah? Funny, I don't feel that way. After all, you were just about to take my head off, right?"

She chuckled as she leaned the sword over her shoulder, her elbow now pointing at Jeremy.

"Yeah, hon, but the trick is, I didn't, remember that." Then she turned and strolled away, giving Rob a wink as she passed him. Rob lowered the Magnum now that the episode was over.

"Hey, Val, wait a second," Jeremy called to her.

She stopped and turned slightly to see him. "What?"

"You really would have killed me?

She nodded. "Damn straight, hon. You get bit, you die, end of story."

"So, what about your mother then?" Rob asked.

"That's different, that's my mother. You guys are just people who came here and messed up my operation." She spun around and walked away.

Jeremy watched her go with a pained look on his features. "That hurts, man. I thought I meant something to her, even a little."

Rob patted him on the shoulder.

"I can't explain women to ya, son, sorry. I was married for almost half a century and I still don't know anything about the fairer sex."

Both Rob and Jeremy turned at the sound of Karen clearing her throat. She was watching them both, her arms crossed.

"What?" they asked her together.

She shook her head sadly and studied the floor for a moment, contemplating the idiocy that was called *man*.

"Glad you're okay, Jeremy," she said simply and walked away, leaving the two men alone.

"See what I mean?" Rob asked.

"Yeah, I guess I do," Jeremy replied

With no reason to stay where they were any longer, they turned and followed Karen while the undead wailed below.

* * *

The next day found Jeremy and Rob at the railing overlooking the CVS store.

Karen was feeling bored, and with Val on the roof she had no one to talk to, so closing the book she'd been reading, she'd decided to see what the men were doing.

As she approached them, she could see the blood pool where the zombie had been gutted for its insides, but the actual corpse was gone now, tossed over the railing hours ago. Looking up from the congealing blood on the floor, she saw Rob dropping a rope with a large hook on the end.

"Oh, so close; almost got one that time," Rob said as he pulled the rope back up and then tossed it down again, the hook clinking on the floor over the moans of the undead.

"Careful, one of them is gonna grab the rope," Jeremy told him as he watched the undead below.

"I see him, I see him, relax," Rob said as he pulled the rope back and then went through the process again.

"What're you guys doing?" Karen asked when she was close enough not to have to yell.

Jeremy glanced her way and shrugged. "Fishing," he said flatly, as if that said it all.

"Fishing? For what?" Karen asked perplexed.

Jeremy pointed to the CVS store and the baskets of food and bottled beverages at the front of the store.

"For them. Rob thought it was a shame we were so close to getting all that stuff and he came up with this idea. Pretty cool, huh?"

Karen watched Rob manage to hook a basket on the handle, then he began pulling in the rope, the basket sliding along the floor.

"Hey, you got one!" Jeremy exclaimed happily.

"Of course I did. Why, you doubted me?" Rob asked annoyed.

Jeremy smirked widely. "Well, yeah, kinda, I mean, we've been at it for almost an hour and that's the first one you landed. I thought you said you knew how to fish."

"I do know how to fish, son, but in case you haven't noticed, this ain't fishin'."

He pulled back the rope some more, the basket weaving in and around the ghouls, but then one of the ghouls found the basket curious and it reached down and stopped it, holding the basket from moving. Rob didn't want to pull it anymore or he would risk tipping the contents out and that would do none of them any good.

"Looks like that one's gonna get away," Karen said idly.

Rob handed the rope to Jeremy, made sure the younger man was holding it tightly, and then pulled his Magnum from his waistband.

"We'll see about that," he said and lined up the head of the ghoul holding the basket in his sights. He took his time, as there was no need to hurry.

"Like shootin' fish in a barrel," he said dryly and squeezed the trigger.

The shot was loud in the shopping mall and Karen winced from the echo, but the bullet found its mark.

The ghoul's head imploded and the back of its head erupted outward, spraying the floor and a few ghouls too close to it with blood and gore. The zombie slumped to the floor, dead for good, and the basket was free again.

Rob took the rope back and began pulling it again, the basket sliding without a problem. The other ghouls below never flinched, never so much as tried to escape when they heard the gunshot and watched one of their own be gunned down. That was their greatest strength and their greatest weakness, their apathy for self-survival.

When the basket was directly below him, Rob began to pull it upward, the basket swinging back and forth. A dead man with red hair and cracked lips tried to grasp the basket as it rose, but then it was out of reach and Rob was smiling. Jeremy reached out and grabbed the basket, pulling it to him with a cheer.

"Oh, sweet, look at all this shit!" He yelled as he inspected the juice, cookies and small bags of potato chips.

"Watch that mouth, son, I mean it. I don't like cursing, it's the devil's work," he said in a stern voice.

Jeremy looked up, saw Rob's serious countenance and nodded. "Yeah, Rob, sorry 'bout that. Got excited is all."

"Fine, but remember next time. Now, let's see if we can land a few more baskets today before we give up for the night."

Karen moved next to Jeremy and he handed her a bottle of water. She smiled, took it and drank half in one gulp, the flavorless water tasting like the sweetest nectar on her tongue.

"He never tells Val to stop swearing, you know that?" Jeremy said to her while Rob was occupied.

"Yeah, I know. I think he's scared of her, though he wouldn't admit it to us, or maybe even to himself."

"Really, ya think so?"

She nodded. "Yes, Jeremy, men like Rob are stuck in the fifties. He respects women and all, but at the same time feels a women should stay in what he thinks is their place in this world. I'm sure he was a great husband, took care of his wife and everything, but if she wanted to go out and work for herself, you know, get a job, I bet he wouldn't let her."

"What're you two gabbin' about over there like a couple of old hens?" Rob asked as he tried to land another basket. The hook went wide and he had to try again. Still, he was hopeful now that he had actually landed one.

"Nothing, Rob, just talking about stuff, you know, about everything that's happened to us. It's still all pretty crazy, huh?"

"I know what you mean. Just look at them down there and tell me this isn't the most ridiculous thing you ever saw. I mean, zombies? It's impossible right?"

"It's supposed to be," Karen said as she finished her water.

"Here, let me take that for you," Jeremy said and she smiled while handing it to him.

"Thanks, Jeremy, that's very nice of you," she said, expecting him to hold it until he could find a trash barrel. So when he casually flipped it over his shoulder to fall down to the first floor, she frowned deeply. The bottle bounced off the head of an old man and the ghoul blinked, but then continued to go on about its business of moaning and stumbling.

"Now, why did you do that? Hell, I could have done that," she told him.

"Then why didn't you?" he asked.

"Because it's littering, that's why."

He chuckled. "Littering? You can't be serious, Karen, look down there, will ya? There's body parts and corpses everywhere. I really don't think one water bottle is gonna matter."

"Well, still, just because things are rough right now doesn't mean we have to degenerate into slobs."

Jeremy was about to give her a witty rejoinder when Val came charging down the hallway, her arms pumping like she was running a marathon. Her sword was strapped to her back, the sheath slapping her shoulder blades as she moved, but she ignored it.

"Hey, guys, there's something happening outside, come on, you need to see this," she called as she slid on the floor, spun around, and dashed back the way she'd come, not looking to see if anyone was following her.

Rob pulled in the rope and dropped it to the floor. He could come back to the fishing thing later. Slapping Jeremy on the shoulder, he glanced at Karen.

"Come on, whatever's happening sounds interesting. Especially if it got her worked up like that," Rob stated and was off, jogging slowly down the hallway towards the stairwell that would lead to the roof.

"Well, I don't want to be left out, how 'bout you?" Jeremy asked.

"Let's go see what's so interesting," Karen said and the two ran off behind Rob, quickly catching up to him and then passing him by.

"Come on, old man, hurry up or the show's gonna be over by the time you get there," Jeremy teased when he passed Rob by.

"I told you not to call me that, now knock it off," Rob snapped at him, but then he was saving his breath for running, regretting once more how out of shape he was. While he ran, he couldn't help but wonder if Val had spotted the army or National Guard and that this was the help, the rescue, he'd been holding out for. Though it felt like months, it was hard to believe it had only been weeks.

* * *

Rob was the last one to reach the rooftop and he saw the other's attention was focused on something happening down below in the parking lot.

As he moved across the roof, he saw in the distance the fires that had been burning since he'd been at his house were at least moving the other way, the wind blowing the conflagration away from the shopping mall.

At least they had the luck of nature, if nothing else, he thought.

That was when he heard the first sounds of automatic rifle fire and the roar of automobile engines and the screech of tires.

Picking up his pace, now very interested in what was happening, he slowed when he reached the edge of the roof, the others askance of him.

"Look down there, Rob, it looks like someone's in a gun fight," Jeremy said as he watched the tableaux play out before him.

Rob saw what he meant instantly as the three cars drove around the parking lot while two others, luxury cars by the looks of them, followed.

The three cars that were trying to evade the latter were driving erratically, and appeared to have no firearms as they never shot back, not even once. As for the chasing cars, men hung out the sides with automatic weapons and one man was propped in the middle of the roof, the sunroof now missing, as they fired shot after shot into the escaping cars.

What had led the first driver to the shopping mall was unknown, but the other two had followed and now they were trapped inside the parking lot.

Zombies were everywhere, some trying to chase the cars while others were either run down or blown away by the chasing vehicle's occupants.

"What're those people doing?" Karen asked as she watched the three cars being pummeled by bullets. The rear windshield of one car was shattered, while the side window of another imploded, the condition of the occupants unknown.

The three vehicles tried to leave the parking lot, but one of the two luxury cars turned and blocked the entrance.

While the driver of the lead escaping car didn't try to leave another way was just one more unknown, but when the first car tried to back up and escape, he accidentally crashed into the car behind him, the last one following the second like ducklings to a mother.

With the three vehicles locked together, the two chasing cars took the opportunity to close their trap and the men jumped out of the vehicles and began firing into the cars, bullets riddling the metal until it resembled Swiss cheese.

From up on the roof, Karen went ashen and she grabbed Rob's arm.

"We've got to do something, Rob, those people are getting slaughtered!"

Rob yanked his arm away from her.

"Don't you think I know that? But what exactly is it you'd want me to do?"

"Well, you've got a gun, you could stop them," she replied.

"Are you serious? I have one gun and they have automatic weapons. No way, Karen, I'm sorry for those people, but there's nothing we can do for them."

"He's right, Karen, we need to think about ourselves right now," Val added, supporting Rob.

Down in the parking lot, the gunfire had ceased with the exception of the occasional sporadic gunfire as one of the men shot a ghoul moving towards them.

While the men kept guard, the others went to the three bullet-riddled cars and opened the doors.

Bodies spilled out, bloody and dead; there was no question of that. The men dragged the bodies away from the cars and began rooting through the insides, each of the trunks being popped open.

On the roof, the four survivors watched as the men below began taking boxes and bags from the trunks of the cars and packed them into their own vehicles.

A scream came to Rob and he saw a woman being dragged out of the last car. For whatever reason, she had avoided being shot to death, perhaps shielded by another body, and now she was pulled from the car and dragged by her hair by one of the men.

All the men were laughing and a few moved to the woman and squeezed her buttocks and breasts, making rude noises and gestures.

Rob hadn't seen any women with the raiders and he knew the fate of the lone surviving woman. His heart went out to her, but there was nothing he could do without risking their discovery and then their lives.

One of the men paused, then turned to stare at the shopping mall.

"Dammit, get down!" Rob hissed as he dropped to the roof, grabbing Karen's sleeve as the woman stood there flabbergasted.

Val and Jeremy followed him almost as fast and the four lay prone on the roof, while Rob stared at the man who was now inspecting the roof of the mall.

He could see the destroyed glass doors where Rob had crashed through, and then saw all the ghouls, so he decided the mall wasn't worth the fight.

The man's hard eyes scanned the rooftop slowly. For a moment he could have sworn he'd seen someone up there.

His cold eyes remained riveted to the roof.

On the rooftop, Rob slid his hand down to his Magnum; despite the fact he was too far away from the man to use it.

If they were discovered on the roof with two women, Rob had no doubt the men would consider the mall worth the risk.

There was a tense minute while Rob and the others watched the man, the one man below never removing his gaze, never wavering his steely stare, but then one of his men walked up to him and slapped him on the back, distracting him. The man turned away from the mall to see what his friend wanted. They chatted for a second while the second man pointed to the woman who was even now being tossed into one of the luxury cars.

The man nodded curtly, and then with one last glance to the shopping mall's roof, he spun on his heels and returned to the lead car.

He blasted the horn of the vehicle and the other men began piling back inside, whooping it up and shooting into the air when they weren't shooting the shambling zombies.

When the last man was inside, the two cars turned and drove out of the parking lot, leaving the three cars behind and the corpses of more than a half dozen people.

No sooner were they gone then the undead converged on the three vehicles, pulling out the bodies still inside while others descended on the still warm corpses of the slaughtered men and women lying on the warm asphalt.

Rob could see some of the bodies being pulled from the cars were children and he found he couldn't watch any more as dead hands ripped small limbs from fragile forms. A small blonde girl, no more than five, was ripped to pieces as four ghouls each grabbed an arm and a leg. Then another went for the small head, and as one group they pulled, the body coming apart like an old cloth doll with frayed stitching.

"Oh my God, it's horrible," Karen said as she covered her eyes with her arm as she lay prone on the roof. "I can't look anymore."

"Man, that's not right," Jeremy said as he watched the carnage below. "Why'd they do it, Rob? Why'd they kill those people like that?" He was in mild shock, the butchery so horrific it was hard for any human being to comprehend. How could one person be so cruel to another, especially when the world was in such a state?

"They were looters and raiders, son, plain and simple. They take what they want, and if they have to kill for it, then so be it. They've probably been surviving all through this thing the same way." His voice lowered and he caught Val's eyes on him. "Just be glad they didn't see we were up here. If they did, we might have ended up the same way those poor people did."

"Shit, Rob, I could have taken those bastards if they'd tried to get at us," Val said confidently.

"You keep thinkin' that, Val, but we both know that's not how it would have gone down."

She opened her mouth for a rebuttal, but Rob held his left hand up, palm facing her to stop her.

"Look, Val, I don't want to argue with you, all right? Not now, maybe later, okay?"

She saw the emotion in his eyes after witnessing the slaughter below and she nodded, for once understanding where the older man was coming from.

"Fine, Rob, fine."

Karen backed away from the edge, and when she was far enough away, she went to her knees; despite the fact the two cars were long gone.

"I'm going back inside, I need to lie down," she said and without waiting for an answer from the others, stood up and left, her head held low.

Down in the parking lot, there was nothing but blood and body parts as the zombies feasted on the dead bodies. Some had taken arms or legs, one with a head, and had moved off to feed in peace, while some followed their brethren, wanting to take what the others had. There was no sharing amongst the dead, each one out to satiate his private hunger.

"There's gonna be more people like that, ya know. The worse things get the worst humanity will fall. Man is an evil animal at heart and it's only the thin veil of civilization that keeps that animal in check. Take away that and man is free to let out the beast and be free. It's just the way it is," Rob said quietly.

"So what do we do about it?" Jeremy asked.

Rob turned his head so he was staring directly into Jeremy's eyes.

"That's just it, son. There's nothing we can do but wait and deal with it, if, or rather, when, it happens."

Without waiting for an answer, he stood up and walked away, the images of the bodies being ripped to shreds still prominent in his mind. The image of the children being torn apart something he believed would be with him for far longer than he would have liked.

* * *

That night, while everyone was sleeping, Rob was woken up by the sound of breathing coming from next to him.

Opening his eyes, his hand went for his Magnum lying beside him.

He could see only a dull shape standing over him, and for a second, he thought it might be Val's mother. Had she escaped her bonds and was now looking for a late night snack?

The dark shape let out a small sob and Rob recognized the voice as Karen's, so he lowered the gun and sat up, his eyes still blurry from sleep.

"Karen? Is that you? What's wrong? Is there something happening?"

She moved closer and sucked in a breath, then let it out.

"No, Rob, everything's fine, it's just… I can't get the thoughts of those poor people being killed out of my mind. I mean, those children…"

"Here, come sit down on the edge of the bed," he said and moved until his feet were on the floor.

He could hear the moans of the dead floating through the furniture store and from off to his right somewhere, Jeremy's snoring.

"I don't know what to say to make you feel better," Rob said.

Karen was all shadows, the furniture store dark. The only light came from a small candle near the front of the store.

"You don't have to say anything, Rob. It's not your fault, but…"

"But what?"

"I'm lonely, Rob, and scared. I…look, I think it was a mistake me coming over here." She stood up and prepared to leave. "I'm sorry I woke you, I'll go back to my bed now."

"No, wait a second, Karen, Don't go. I know how you feel, it's just…my wife's been dead for a long time and I'm a little rusty."

She moved closer to him and he could smell her. She smelled of lilacs and honey. She must have found some perfume, he thought.

"That's okay, Rob. I don't know what you thought I wanted, but it's not that." She sat down next to him again.

"Can I just lay next to you for the rest of the night? I just want to close my eyes and feel another person near me. I want to pretend I'm home in my own bed and everything's fine. That all this is just a horrible dream and when I wake up in the morning it'll all be gone."

"Oh, ah, okay, sure," he said, now feeling embarrassed.

He stretched out on the bed again and Karen stretched out next to him. He didn't move, not knowing what he should do until she spoke.

"Put your arm around me, Rob, I don't bite," she said softly.

"Ah, okay," he said and placed his right arm over her waist.

She placed his hand in hers and pulled it close and Rob could feel her belly rising and falling as she breathed. Her hair was next to his nose and he breathed in her scent.

It had been a long time since he'd been this close to a woman.

"Thank you, Rob, goodnight," she said softly.

"'Night, Karen."

He remained still, not doing anything and in a matter of minutes Karen's breathing became more steady as she drifted back to sleep. With a gentle sigh, he got more comfortable, and as he dropped into the darkness of slumber, he also pretended he was back in his home and it was years ago and his wife was alive and now lying next to him. And though he knew the dream was false and in the morning he would have to face his unpleasant reality, he still relished the few hours where he could pretend, because in the end, sometimes that was all God would give you.

* * *

The next seven days went relatively smoothly, with the four survivors trying to keep busy while dealing with the constant presence of the undead on the first floor.

When Jeremy got bored, he would take a bucket of golf balls pilfered from the sporting goods store and go to the railing with them. There, he would make a game out of trying to see how many golf balls he could get inside the mouths of the ghouls.

By the time he was bored with the game, he'd gotten pretty good at it and there were more than a dozen ghouls with golf balls now lodged in their throats, the round balls protruding like misshapen Adam apples.

Karen kept busy knitting. There was a yarn store on the south side of the mall and she had her pick of colors and needles. She'd decided to knit a sweater for Rob, the two growing closer with each passing day. Though they had not slept together since that night days ago, the event had softened him some to the possibility of perhaps being with another woman besides his late wife.

Karen was a patient woman and knew not to rush him. If it was going to happen then it would.

Rob went fishing for more of the baskets at the CVS, and with what he could hook, plus the supplies Val had already accumulated, they were doing fairly well with food and water.

One night it even rained, filling all the bowls and buckets with almost a half inch of rainwater, which was collected and brought inside and stored in larger buckets.

Every night one of them would make sure to put down the metal grating at the front of the store, no one wanting to take any chances. It was their last line of defense against the ghouls getting on the second floor, though none of them wanted to test it.

Late in the night, with everyone fast asleep, a large crash filled the shopping mall, overriding the steady moaning of the dead.

Rob was the first to snap awake and it wasn't until the crashing came for the second time that he knew he wasn't dreaming, and that in fact the noise had been real.

Climbing out of bed, he quickly dressed and moved to the front of the store. Once there, he was greeted by the others, all with bleary eyes and small wrinkles on their faces from the sheets pressing into their skin.

Jeremy had an aluminum baseball bat taken from a sporting goods store strapped over his back and a crossbow with a dozen or so quarrels hanging from a sling, and Val had her sword, while Karen held a titanium golf club.

All knew what the loud noises might mean and plans had been made days ago in case there was an emergency.

It looked like that emergency had come tonight.

"What's going on? Did you hear all that noise?" Jeremy asked as he glanced at the others."

"Don't know what it is, but it can't be good," Rob said.

More crashing could be heard and it was Val who realized what was happening.

"Oh, no, those are the cans and shit I put on top of all that stuff piled on the east stairwell. There's something going on over there."

"Well, what do we do?" Karen asked, gripping the golf club tighter.

"We go check it out, what else can we do?" Rob said. "Come on; let's go before it's too late to do anything."

While they waited at the metal grating at the front of the store for Val to unlock the padlocks and open it, Rob turned to Karen, placing a hand on her shoulder.

"Karen, you stay right here and wait for us. If anything comes down that hallway that's not us, close the gate. Otherwise, just cross your fingers.

"Okay, whatever you need me to do," she said, her face filled with concern and a touch of terror. "Just be careful."

"We will," he said, and with a glance to Val and Jeremy, they turned to exit the store.

"Wait, Rob," Karen called and ran to him. He stopped, turned, and was surprised when she jumped at him and kissed him square on the lips. It wasn't passionate as it was rushed but the point was made.

"I mean it, Rob, come back to me," she whispered so only he could hear her.

Swallowing hard, he was taken aback, but he nodded, smiled slightly at her, and then he took off with the others nearby. Karen watched them go, and when they had rounded the far corner, she stepped back inside and waited with one hand on the grating to close it if need be.

As they moved down the hallway, the mall had taken on a different look from when it was daytime. With only the dull moonlight for illumination, the storefronts and stone pillars were now all sharp angles and shadows.

While Jeremy ran alongside Rob, he had a wide smile on his lips. Rob saw this and pointed a finger at him warily.

"Not a word, son, I mean it," he said coldly.

"I wasn't gonna say anything, I swear!" Jeremy replied, defending himself.

"Good, keep it that way," Rob told him.

"Val, wait up!" Rob yelled, the woman sprinting forward while holding her sword out in front of her.

"Damn, she's fast," Jeremy said as he put on a burst of speed and left Rob chugging along alone.

"Curse youth and their extra energy," Rob muttered, but then decided to save his breath for running.

By the time he rounded the last corner of the hallway, he realized they were in for more trouble than they could handle.

Val was even now at the stairwell, and as she raised her sword to take out the first ghoul even now crawling over the debris on the stair, Rob knew they were in for a fight they couldn't win.

* * *

Val never hesitated, never slowed as she swung her sword at the first zombie stumbling up the stairs. The blade sliced deep into the ghoul's neck, severing half of it from its shoulders, causing the body to stumble away, the ghoul now looking at the world sideways. Behind that one, more than a score were surging up the stairs, almost all the debris once piled there now removed and pushed to the side. On the floor below, the pots, pans and shattered glass was kicked and pushed around, the early warning system left by Val now useless.

She couldn't help but wonder how this could be? How did the zombies manage to figure out how to get up the stairs?

But the time for contemplation was forgotten as a swarm of undead came at her.

She slashed sideways, taking off the gnarled, arthritic hands of an old woman, and then thrust forward, stabbing another through the heart. A dead man came at her from the right and she knew she wouldn't be able to get her sword free in time to save her when a *thwack* sound cut through the air.

A quarrel appeared in the dead man's left eye.

The zombie swayed on his feet for a moment, an icky, bloody ooze seeping from the punctured eye and then the body toppled over, slowing the ones behind it for a fraction of a second.

She knew Jeremy had saved her ass, but there was no time to thank him as more bodies were creeping up the stairs. Then she heard Rob's large handgun sounding and ghouls were knocked off their feet, some thrown from the stairwell and over the railing to fall to the hard floor below. Necks cracked and skulls exploded as the three warriors battled to save what they now called their home.

Jeremy saw a small child with more than half its face missing coming at Val and he lined up his shot and let fly.

The quarrel struck the small ghoul in the mouth, the pointed tip sticking out the back of the head, but the child continued onward, barely fazed by the new protuberance. The child gummed the wooden shaft, trying to bite it off, but like a lion with a splinter, it didn't know what to do. Val solved the small ghoul's dilemma by hacking at its head, slicing into it like she was splitting a melon.

Any sympathy she had was long gone now, only the fire to survive burning brightly.

Yes, she still saw the zombies as people who once had lives, families and dreams, but she also knew if she let down her guard for even one second, those very same people would rip her apart, and she was not going to let that happen.

So, already covered in gore, she chopped, stabbed and hacked, leaving a bloody trail of body parts in her wake.

But despite this animal ferocity, her skill with the blade, it was not enough and Rob was the first to yell the retreat, knowing if they stayed for a minute longer they would find themselves overrun.

He emptied the spent brass from his gun and reloaded while backing away from the stairwell, his boots sliding on the polished floor.

"There's too many of them, Val, we've got to get back to the store!" he yelled as he closed the cylinder and readied the gun for six more shots.

"No, we can take them!" she screamed, taking off the head of a teenage girl, her pony tails flopping away as the head was kicked around by other feet. "This is my place, I took it from them and I won't give it back!"

"No we can't! Damn it, woman, there's too many of them. This is just a place, we can find another one!" He glanced to Jeremy who was reloading his crossbow.

"Talk to her Jeremy or she's dead, and us right behind her!"

He shot a ghoul coming for him, the bullet taking out a massive hole in the torso, but the zombie continued forward and Rob raised his aim, this time shooting the ghoul in the face. He told himself to watch that, only head shots would do the trick and even then it was sometimes iffy if he didn't hit the skull just right.

"He's right, Val, this is one place out of a million. We can find another if we have to. Please, don't let them kill you, too, Think of your mother!"

That sunk into Val's brain as she fought the dead. Her mother wouldn't want her to die here; she knew that for a fact. One of her mother's last words to her before she died was, "Don't give up, keep fighting."

She slashed a dead man in the face, slicing off his nose, the gaping orifice now an open maw where phlegm, blood and pus seeped forth.

"Okay, all right, goddamn it, we'll leave. Shit," she snarled in anger and sliced at two more ghouls, taking their arms off with one swipe of the blade. The ghouls still tried to grab her, but didn't understand why they couldn't.

She turned around and ran to Rob and Jeremy who had taken a wider stance from the approaching undead army. Jeremy had been firing quarrel after quarrel, a few bodies now resembling pincushions.

While Val ran, she hacked at zombies from behind them, the ghouls never seeing their ultimate end until they felt the deadly touch of her blade.

Rob shot two more in the head and Jeremy sent another to oblivion with his last quarrel, then he grabbed Val's hand and the three of them took off at a fast run.

Behind them, the ghouls swarmed onto the second floor, nothing stopping them now. Like a parade, the undead moved forward, all following after the three warriors.

They rounded the far corner and Karen perked up, her face filled with worry. She had heard the screams, the gunshots and moans of the dead and was frazzled with concern, especially as she didn't know if they were still all right.

Relief flooded her eyes when she saw her three friends dash around the corner like the demons of Hell were on their tails.

And no sooner did she think this, then the first ghoul rounded the corner, followed by a horde of stumbling bodies, all shambling at a good clip.

"Get inside, and get ready to close the gate!" Rob called when he saw Karen standing there.

She was ready, and as the three of them charged into the furniture store, she reached up to pull down the gate, but it wouldn't go down and though she tried again with all her might, the gate remained up.

"It's stuck! It won't go down!"

"Shit, get out of the way, damn you!" Val snapped as she shoved Karen to the floor and reached up to grab the bottom of the gate.

"It gets stuck sometimes and you have to jiggle it a little," she said, as if that said it all.

She was calm on the outside as she wiggled the grating, but inside she was fraught with fear. As she wiggled the gate back and forth to break it free, the ghouls were coming closer and she was beginning to worry she might not make it.

Then it was free and she was bringing it down, but not fast enough to keep all the zombies out. As the grating hit the floor with a clang, one ghoul became trapped under it, and the long opening was enough for others to attempt entry.

"Help me, you guys, before they get in!" Val screamed as she kicked a ghoul in the face.

Rob and Jeremy ran to her and began stomping on hands and punching faces. Val reached down and grabbed the ghoul half in/half out of the store and dragged it inside by its stained shirt collar. Once the body was free, she ignored the prone ghoul and ran back to the grating. Using her foot, she stuck her toe into the grating and pushed downward, the grating almost making it to the floor. But there were still a few arms and hands in the way, plus one zombie had its head stuck, the grating trapping it by the neck.

"You, two, hold the grating down!" she screamed as she picked up her sword and turned to the obstructions.

Rob and Jeremy did what they could, but they had to be wary of snapping teeth, which wanted their fingers as they held down the grating.

More than thirty ghouls were at the grating now, with more coming up behind and the stench of death was overwhelming. Bloated bodies bounced off the gate, flies buzzing around like angry hornets.

Val went into action, raised her sword high, and began chopping off the limbs sticking out from under the grating. When she got to the ghoul with its head in the way, she tried to hack it off, but the angle was wrong. She had to kneel down, place the blade on the top of the neck and then sawed at it like she was cutting bread. As she did this, blood, deep red and black in places, squirted upwards, hitting her in the face and torso, but she ignored it, and forced the steel through the pale flesh.

When she had hit bottom, she slid the blade across the floor like she was clearing a cutting board of fat trimmed from a steak, the head rolling away.

And then the grating was closed, slamming down hard, a few twitching fingers still underneath.

"Get it locked, now!" she yelled as she wiped blood from her forehead. She was lucky and didn't get any in her eyes or mouth. Not that she knew if that would matter. Her mother had died after being bitten, but if whatever had killed her, *changed her*, was like a virus, like Aids maybe, then the blood was deadly.

Only way to know would be to find out if she got sick later, she supposed.

Rob had the padlock and he snapped it shut; the click loud despite the moaning of the dead.

Pale, dry fingers were wrapped in and around the holes in the grating as the ghouls shook the gate back and forth. Behind Rob, Karen finished whacking the prone ghoul over the head with her golf club, smashing the skull to mush.

For the moment the grating was holding, but as Rob watched the top and sides of the metal gate, he severely doubted it would hold forever. There was simply too much mass on the other side, the constant pushing of dead bodies more than enough to weaken the hinges and metal hooks holding it in its frame.

"We can't stay here for long," Rob said as he went to Karen and hugged her.

"Ya think?" Jeremy said as he stared at the wall of undead before him. Faces of all sizes, shapes, and color stared back at him, the only unifying thing they had in common now that of being dead.

It sent a chill down his spine and he wondered if he would just go crazy right now and save himself the aggravation of trying to survive another minute.

"We can't leave, I won't leave, dammit. My mother..." Val stated coldly.

But then the problem was taken out of her hands when a vase was knocked over behind the four scared people and they spun as one to see what had caused it.

Val was the first to gasp and let out a cry of despair at what greeted them.

Coming from the now empty bed was Val's mother.

Somehow she had broken free of her bonds, the bindings still hanging from her wrists, and now she slowly moved towards Val. Whether the old woman still recognized her daughter or if it was just because Val was the closest to her, the dead woman lifted her hands high, opened her mouth to expose the dry, cracked tongue and began moving towards Val.

Rob let go of Karen and walked over to the old woman, raising the Magnum as he did so.

Just before he was going to shoot her, Val touched his arm. He glanced at her and she nodded no.

"It's my mother, Rob, let me do it. It's the least I can do for her."

"So you agree it has to be done then?" His words were low, knowing what Val must be going through.

She nodded curtly. "Yeah, and I need to be the one who does it."

"You're sure? I can do it if you need me to."

"No, I'll do it. I think she'd want me to if she could tell me."

"Okay, have at it, but be careful," Rob said and stepped back while lowering the Magnum, but only a little bit. If Val lost her nerve, he would do what had to be done.

Val nodded and then turned to the others. "Could you guys leave me alone with my mom please? The gate will hold for now and I'll call you if there's a problem. I need to do this by myself."

Rob nodded, lowered the Magnum the rest of the way, and moved to Jeremy and Karen.

"Sure, come on, guys, we need to get together what food and water we can, anyway." As they moved to the rear of the furniture store, Rob paused "Shout if you need us," he said, not wanting to leave the woman alone, but knowing he had no choice.

"Go, I'll be fine," Val told him. Rob stared at her for another three seconds and then, seeing the resolve in her eyes, turned and moved away with the others who had been waiting for him.

Val waited with a breaking heart as her mother reached her. Val pushed her away, dodging snapping teeth when her mother tried to bite her. The old woman was fast and Val realized she needed to smarten up or she could actually find herself bit.

Wrapping both hands around the shaft of her sword, she sighed heavily. Her mother flashed brown teeth at her and snarled low in her throat and Val nodded to her.

"Okay, mom, I love you, just know that. Okay?"

Her mother didn't acknowledge the sentiment, and came at Val with her head low and arms stretched wide. Val gritted her teeth, closed her eyes tight, and when she knew it was time, brought the sword down hard, severing the head from the frail shoulders in one swipe.

The headless old woman continued forward and ran into an oak bureau before toppling sideways to the floor. The head dropped to the floor with a thump and rolled back and forth like an off-kilter weeble, then slowed to a stop. The eyes still blinked and the mouth still moved.

Val went to the head and picked it up, finding it hard to look at the pale-brown face of her mother.

The teeth clicked shut, opened and clicked again as the severed head tried to bite her.

Val felt the sadness in her become anger as she stared at the head of her mother.

What had happened to her wasn't fair, it wasn't right! She wanted to take that anger out on something, anything.

With the head in her hands, she walked over to a table and sat down, then placed both thumbs over her mother's eyes.

"You're not my mother anymore," she hissed through clenched teeth. "You're evil."

She pressed her thumbs deep into the eyes, the mouth still moving up and down. Pushing as hard as she could, the eyes squirted a clear viscous fluid, the syrupy liquid seeping around her thumbs and down onto the table top. Still Val pressed, all her anger being vented at the head of what was once the only person in her life she had loved unequivocally.

Her thumbs pushed deep, until she could feel the meat within and still she pressed, mangling the frontal part of the ghoul's brain. Finally, she must have crushed the right part of the brain because the mouth stopped moving and then went slack.

Slowly, Val took her hands off the head, shaking her thumbs free of the gore now stuck to them.

"You're not my mother anymore," she said in a whisper while tears ran down her cheeks.

She felt ashamed now as she stared at the destroyed face of what was once her mother, but there was something more there, too.

She felt free, as if whatever had been holding her to this place was now severed.

Picking up the head, she carried it to the bed her mother had died in, then she dragged the headless body there, as well.

She placed the body with the head and covered it all with a sheet,

"I love you, Mom," she said quietly and then she turned and walked away, barely glancing at the undead shaking the gate like teenagers at a rock concert as they waited for the gate to go up to let them inside the main hall.

Val took a second to wash her hands and face, making sure the tears she'd shed were no longer visible. Then she joined the others in the middle of the store.

"You okay?" Rob asked.

"Yeah, Rob, I'm fine."

"Is it...?" Karen asked as she hugged herself.

"Yeah, it's done. She won't be bothering us again," Val said coldly. She moved to the others and picked up a bottle of water, seeming to study it."

"You're right, Rob, we need to leave here and leave here fast before they get past that gate."

"We were just talking about that very thing, actually. Trouble is, once we leave here, we don't have any transportation. And without a car or truck we'd be dead in minutes out there."

Val smiled then, a wide smile that said she knew something the others didn't.

"Well, maybe I can help with that," she grinned. Then she began to fill them in on what they would do next.

* * *

Just as Rob said it would happen, it did.

Rotting hands and faces pushed at the metal, teeth clamping on the open spaces, the rungs becoming covered with drool and blood. Hands shook the grating as hard as atrophied muscles would allow, dried skin cracking from the exertion. Their strength was in their numbers and that was something they had in abundance.

The metal hinges on the gate soon weakened, not able to take the abuse thrust upon them and twenty minutes after Val had slammed the metal grating down for the furniture store; the undead forced their way inside with a crashing of metal and a cacophony of moans and wails.

Like a ransacking army, they rampaged into the store, moving amongst the furniture on their search for the humans. The dinner table the four survivors had sat and dined on was knocked over, the plates and dishes sitting on the top dashed to the floor like so much garbage, the one unlit candle knocked over to roll onto the floor.

Even in their fugue state, the ghouls knew the humans had to be hiding in the store somewhere. Cabinets were opened and bureaus knocked to the floor. Beds were ripped of their sheeting and Val's mother was tossed to the floor, ignored, her rotting body unappetizing to the dead.

No, they wanted fresh meat, warm blood, and they knew their prey was in here somewhere. The trick would be to find them.

A few ghouls became confused, tumbling onto beds and falling onto sofas. A dead man and woman dropped onto a couch, their arms entangling, and from a casual glance they looked like a young couple taking a moment to snuggle. But if the viewer moved closer, he would have had an eyeful of rotting flesh and a putrid stench that would make even the heartiest soul gag.

As the ghouls swarmed into the furniture store, the din was enormous, and if the humans were trying to escape, they wouldn't get far.

There was nowhere to run. Even the zombies knew this in their dull minds, but if that was so, then where was the prey?

Where were they and how could they have escaped the trap of the dead?

The answer was they hadn't, and in due time they would be located, and the first ghouls lucky enough to find them would feast heartily on their warm organs and tender flesh.

*   *   *

In a small passageway behind the furniture store that ran parallel with the long hallway that criss-crossed the shopping mall, four people moved with careful precision. The passageway was barely five feet high, the extra foot that would be for the ceiling filled with ductwork, heating pipes and electrical wire.

The passageway was a service tunnel and wasn't for traversing normally. It was only for the maintenance and engineers of the mall, who would need to check on various gauges, dials, and vents to make sure the internal machinery of the large building was working properly.

Val was in the lead with a flashlight, as she was the only one who knew the way to their present destination.

She had taken the time to scout the service tunnel back when she'd first holed up in the shopping mall with her mother, knowing she might need a back door out.

Behind her was Rob, followed by Jeremy and Karen.

All of them carried packs filled with all the food and water they could carry.

"How much longer?" Jeremy inquired as he ducked below some low hanging wires. He ended up getting his face caught in a spider web and he wiped the sticky filaments off his face, grossed out. He thought it funny how he was fighting rotting, blood-covered bodies of the walking dead, but a small spider the size of his thumbnail still grossed him out.

"Not long, hon, keep your panties on for a few more minutes," Val said from the front of the line.

"Are you sure about this, Rob?" Karen asked from the rear of the line.

He slowed and let Jeremy pass him, then moved forward again with Karen right behind him. They hadn't talked about the kiss they'd shared yet, there had been no time, but he knew she wanted to, he could tell by the way she looked at him now.

"No, I'm not sure, but we don't really have a choice now, do we," he said in a low voice,

A loud crashing sounded from behind them and they all stopped walking.

"They got in," Rob said loudly to Val and Jeremy.

"Then let's get a move on," Val said turning slightly to see him. "If they find the door to this tunnel it's possible they could get in here, and I don't want to deal with them in this place, that's for sure." She turned around, and without waiting for a reply, began moving onward, her flashlight beam bobbing up and down while she walked.

Rob took Karen's hand. "Come on, Karen, she's right, let's keep moving.

They all began walking again, now with Jeremy and Val a little ahead of them. After a few minutes, Jeremy slowed until Rob was right behind him and he turned so he could see the older man in the dim light of Val's receding flashlight.

"Hey, Rob, I wanted to ask you something."

"Sure, go 'head, just do it while you walk, okay?"

"Yeah, cool, okay." He began walking again. "I wanted to ask you about what you said while we were at the stairs, when Val wouldn't leave."

"Yeah, and that is?" Rob asked.

"Well, you said *damn it*, remember? I thought you didn't believe in cursing. Hell, you give me enough grief about it."

Rob smiled slightly, but Jeremy couldn't see it in the gloom.

"Well, son, for your information, you're right. It was a moment of weakness and I've already asked God for his forgiveness in my lapse of judgment."

"And did he?"

"Did he what?" Rob asked, perplexed.

"Forgive you, Rob. Did he forgive you for swearing?"

"Yes, son, he did."

"So let me get this straight. You thought to yourself that you were talking to God and then you thought he said he forgave you. So tell me, Rob, did you actually hear his voice? Was it like a loud booming voice said '*I forgive you, my son, go in peace.*' Or did you just say to yourself, '*yeah, it's cool, I forgive myself*'."

Rob's face took on hard look. "What're you implying, son?"

"Nothing, nothing, don't get worked up. I'm just sayin', unless you got a phone call from God saying it's cool if you swear once in a while, I just don't see how you can say he forgave you."

"Well, he did, now why don't you concentrate on walking forward and less on my faith in the Lord."

"Fine, I'm just sayin'."

"Yes, you've made that abundantly clear. Now turn around and keep walking," Rob said, the annoyance in his voice clear for anyone to hear.

Jeremy either was done teasing or got the point, but he turned and began moving forward, walking a little faster.

"Hey, Val, wait up, will ya?" he called and tried to catch her.

In the gloom of the tunnel, Karen reached out and touched Rob's arm.

"Don't listen to him, Rob, he's young. He doesn't understand what faith really means yet."

"Maybe, or maybe he's just a jerk," he replied.

"Yes, there is that," she smirked, but he didn't see her.

The two moved forward, ducking under vents and pipes, while Jeremy's voice floated in the tunnel as he began bothering Val, asking her questions she didn't want to answer.

* * *

"Okay, we're here," Val said when she stopped by a small door with a large X scratched in the middle of it.

The others joined her, and the instant they were next to the door, their noses scrunched up and each of them took on a look of disgust.

"Oh, man, what's that stench?" Jeremy gasped as he covered his nose with his sleeve.

"He's right, it smells like something died on the other side of that door," Rob answered as he did the same gesture, covering his nose.

Karen said nothing, but immediately tried to breath through her mouth.

"Oh, yeah? You think it's bad now, wait until I open this door," Val said as she prepared to do just that.

"Why, what's on the other side?" Jeremy asked, his voice muffled now that his arm was covering his mouth.

Val smirked at him, then the others.

"Why don't you just see for yourself," she said as she turned the handle and pushed the door open.

The instant the door was opened, a miasma of death, a redolence so foul it took all the three survivors had not to gag and throw up right then and there. Only Val seemed immune to the stench of decay and rot, and with an amused glance at each of them, she stepped out into the dim gloom of the loading dock.

"Well, let's go, standing here isn't gonna make it any easier," Rob told the others and then exited the service tunnel, a foul taste coating his mouth.

"Oh, I don't know about that one. I think I might just decide to live in here. That is, if I can get the door closed and get this smell out of the air," Jeremy said, his eyes watering slightly.

Karen pushed past him. "Rob's right, Jeremy, the sooner we get through it, the sooner we'll be outside. Though if that's any better than what's in here, I don't know." Then she was past him and he was alone.

A low moan echoed in the tunnel and Jeremy peered into the darkness from whence he'd come. Deciding it was safer to stay with his friends than stay in the tunnel with who knows what was following him, he exited the tunnel and slammed the door closed behind him.

After all, nothing could be as bad as it smelled in there.

* * *

Jeremy was wrong on that count and he began coughing and gagging as he tried to suck in a breath from the foul air of the loading dock.

In front of him by only a few feet were the others.

They weren't moving because none of them had a clear path through the pus-filled, sludge-covered, blood-soaked loading dock floor.

Finally, Jeremy's insides couldn't take it any more and he leaned forward and puked, spitting up the entire contents of his stomach. Near him, both Rob and Karen were doing the same, their sounds of displeasure filling the loading dock, overriding the buzzing of insects feeding on the rotting corpses.

When he was finished for the moment, Jeremy looked up again and his eyes stared at the absolute, most disgusting thing he'd ever seen. Hell, ever imagined.

The entire floor of the loading dock was covered in rotting, putrid bodies. Val had said she'd brought all the ghouls she'd killed to the loading dock, dumping them there day after day until there were mounds of diseased flesh in all directions.

After weeks of sitting in the warm temperature, the flies and maggots had grown to unbelievable proportions, feeding on the once human remains. Blowflies filled the air and hopped from body to body, while rats burrowed deep into the cadavers, feeding on the black and blue meat. Stomachs filled with decomposing gas and resembled swollen bladders were everywhere, and more than one had ruptured, disgorging yellow pus and bile across the floor. More than half the corpses appeared to undulate and bubble as maggots and other insects burrowed under the skin, the pieces of flesh flexing and retracting like a balloon being blown up and then deflated.

A liquid resembling pea soup covered the floor with more of an inch of fluid, and as the four survivors moved through the syrupy concoction of soupy flesh and dissolving organs, their feet splashed and stirred the stench up even more, if that was possible. The stench of decomposition was all pervasive and all of them but Val threw up more than once.

Halfway through the loading dock, Jeremy didn't see where he placed his left boot and he ended up stepping inside the body cavity of what was once a middle-aged woman.

Like stepping into a mud puddle, the yellow and pink, rancid pus splashed on his legs, causing him to throw up yet again. When he pulled his foot up, tendrils of goop stuck to his sole and he truly felt like he was in Hell.

Val was the only one unaffected by the utterly unimaginable carnage and she hopped between bodies until she was at the side door that would lead out to the rear parking lot.

Flies buzzed in the air and landed on the heads and faces of the four survivors, and constant waves and slaps of their hands were all they could do to fend them off.

Maggots writhed everywhere, crawling on the walls, ceiling and every conceivable surface in between. More than once the white larva dropped from the ceiling to land in hair and under collars, and a wiggling dance was needed to extract them. By the time all were at the door with Val, Jeremy had more than two dozen maggots in his hair and he bent over and brushed them free, knowing there were probably more which had burrowed into his hair and were even now crawling on his scalp. He tried not to think about it or risk totally freaking out.

Val peeked through the small window that looked out onto the back parking lot wreathed in darkness, and when she was satisfied, she turned back with a frown.

"I was afraid of this," she said.

"Afraid of what?" Rob asked.

"There's too many of them out there, that's what. That why I never tried to leave before. 'Sides, where would me and my Mom have gone to? For all I knew, it was like this everywhere."

"Shit, Val, that's not far from the truth," Jeremy said and then apologized for cussing when Rob flashed him an annoyed look.

Suddenly there was banging on the tunnel door across the loading dock and all eyes went to it, Val cursing under her breath.

"Looks like they figured out where we went to," she said and then peered out the window one last time. "Well, guys, there's only one way we're gonna get to my car in one piece and you're not gonna like it," she said with a grin.

Jeremy was the first to figure out what she meant

"Oh, come on, Val, no way. I just got the smell out of my hair from the last time," he whined.

"Sorry, hon, but it's the only way to make it there safely."

Val went to the closet corpse and knelt down. Picking up a mess of rotting organs, even she had to turn her head away from the smell.

"It won't be so bad once you get used to it," she said while trying to ignore the maggots squirming between her fingers.

"Uhg, says you," Karen added as she tried to keep what was left of her insides down.

With a heavy sigh, Rob set down his backpack and bid the others to do the same. There was a small clear spot near the door that would lead them to freedom and at least the backpacks would stay relatively clean.

"Come on, folks, the sooner we do it, the sooner we can leave this awful place."

"Oh, man, this sucks," Jeremy said, but knew he had no choice. Better to wear a meat suit than become one.

Moving to Val, she picked up a large handful of intestines and began draping them over his shoulders. The mucus and pus dripped down his arms and dribbled under his collar, the feeling reminding him of crawling worms. The bile and gore was warm in some places, but cold in others, and it felt like she was spreading pudding on him.

When she was done, he was covered from head to toe in gore, black and red guts and intestines. Just for fun, she stuck a bubbling kidney into his jacket pocket and then slapped his side hard. The kidney popped like a balloon, his pocket now seeping a brownish liquid. Maggots wiggled and squirmed everywhere, annoyed their home and food was taken from them.

"Okay, next," Val said with a mischievous grin. Then she had to look away and try to hold her breath. The stench of rotting meat was unbearable and there were times she couldn't see, her eyes watering so badly.

Karen was next, and in no time she was adorned in the new apparel of the land. Her meat outfit was outfitted with a live scarf and matching severed legs ensemble. She looked dashing as she striated across the loading dock, the intestines wrapped around her arms like a shawl dripping blood and slime.

She was ready for the runway of the dead.

Rob was next and Val really had fun with him. She picked up a large, bloated stomach and dropped it down on his head. The lining ruptured and he was bathed in stomach acid, maggots and bits of whatever the corpse had eaten before being killed by Val. Rob stood perfectly still, his eyes closed, his mouth a slit as he sucked in air through his teeth.

"Oh, man, some of it got in my mouth," Rob said as he began spitting the foul taste out.

"Hold on, Rob, almost done," Val grinned as she tossed organs at him and draped a long cord of lower intestine around his neck like a scarf.

Finally, Rob couldn't stand it anymore and he turned to the side and threw up the rest of his dinner from the night before. When he was done and was about to wipe his mouth clean, Val stopped him.

"No, leave it. It adds to the disguise. In fact, next time just puke on your shoes. Anything to cover the smell of being alive." She pushed him away from her. "Go, you're done."

He moved away without making a sound other than splashing and squelching. His throat hurt from vomiting and his eyes were watering from the stench. He could feel dozens of maggots squirming on his neck and in his hair and he thought a few had crawled into his ears.

Across the room, Val was getting into her own rotting disguise of decayed meat. She picked up handfuls of gunk, dripping tendrils of pus and ooze and slathered her body with it. She ignored the maggots and shooed away the rats until she was so covered in gobbets of flesh her skin color would be unknown to anyone seeing her, and the fact she was female was only a guess.

Sloshing forward, she picked up her sword and looked at the others.

"You guys ready?"

"Let's just do this," Rob said quietly.

"I'm beginning to think letting them catch me isn't such a bad idea," Jeremy added.

Val opened the door and the warm, night air filtered in, causing them all to breath only slightly easier.

The moon was high and there was more than enough illumination to see by. With Val in the lead, the four gore covered survivors stepped out into the parking lot, their backpacks hanging from their arms. Rob held his magnum out to his side and had made sure Val didn't get any gunk on it. But the hand holding the weapon was still covered and he knew the grip would need a good cleaning when they were safe somewhere.

Slow moving, shadowy forms were everywhere, sluggishly moving around the parking lot like shoppers who'd forgotten where they had parked after a long day of shopping.

As the four, gore-covered people moved across the pavement, it was Jeremy who ended up slowing down when a particularly nasty maggot found out it liked his right ear very much. As he stopped and began digging at his ear with his right pinky, the others passed him, all following Val.

Val led them to the third row of cars, and when she found hers, she pointed happily.

"There it is," she said softly, not wanting to be overheard by the nearby ghouls.

"Really? That's you car?" Rob asked in a low voice. He wore a quizzical expression on his blood-covered face.

Val looked hurt.

"What's wrong with my car?"

"Nothing, nothing, it's fine. As long as it runs, that is," he said as he glanced at Karen. She only shrugged, not having an opinion.

As the three moved to the old, beat-up, rusted fenders and peeling paint, worn tires and falling headliner of a VW Bug, none of them realized Jeremy wasn't with them. And worse, he was slowly being surrounded by ghouls, the young man oblivious as he continued worrying at his ear.

* * *

Jeremy didn't realize he was in trouble until it was too late to do anything about it. One second he was getting the maggot out of his ear, and the next he was staring at more than a dozen dead faces, all in similar signs of decay. One ghoul had a large scalp wound; the black and crusted blood covering the open sore like it was a leper. Another was missing all the skin on its face, the tendons and tissue underneath glistening red in the moonlight. Another had small boils on its flesh that pulsed and moved of their own accord. It made Jeremy think of the maggots and he felt his stomach rolling again.

A few were children, the small girls still wearing their pajamas or night dresses, the boys wearing pj's or just their underwear. Jeremy figured they'd been attacked while sleeping, and images of their demise flashed through his head when he thought of the children's parents, now infected, crawling up the family stairs in their homes to feed on their own sleeping children.

Then a middle aged-man in his late fifties moved up close to Jeremy. The dead man showed no signs how he'd become a zombie. His clothes were relatively clean and there were no apparent wounds that Jeremy could see.

But the pale complexion and white eyes gave it away immediately. This wasn't a live human playing dead like Jeremy and the others. Oh, no, this was a ghoul, and for some reason it had now focused its attention on Jeremy.

The dead man moved in close, pushing past the other ghouls who were basically standing around. At the moment, none of them thought of Jeremy as anything but one of them. Not this dead man, though. This ghoul seemed to know there was something off about Jeremy and he moved in closer and touched Jeremy's jacket, puling away a large chunk of rancid meat. The ghoul sniffed the meat and then popped it into his mouth, the pungent juices squirting out the sides of his mouth while he chewed.

When the meat was consumed, the man moved so close to Jeremy the younger man could smell him and Jeremy had to fight to remain calm, to not show emotion that would give away his disguise.

The dead man began sniffing him like an animal and Jeremy wanted to mumble an, "Oh, no, here we go again," as he thought about the blonde woman in the mall who had figured out he wasn't like her.

But he knew if he opened his mouth and uttered one word that wasn't a moan, wail or growl, his costume would be useless, and in less time than it would take to call for help, all the ghouls would pounce on him and tear him apart.

As the dead man investigated Jeremy further, others now took an interest, and they began moving closer to him, some reaching out and touching him. Dead hands went to his face and a finger slid into his mouth. He fought the urge to gag on the fetid digit and sighed happily when it was pulled away.

As he stared at the dead eyes of the surrounding zombies, he then glanced down at himself and realized he wasn't covered with as much gore as the others. A lot of it had sloughed off to the point it wasn't an impossibility the ghouls would know he wasn't like them.

As if the dead man who had begun the whole thing sensed his thoughts, he let out a growl and raised himself to his full height of about six feet and change.

Jeremy gazed up into the grim visage of what he had a good feeling was going to be his death, and just as he opened his mouth to scream, knowing teeth were about to get busy munching on his ass, a loud gunshot filled the night and the dead man's head blew apart like the inside had been stuffed with dynamite.

The head flew off in dozens of pieces and the now decapitated body swayed on legs that no longer had a leader. Then the body toppled to the side, and after twitching slightly, remained still, a black ichor seeping from the neck wound.

Jeremy was sprayed with brains and gore and he blinked his eyes clear, a little shocked at what had just happened, then he heard Rob call out from his side.

"Time to go, son!" Rob yelled and then shot another zombie moving towards him, the body falling away between two parked cars.

Jeremy snapped out of his stupor, and as the other zombies moved in, he pushed one aside and dashed for the others. While he ran, the others realized he wasn't one of them and all turned and began to follow, their sluggish movements picking up speed now that food was in sight.

Val pulled her car keys from her pocket and opened the driver's door, climbing in and unlocking the other doors. Karen jumped in and Rob fired two more shots at the closest bodies, and then, with Jeremy racing up to him, he let the younger man jump in and then followed suit, slamming his door closed as hands and faces pummeled the glass.

"Seems like this is where we came in," Rob said as he waved the barrel of the Magnum at the undead faces, but he wouldn't shoot, that would be insane. The glass was strong and should protect them nicely. One ghoul scraped fingernails against the glass and they all stared in disgust when the yellow nails bent backwards and then fell off the decayed fingers, leaving red and yellow streaks on the glass.

It was only when the car began to shake, rocked on its shocks by the bodies pushing on it that Val snapped out of it and put the key in the ignition.

Starting the engine, the motor whined, but didn't catch. She tried again and other than a whirring noise, there was nothing.

"Are you kidding me?" Rob asked from next to her. The VW was small and the four survivors were cramped. Jeremy and Rob were in the backseat, both huddled together. In the small vehicle the stink of their meat disguises was almost intolerable, but there was more to worry about at the moment.

"Relax, Rob, it'll start. Remember, the car's been sitting for a while now. Just let me get some gas to the carb."

"Don't flood it," Jeremy said from the backseat.

"Thanks, hon. I know how to start my own car, thank you very much."

Val tried again and was greeted to more whirring. She pumped the pedal again and this time there was a small sputter, but then more whirring.

"You're gonna kill the battery if you keep this up," Rob snapped at her as he stared at the faces surrounding them.

Val ignored him, mumbled a few words to the car and then tried again. The whirring continued, but then the engine began to sputter more than before. She kept the starter spinning and slowly the engine began catching, though it was a battle the entire time.

"You're gonna fry the starter!" Rob yelled at her, but she paid him no mind. Then, when Rob was about to make her stop, the engine caught and a large black cloud of smoke blew out the rear tailpipe.

A ghoul had been crawling in front of the exhaust pipe and its pale face turned black, looking like Alfalfa from The Little Rascals. Inside the car, a cheer went up and Val shifted the car out of park, and when she was confident the engine was steady, she stepped on the gas.

At first the car didn't move, the bodies surrounding the small vehicle holding it fast, but then one ghoul lost its footing and fell to the ground. Val put the car in low gear and it began rolling. The left front tire drove over the fallen ghoul's arm and there was a loud crack, the sound resembling a tree branch snapping. Then the car was rolling forward, knocking the decayed bodies to the side like stray branches lying on an overgrown back trail.

Val swung the car around and drove for the parking lot exit, the ghouls following behind like sheep being herded to pasture.

She slowed when she reached the three cars that had arrived and then been attacked. All that was left of the slaughtered victims were bloodstains on the vehicles and on the pavement, a few tatters of clothing here and there.

No one spoke, almost as if the cars had become a shrine to the lost souls here and everywhere else, an image they were sure they would see again and again now that they had left the safety of the shopping mall.

In no time the VW was out of sight and leaving the shopping mall behind, the wails of the dead soon fading away.

"I don't believe it, we actually made it," Rob said to them all in slight astonishment.

"Never had a doubt," Jeremy said, acting more confident than he felt.

"We were lucky, that's all," Karen said as she turned to see behind them. The road was empty, the mall already behind them.

Val turned onto the main road that would lead into town and she frowned deeply as she studied the gauges on the dash. Rob saw this and leaned over to see what she was looking at, but he rolled his window down a little before he did, hoping the night air would help dissipate the odor of death and decay filling the inside of the car.

"What's wrong? I saw that look," he told her.

She shook her head and pointed to the gas gauge.

"I forgot I needed gas when I got to the mall all those week's ago. Gas was almost four dollars a gallon and I was putting it off for as long as I could. We're on fumes."

"So, can't we just get more gas?" Karen asked.

Rob shook his head and glanced over his shoulder to see her.

"It's not that easy anymore, Karen. With no power, the gas stations won't be pumping and if we try to siphon gas from a car or truck we'll be vulnerable to attack. And if we get surrounded while we're doing it, we're screwed."

"How much gas do we have?" Jeremy asked.

"Not much, hon, maybe five or six miles, tops," Val told him.

Jeremy nodded and then pointed south towards the city. "So why don't we go onto James Street and see if we can park in one of those underground parking lots. There's lots of cars in there. Or there should be, and we can make sure it's clear before we try."

Rob smiled, giving his idea some thought.

"That's not a bad idea, son."

Jeremy leaned back in his seat, grinning.

"Thanks, old man, I get one now and then. Figure I was due."

"I told you not to call me that, now stop it, ya hear me?" Rob said in an annoyed tone. It only made him look angrier than he was as his face was still covered in gore and blood from his disguise.

"Sorry, Rob, it slipped out. Won't happen again," he replied.

"See that it doesn't," he said and turned around to talk to Val. She agreed with the idea and turned at the next left to take them into the city. The office buildings with the parking garages underneath them were on the edge of the city limits and, with luck, the undead wouldn't be there in any form of large numbers.

Jeremy glanced at Karen and his eyes asked what was up with Rob. She only shrugged her shoulders, pieces of meat falling off her to land on the floor and seat of the car.

With a destination in mind, the four weary people remained silent, only the purr of the small engine filling the night as Val drove through the dark streets.

It would be dawn soon, and hopefully, with the coming of a new day, they would find the fuel they needed, but even when they did, they still had no idea where to go or what to do next.

Jeremy brought this up and Rob only nodded, agreeing with him.

"One thing at a time, son, one thing at a time."

As if that was good enough for all of them, the rest of their trip was in solitude, each of them lost in thoughts of *what ifs* and *what might have beens.*

* * *

Val veered around another derelict car and slowed at the city limits. Though the road was choked with cars and trucks, there was still room on the sides, the breakdown lanes mostly empty.

That was amusing to Rob. Given the state most people would have been in, he found it odd that most people wouldn't have simply ignored the rules and just driven in the breakdown lane, but even with the world crumbling around them, it seemed the average man or woman followed the rules. Perhaps even feeling comforted by knowing they were in place.

Val glanced at Rob and Jeremy in her rearview mirror, as if waiting for someone to tell her to go. Finally, Rob tapped her headrest impatiently and pointed forward. She nodded, steering the car into the breakdown lane and slowly driving down the road.

As they passed the cars, the four survivors saw much of the same carnage and death as before.

Blood splattered windows and car doors hanging open were the common denominator, and added to that was more than one accident.

A large bread truck had pummeled a small Toyota, the driver of the Toyota now stuck in the front windshield.

As the VW drove past, Karen stared at the face of the dead man adorning the hood, his glazed eyes still open wide like saucers, the mouth slack, the lips creased in the last look the man had as he flew through the glass, which was one of shock and pain. A dried pool of blood was spread out around the corpse's face, a few small footprints in the viscous fluid from where rats had fed.

As if on cue, a large rat the size of an average housecat popped up from the middle of the corpse. It was then Karen realized there was a large hole in the body's back. The rat had burrowed deep, searching for the meat within, and she had to look away when the rat's face, matted a dull-red, looked at her; the small eyes blinking while whiskers flicked in the night air.

"Oh, how horrible," she said as she moved closer to Val.

"We're gonna see a lot more of that before this trip's over," Rob said as he cast a glance at the corpse. Then the car was past and rolling onward.

By the time they reached the edge of the city itself, all four of them were anesthetized to the horrors around them.

Val pulled to the side and slowed, the engine ticking softly.

As they had made the trip from the shopping mall, the ghouls had tried to reach them as they stumbled about without purpose. Now was no different. The moment the car slowed, ten ghouls in the immediate area began moving towards them. So far, they'd been spread out, but Val knew if she stayed still for too long they would have an army to deal with.

"So, we're here. Where to now?"

Jeremy leaned forward and pointed straight ahead.

"Go that way. There's a few office buildings with lower underground garages on High Street."

"Sounds good," she said and began driving. A zombie was in her way and she struck it with the left bumper. The ghoul went sprawling across the pavement, now with a snapped hip. Not able to stand any longer, it began crawling after the car. Not that it mattered. In less than a minute, Val had turned the corner and was on her way.

Here, the streets were worse off than the main road. With only room for one car to drive on each side of the double line, there was more congestion thanks to stalled, miscellaneous vehicles and cars. An overturned police car lay in the middle of the road, a large part of it a blackened mess from a fire that had burned itself out, and as Val pulled up to it, two dead cops came out from around the undercarriage. Both were horribly burned, their faces nothing but scorched flesh. White teeth gleamed without gums in the night, and with a chill, Val continued on, the left side of the VW scraping the police car.

"Sooner or later there's gonna be a place we can't get past," she said to Rob.

"Yeah, I was thinking the same thing." He pointed to the right when they approached the next intersection. "Go that way. There's a bank there and I know for a fact they have an underground parking garage."

She did as he suggested and swung the car to the left, a few ghouls bouncing off the front end. One reached out and grabbed the rear bumper, wrapping pale, dry fingers on the end. As the car moved past, the fingers were ripped from the hand and the ghoul raised its fingerless hand to its face, not understanding what had happened. Then the VW was gone and the ghouls were alone again. A few still followed, more joining them, but they weren't fast enough even for a slow moving car.

Val slowed when she approached the bank. A Brinks truck lay on its side in front of the bank, the rear doors open. Money was everywhere, blowing around like confetti after a city parade, the bags that held it torn open and lying on the street like deflated balloons. At the moment, the currency was worthless to any of them and they barely paid it any attention at all. All four of them realized money couldn't protect them or feed them in any way. It was just another lost relic of what was.

"The garage entrance is on the other side of the building," Rob told her and she drove around the Brinks truck. There was a corpse in a guard's uniform lying half-in/half-out of the driver's window, most of his face and neck missing. They all turned away, having seen more than their share of carnage for the night.

As Val rounded the building, she suddenly slammed on the brakes.

Rob looked at her, not understanding what was wrong, but that was because he was looking to his left. When the car stopped, he looked to Val and then out the front windshield, gasping at the sight that greeted him.

There had to be a hundred zombies in the street, all seeming to be shambling about like lost souls. More than half the men wore suits and ties, the women wearing power suits. All the clothing was covered in gore and puss, not to mention a good amount of bile and dung. Though an unattractive thought, when these human beings died, they evacuated their bowels and bladder, and once revived, they obviously didn't get a new change of clothing.

Many ghouls had shoes covered in shit after it had dribbled down their legs after dying. Just one more distasteful thing about dying and returning. After all, who wants to walk around for eternity with a dirty ass?

"They're blocking the ramp to the garage," Val stated as she watched the ghouls. Already they were coming for the car, their feet dragging like they were lead weights, their arms swaying slowly as they strode with ungainly movements.

Rob glanced to the other buildings, but there was nowhere better to go.

"Oh, no, look behind us," Jeremy said in a concerned voice.

Rob, Karen and Val turned and glanced over their shoulders and spread their eyes wide. More than two dozen ghouls were appearing, the bodies coming out of doors and alleyways.

They were surrounded.

"What are we gonna do?" Karen asked as she stared at the slowly moving bodies. Like a procession of drunken soldiers, the undead moved towards the car, all a mixed bag of humanity. Many wore rags, signifying they had been homeless in life while others wore two thousand dollar suits. All were equal in death, no more prejudice amongst one another.

The dead knew not pride, or greed, or jealousy, only hunger.

And they were hungry for the four survivors.

The first zombies had reached the VW and their hands began a staccato of drumbeats on the hood and fenders.

"Go! Go! We don't have any choice! Try to plow through them!" Rob screamed to Val as he pointed to the opening of the parking garage.

"This isn't a goddamn tank, Rob. It's a VW, for Christ's sake!"

"Watch your mouth, woman, and it doesn't matter. If we stay here, we're dead. Any more of them reach us and we'll never drive through them. Now, go! For the love of all that's holy, go!"

Karen decided she agreed with Rob, and before Val could stop her, she reached across the floorboard with her foot and slammed her left sneaker on Val's which was on the gas pedal, the car surging forward. Large thumps filled the air as bodies were knocked to the side, rolling off the small hood. One went straight over the hood, its left cheek smashing against the glass. As it slid off, it left a slime trail that screeched like nails on a chalkboard. Then the body was gone, but there were plenty more to replace it.

Val fought the steering, the bodies making it impossible to drive straight. But she slowly made progress. One of the reasons for this was that as the dead rotted they were slowly losing body mass. While some were in good shape, others were nothing but emaciated corpses that looked as if they would blow away in a stiff wind.

With everyone on the edge of their seats, Val forced the car through the undead mob until she was at the opening to the underground parking lot. The gate was almost half up and the ramp led into darkness like a cave beckoning adventurers to their deaths.

Only a few bodies stumbled about below in the shadows and Rob nodded. The car couldn't get into the garage, but they could, crawling under the gate.

"Good, that's good, it doesn't look like there's that many of them down there. We can make it."

"But how? The instant we get out of the car and run for it, they're gonna attack us," Jeremy stated as he stared at the pale faces passing the car's windows. More were arriving with each passing second.

"You're right. We need a distraction," Rob agreed.

"A distraction? Like what?" Val asked as she backed up the car, knowing they needed to keep moving or become surrounded. She ran down a five-year-old with red pony tails. The small body caused the car to rise a few inches into the air, like she'd driven over a speed bump, then the car was down and moving on.

They were almost at the point they would need to make a decision on what they were going to do, the fuel gauge on **E** for a while now. Val was shocked the engine was still running at all.

"That's easy," Rob said. "We're sitting in it. Now, Val, get us out of here and we'll make plans."

Val turned off the road and drove away from the bank, while inside the car, the others listened with mouths agape, as Rob filled them in on how they were going to escape the car and reach the underground parking garage.

* * *

"This is so crazy; you know that, don't you? It's never gonna work," Jeremy said as he shifted to the side of the backseat so Rob could get at the engine easier.

"Well, if that's true, then we're all gonna die. You do know that, right?" Rob asked.

Jeremy frowned. "Well, yeah, but when you put it like that I don't think I wanna be right anymore."

Rob chuckled a little, his head and shoulders inside the engine.

The VW was parked on a small side street in an alley, a block from the bank. Night was slowly fading away to morning, but in the gloom of pre-dawn there was still enough lack of light to hide them fairly well.

As they all sat silently in the car, bodies of the walking dead slowly moved past the opening to the alley, resembling homeless people; all aimless in their journey.

The back seat of the VW was torn and sliced, then bent back allowing Rob access to the engine. If the car had been American made he would have had to risk going outside of the metal and glass of the car, but with the engine in the rear, that wasn't an issue.

"I sure hope this works," Karen said from the front seat. Rob was still busy working so only Jeremy and Val heard her.

"It's got to, hon, if not, Rob's right, we're all dead, Val said. "There's too many of them out there to fight. All we can do is hope this works and then run for it when the fireworks start."

Karen nodded and no one spoke for a few seconds, Rob's tinkering inside the engine compartment the only sound.

"Where do you think all the people went?" Karen finally asked, wanting to break the silence. Plus, when no one was talking she had time to think about everything and she didn't like that. Distractions was what she wanted, needed, so she wouldn't go crazy.

"Probably got evacuated when everything began to fall apart," Rob said as he backed out of the engine compartment. He had a few spots of grease on his face along with the dried blood he'd used for a disguise and he looked just like a grease monkey from the local garage.

"Or worse," Val said in a low voice.

"Worse?" Karen asked.

"Yeah, hon. It's not improbable that everyone in this city who didn't get out has been eaten and turned. You saw how many of them are out there. There's probably an entire city of dead people just waiting to chomp on our asses."

"Val, please, language," Rob pleaded as he wiped his hands on a corner of his shirt. It was late summer and it was warm in the car and they all smelled like road kill, but they all agreed the windows would remain closed for safety.

"Well, it's true, Rob, sweet words or not. Truth is, there's an entire city of dead people out there and we're smack dab in the middle of it." She shook her head. "Maybe we should just hightail it back to the suburbs and see what we can find."

"Oh, okay, let's say we do that," Rob rationalized. "What happens when we run out of gas somewhere on the road?"

Val opened her mouth to answer and then closed it, knowing he had a point.

"There must be somewhere we could get gas," Jeremy suggested. "What about a cab company or a bus station."

"No way, son. Wherever we go, they'll be waiting for us, it's simple math. Besides, you see the way they wander around. All they do is walk it seems. They're everywhere by now. No, we need to find someplace strong to hole up in. The mall was good, but there were too many exits and the dead were already in there good. Maybe the parking garage is better. It didn't look like there were many at the bottom of the ramp. I don't think they've figured out they can go down there."

Karen nodded. "It is possible. When I was on the roof of my house I would watch them, and sometimes a few tried to reach me by climbing out the window. They aren't very smart and they always fell off."

"Exactly," Rob said and then looked to Val. "Okay, it's done. All I have to do is pull on the gas line and it'll pop right off."

"Is there enough in there to do what you want?" Val asked.

Rob shrugged. "That, I don't know, but all we can do is try."

"So we're ready?" Val asked.

"Let's go, the sun's comin' up and I don't think daylight is our friend. At least when it was dark, they couldn't see us that well."

"Yeah, but they saw the headlights," Jeremy stated, wanting to be part of the conversation.

"True, son, true, but all they saw were headlights. The beams blinded them."

"Well, then let's go, the sooner we're off the streets the better." She started the engine and the car surged forward. A zombie happened to be in the middle of crossing the alley opening and its rotting face turned at the last second to see the small car barreling down on it. It had time to raise its arms in either defense or attack and then it was rolling off the hood to fall away, battered and broken.

Val swerved around the turn and headed back to the bank, the bodies on the streets silhouetted by the coming dawn.

As they were only a block away from the bank, Val got them there in no time. Traffic was light, obviously, and if it wasn't for the abandoned cars and corpses lining the street, she would have made it in less than a minute.

As the VW approached the bank again, the bodies were now more spread out. When they had left the bank to retreat as Rob planned their escape, there had been a time when Val thought they might not have been able to extricate themselves from the mob of bodies. But luck, fate, or both had intervened and she'd found an opening.

Now they were going back to the crowd and she wondered for the hundredth time if she was crazy. After all, it was her car they were in. She was ultimately in charge at the end of the day, but deep in her mind she knew she had no clue what to do. Though slightly overbearing, Rob seemed to have a handle on things. Now, whether that was a false facade or not was unknown, but so far he'd done a good job of getting them out of scrapes. Not that she had done such a bad job herself. It had been her idea to get them from the shopping mall and then to her car.

The bodies began to congeal around the car and she had to focus more, thoughts of everything else pushed to the back of her mind. The engine surged as it powered through the crowd, knocking the cadavers to the side like tenpins.

"There's an opening! Go over there, right near the ramp!" Rob yelled and pointed to the top of the ramp leading deep into the underground parking garage.

Val swung the car in the direction he was pointing and bodies went flying, but there were plenty more to take the place of the ones tossed aside and it wouldn't be long before the car would simply be bogged down by the simple weight of the walking dead.

"Everyone, get your stuff together," Rob ordered them. "As soon as she reaches the top of the ramp, we all make a run for it. If any of them get in your way, just push them aside. Don't try to hurt them, that's not our goal. Just run down the ramp and wait at the gate. When we're all there we'll get it closed the rest of the way and go inside together."

"Have you really thought about what's gonna happen if there's a shitload of them inside the garage, Rob?" Jeremy asked as he held on to the handle of the door as Val crashed through more bodies.

"Positive thinking, son, that all we can do, now watch that mouth, I'm not gonna keep telling you."

Jeremy rolled his eyes upward. "We're probably all gonna die in a minute and this guy's worried about swearing, gees," he muttered.

"Heard that," Rob said from his side.

"Good, I wanted you to," Jeremy replied, and thought that was why he said gees and not Jesus.

Dead hands slapped the car from all sides and the four survivors gritted their teeth as Val slowly made her way through them.

Val floored the gas pedal and the vehicle broke free of a large knot of corpses, the tires screeching on the pavement.

She slammed a few more aside and then the VW was at the top of the ramp.

"Move, move, let's go, now!" Rob screamed as he kicked open his door and climbed out, Karen already out of the car and by his side.

Val and Jeremy did the same, the engine still running.

Just before Rob climbed out, though, he reached inside the engine compartment and yanked on the gas line. With the fuel pump still pumping fuel, gas shot out and began to drip onto the seat and rear floorboards.

It wasn't much as the tank was about dry, but they couldn't be fussy. Reaching into his shirt pocket, Rob pulled free a small Zippo lighter. All of them had one, just one of the many items pilfered from the shopping mall. He flicked the cover open and lit the flame, then tossed it back into the VW's back seat.

With the four survivors dashing away, the interior of the car caught almost immediately, bright yellow flames erupting like living tendrils.

Val had her sword up and she slashed and hacked at the bodies closest to her while Rob shot two foes in the face and kicked another away. Even Karen was fighting, knowing they all had to chip in or else be swarmed by the rotting bodies. Jeremy pushed two away and then felt teeth on his leg. Luckily, the heavy material of his jeans kept him from being bit and he yanked his leg away, his pant leg tearing. The ghoul spit out the material and tried to reach him again, but Jeremy was gone, already on the move.

The only saving grace for the four fighters was they had picked a spot not heavily compacted with bodies. All the dead had to do was surround them and all would be lost, but they were spread out and slow, the survivors able to dodge and weave and continue moving forward.

Just as the four people reached the ramp to the garage, the VW exploded; sending smoking wreckage in all directions and knocking bodies to the ground and giving Rob and the others the chance they needed to escape.

Flaming debris splashed onto the ghouls, their dry clothes like kindling for the flames. The zombies became walking crematoriums, their immolated bodies staggering about with arms held high. Eyes melted inside sockets, the goo dripping down cheeks to sizzle in the flames and the sickly sweet smell of cooking meat saturated the area. A few of the ghoul's opened their mouths wide and high-pitched screams filled the night. Rob wondered if the scream was from pain or just air being expelled from the roasting cadavers, but either way it was a chilling sound.

Like blind men and women, the ghouls with burned out sockets stumbled around until there wasn't enough left to feed the flames, then they dropped to the pavement to remain still, the rest of the forms still smoldering. But the four survivors didn't see that part, as they were charging down the ramp and hopefully to the safety of the underground parking lot.

More ghouls were following them and when Rob glanced over his shoulder, he saw a line of pale faces in the gloom of the coming dawn.

"Hurry up, we've got no time!" Rob called to the others, their feet slapping the cement as they charged down the ramp. Upon reaching the half-open gate, the others scooted under and Rob tossed his backpack to the other side after them and reached up for the lip, trying to pull the gate down.

It wouldn't budge, and as he pulled again, he looked back up the ramp into the eyes of the dead.

They were close, twenty feet and closing fast.

"It won't go down, help me you guys!"

Val, Jeremy and Karen all joined him and each one reached up, grabbed the metal links, and began to pull.

"It's stuck, goddamn it!" Val screamed as she struggled to pull the immovable object down.

"Oh, shit, we're so dead," Jeremy said with finality.

"No, we're not, now keep working at it!" Rob yelled at them him, his eyes wide with the stress of the moment.

With grunts and groans to mimic the dead, the four people pulled as hard as they could, and just before the first dead man reached them, the gate released with a groan of its own, whatever linkage holding it snapping under the strength of the four determined people.

The gate dropped closed so hard it jumped a foot in the air after connecting with the cement, but Rob forced it back down. No sooner was the gate down then undead bodies crashed into it, bouncing off it with a clatter.

"How're we gonna lock it?" Jeremy asked as he stepped away from the gate to avoid fingers reaching for him.

Rob shook his head. "Don't know, but I don't think they're smart enough to lift it up."

"Maybe, but excuse me if I don't want to wait and find out," Val said and took the sheath for her sword and walked over to the edge of the gate. She jammed it into the slide track and then tried to lift it up. It moved an inch, but then stopped.

There, that should do it until we can find something else," she said.

"Good idea," Karen told her with a grin. She was covered in sweat and dried gore and her face was a mask of fright, but for the moment she actually felt a little safe again. The gate was strong, much more than the thin one that had been used at the furniture store, and there was no way the ghouls were going to get inside with them.

But then there was no way the four of them were going to get out either, at least not the same way they came in. Three more minutes passed with all of them getting back their confidence. All stared at the pale, blank faces on the opposite side of the grating, watching the dead humanity moaning and growling for them.

Finally, Rob stood tall, went and picked up his backpack, slung it over his shoulder, and gestured to the others.

"Well, we might as well see how safe it is in here," he said, gesturing to the darkness at the bottom of the ramp. Only the barest hint of light penetrated the darkness and even that was almost nothing. The bodies in front of the metal grating blocked what light came from outside. The flickering flames from the VW added some, but not much. Val saw what was left of her car through the shifting bodies and frowned.

"I still can't believe you blew up my car," she said to Rob.

"Sorry, Val, it had to be done. Let me ask you a question. Would you have died for that car?"

"No, of course not, that's a silly question."

He nodded. "Then there's your answer."

"So, are we gonna keep talkin' or are we gonna go investigate?" Jeremy asked from the front of the line. He had a two foot piece of wood in his hands taken from a corner of the ramp. There were other, smaller pieces, but they were mostly splinters. It was probably left there from some work truck when the wood had fallen off the bed as the vehicle entered or exited the underground garage.

Now it worked well as a makeshift club for the young man.

"Hold your horses, son, we'll go, but first we need to get some light," Rob told Jeremy.

Val reached around in her backpack and pulled out a flashlight.

"I got one, thought it would be worth bringing along when we left the mall, you know, with no power anywhere."

Rob nodded and took the flashlight. "Good thinking, Val, thanks." He handed it to Karen who was the only one not holding a weapon. Val had her sword, Rob his Magnum and Jeremy the wooden club.

"Here, Karen, you take this and make sure you keep it moving, and if one of us points in a direction make sure you point it the same way."

"Got it," she said.

He flashed her an encouraging smile.

"You'll do great," he said to her.

"Come on; let's get this show on the road. Besides I gotta use the bathroom, unless you want me to go right here," Jeremy said as he wiggled his legs.

"No, wait a few minutes, if you can," Rob asked him.

Jeremy nodded. "It's not that bad...yet," he added.

"Okay, so let's go see what's down there," he said and they all set off, Karen in the middle as she flashed the light back and forth like a blind man would a cane.

As the four survivors disappeared into the ebony darkness of the parking garage, the undead railed at the gate, moaning and shaking it like wild jungle animals.

* * *

The darkness surrounded the four weary survivors like a heavy cloak, as if it was a living entity trying to smother them in its embrace.

Karen tried to point the flashlight in all directions at the same time, but it was impossible.

There was a soft dripping coming from somewhere to their right, and the fan of a ventilation unit spun slowly, the wind from outside keeping it moving. It was in need of lubrication and the echoes of squeaks added to the atmosphere of doom.

"What do we do first?" Jeremy whispered to Rob as they moved deeper into the parking garage. The light from the flashlight reflected off of glass windows and car bumpers, the cars now resembling relics found in a buried cave. Their owners were either long gone or dead, but the end result was the cars would remain in this man made cavern until the end of time. That is, unless humanity could somehow overcome the dead and take back what was rightfully theirs.

"We make sure it's safe in here and then we get some rest," Rob said.

He, like the others, had spent more than half the night running and fighting and was exhausted. When he gazed into their eyes, he saw the same exhaustion there, as well.

Footsteps sounded from the left, near Val, and then were immediately followed by a low groan.

"Give me some light over here," Val hissed and raised her sword.

A dead man in a parking uniform came out from behind a pair of parked cars, his hands reaching out to attack Val. She raised her sword and slashed at him, taking his hands off at the wrist. Before the man could move closer, she spun around in a circle, her sword held high in a wide arc. With all the power of her lithe frame behind it, the blade cut the ghoul's head from his shoulders, the loose head now dropping away to roll into the shadows. The body took a few more stumbling steps forward and dropped to the cement floor, a viscous fluid dribbling from the jagged neck wound.

"Nice," Jeremy said, his heart beating twice as fast from the scare.

"I try," Val said and wiped the blade on the back of the corpse's pants.

"Good job, Val, let's keep moving," Rob said. "One thing we have to our advantage is these *things* don't hide. If they sense us, they'll come out for us."

"So what're you saying? That we should yell out and call them to dinner? Namely us?" Jeremy asked in astonishment.

"No, of course, not. Let's just keep moving around the garage and if there's more in here we can get them one at a time. Just everybody, keep your voice down."

They moved forward again, moving from row to row of vehicles. Val took the lead, with Karen right behind her to shed light if the warrior woman needed it. Rob knew his Magnum was a last resort. If he fired the gun, then every ghoul in the garage would know where they were.

Another head popped up behind a Volvo, the scraggly blonde hair and smeared mascara proclaiming the ghoul was female.

Karen turned and flashed the light in the dead woman's eyes, and for a moment the woman was blinded. Val moved in for the kill. Slashing and hacking, she cut the woman into pieces, the arms and legs dropping to the ground like cordwood. When she was finished, they moved on.

The going was slow, as they didn't want to make any more noise than they had to. The stone walls of the garage reflected any sound, bouncing it around like a massive cavern. Jeremy took out the next ghoul, an old man with a cane still in his hands. He had a checkbook in his shirt pocket, and whether he had been coming or going when he'd been attacked would never be known. A large ragged wound in the side of his neck gleamed in the beam from Karen's flashlight and the dead man lunged for her. But Jeremy was right behind her and pulled her back, whacking the geriatric ghoul over the head with his makeshift club. The middle of the man's skull sank in and Jeremy pulled the wood back with bits of scalp and hair now embedded in it. When the man still didn't go down, Jeremy raised the wood again, prepared to pummel the ghoul good. But then Val's blade appeared and jabbed the old man in his right eye, piercing the white orb and continuing into the brain. She turned the sword to the left and the blade bit deep, the ghoul dropping to the floor like he was electric powered and the power had been cut.

"I had it, ya know, I didn't need your help," Jeremy said angrily.

"I know, hon, but the sooner we take 'em down the better." She grinned slightly. "It's not a contest, babe."

Jeremy nodded slightly, getting her meaning, but he was still perturbed.

"Well, maybe so, but I still had that one."

"Knock it off, you two, this isn't a game," Rob said, and as if to illustrate his words, another ghoul appeared from his right side. Without thinking, Rob raised the Magnum and fired at the approaching shadow, but as he squeezed the trigger, he got a brief glimpse at the face when the light of Karen's beam came around an instant after Rob had fired.

What Rob saw horrified him to the bottom of his very soul.

The face wasn't drawn and pale, and there were no wounds to be seen. The mouth was open, but not in a growl or a moan, but to speak words...real words.

And then the body was flying backwards and bouncing off the fender of a car, blood smears covering the paint as the man slumped to the ground.

"Bull's-eye, Rob, got another one," Jeremy said, not realizing what was happening.

"Oh my God, no, I didn't just..." Rob said and then grabbed Karen's arm. "Come with me, I need to see something," he said in a hushed tone, the trepidation in his voice apparent.

She nodded and the two moved over to the body now prone on the cement, while Val and Jeremy looked at one another curiously.

"What's that about?" Val asked him. Jeremy only shrugged.

Rob dashed to the body with Karen next to him and they both leaned down as Rob gazed down at the man he'd just shot.

"Oh dear God, oh Lord, no, this can't be happening," Rob muttered as he stared at the face of the man he'd just shot. The eyes were closed and a slim trickle of bright-red blood leaked out of the corner of his mouth to flow over his cheek and down his neck.

"What is it Rob, what's wrong?"

Rob turned to her and lowered his head. "This man wasn't one of them, Karen. Look at him. I mean, *really* look at him. His face is clear and I saw his eyes after I shot him. They weren't white like the others."

"So you mean…" she said, leaving it hanging.

"I think so, yes," he replied.

Suddenly the man opened his eyes and wheezed loudly. He reached up and grasped Rob's hands as his mouth spewed a bloody froth, the words he was trying to say not coming out as he choked on blood. Rob glanced down at the massive hole in the man's chest and figured he had a punctured lung, and a lot more damage that was most definitely fatal.

The man's mouth opened and closed as if he was trying to say something, then small whispers began.

"He's saying something," Karen said.

Rob leaned closer to the dying man and stared into his eyes.

"I'm so sorry, sir, I thought you were one of them," Rob said in a halting tone. The guilt Rob felt was unbearable. He was a man of God and believed all life was sacred. To take another life, especially if it was unwarranted, was sacrilege to him. He didn't count the zombies, they were already dead. In fact, he believed he was doing them a favor by sending them all back to the final death they so sorely deserved.

The dying man shook his head, bloody spittle flying back and forth as he reached past Rob's arms and grabbed his shirt. He yanked Rob to him, so his mouth was only inches from Rob's face.

Karen could only watch as the man whispered hushed words and fragmented sentences to Rob. No sooner did he say what he was trying to get out than his eyes fluttered and one last gasp left his lips. The hands holding Rob's shirt dropped away to lay limp on his chest. Rob didn't move for a few seconds, but just stared at the man's face.

The man he had gunned down in cold blood.

The dead man's eyes were still open and Rob reached out and closed them, then he sat back on his haunches.

Karen shone the light in his face as Val and Jeremy moved closer. They' just figured out what had happened, and though keeping an eye out for anymore foes, they still wanted to see what was going on.

"So, what did he say to you, Rob? Could you make it out?" Karen asked.

Rob stood slowly, his knees cracking as he did so.

He looked at each of his fellow survivors and as he took in what the dead man had just told him, his face went ashen.

"He said to leave here immediately. He said we'll only find our deaths here."

"What? That's crazy. He must have been delusional from loss of blood," Jeremy said as he waved his wooden club in the air like a wand. "We've been through almost half of this place and so far it's pretty empty."

No sooner did he finish his sentence then a low guttural moan, amplified by dozens of voices filled the garage, seeming to come from everywhere at once.

"Uhm, guys, what's that?" Val asked warily, her eyes flicking back and forth to try and penetrate the shroud of darkness outside of the flashlight beam.

The sound of footsteps could now be heard, feet slapping the cement, dozens of them, hundreds of them.

Though the echo was confusing, all of them looked in one direction. Namely, to the lower level of the garage.

"Oh, no, I forgot this garage has two levels," Rob said in a frightened tone.

"Your gunshot must have..." Karen said in terror, realizing where he was going with his statement.

Rob nodded. "Yeah, when I shot this poor soul my gunshot just alerted every one of them in this place that we're here."

"So, we can take 'em," Jeremy said with little confidence.

"No, son, you don't understand what I'm talking about." He pointed to the dead man. "He said some other stuff that now makes sense. It seems people went into this garage to escape what was happening in the city, but they were followed by the very thing they were running from. Some must have been infected, probably bitten, and when they *turned*, there was nowhere to run to. The people were torn to shreds and others were killed to come back again. There's more than two hundred people on the lower level right now."

"Uh, not anymore," Val whispered in fear as she took a step back so she was closer to the others.

Karen raised the flashlight and aimed it at the ramp for the lower level across the garage. The beam pierced the darkness and only ended up casting shadows, but it was easy to see what was making its way up the ramp.

Though the bodies were still below, the flashlight beam was enough illumination to throw dozens upon dozens of shadows on the ramp wall.

"I think things just went from bad to worse," Jeremy said in a hushed tone as he stared at the shadows growing larger with each passing second.

No one spoke then, all staring at what would inevitably be their doom.

Like a fortune teller who was always right, the dead man had told the truth.

Rob couldn't help but wonder if this wasn't the grand Maker's design, as if for taking an innocent man's life, God would now let him be torn apart by the demons of Hell themselves.

They were trapped in the garage. The only doors leading to the inside of the building were on the opposite side of the parking garage and the main gate was blocked by countless bodies.

There was nowhere safe to go.

Slowly, with each slap of a dead foot, the shapes and shadows from the lower level grew closer, and all four survivors could only stare in utter shock, knowing there was nowhere to go and that this time their destiny was written in stone.

* * *

Rob might have considered accepting the fate being thrust upon if not for Karen's face. The woman was petrified, and though Rob was prepared to die, he wasn't prepared to let Karen die with him, nor Jeremy or Val.

181

Taking the flashlight from Karen's shaking hand; his eyes scanned the garage, searching for some way to escape their certain doom.

And then it hit him like a bolt of lightning.

"The cars! Oh my God, the cars have all their keys in the guard shack!"

"What're you talking about?" Val asked, askance of him. Her sword was raised high and sweat beaded down her forehead and cheeks as she prepared for her last fight.

"The guard shack keeps all the keys for the cars in there," Rob told her. "When you go to the bank here, you have to give the guard your car keys. He hangs them on a board on the numbered slot that's the same as the number of your parking spot. Then you can go upstairs and do whatever. It's how they've always done it here. That way no one can accidentally block someone else in."

He took off at a run to the north side of the garage, remembering where the shack was when he'd passed it before.

"Come on, it's our only chance!"

"But what happens if we get into one of the cars?" Jeremy asked. "We'll just be trapped in there with no food or water."

"Maybe," Rob replied, "but either way it'll give us some time to think and plan, now shut up, son, and just follow me! All of you!"

With Rob in the lead, they sprinted across the garage, but before they got there the ghouls began to appear from the lower level ramp.

It was obvious the survivors weren't going to make it.

Rob's eyes flicked back and forth like an escaped convict and then he spied an immaculately restored Ford Pinto parked near the ramp, right where the ghouls were appearing. Raising his Magnum, he lined up a shot and fired at the rear of the Pinto.

There was the loud crack of the large handgun and the Pinto exploded in a blazing fireball that lifted it off the ground two feet before it came crashing down. The force of the blast sent the first wave of ghouls flying, more than one now burning like a giant matchstick.

"Whoa, dude, that was awesome," Jeremy exclaimed as he raised his hands in front of his face from the bright flames.

"Yeah, wow, I don't believe that actually worked," Val said, as she too, stared in open-mouthed astonishment.

"Well, it did, so come on, that's not gonna slow them down for long."

They moved forward again while the garage began to fill with a rich, black, cloying smoke that rolled across the ceiling and threatened to choke them before they could find safety.

With the flames burning brightly, there was more light to see by, but in the darkest corners of the garage, shadowy shapes could be seen moving amongst the parked cars.

When they reached the guard shack, Rob barreled inside, knocking items off the small desk.

"Karen, I need more light in here!" Rob called out to her. She ran over to him, squeezing into the shack. She brushed against him and he felt her soft body, and even in the franticness of the situation, he could sense his own body responding.

But there was no time for that now.

"Here, point it on the wall over here," he told her, and when she did, he began searching the small tags. As he glanced out the dirty, plexiglass window, he could see the cars were labeled easily and it didn't take him long to figure out the gist of it. But he wasn't sure what vehicle went to what key, so grabbing a dozen, he exited the shack and handed each of them three key rings.

"Here, take these, and press the alarm buttons. Maybe we can find a good one and not something like Val drove."

"Hey, that car was damn good. It saved your ass," she said defensively.

"Fair enough," he replied and then they moved off to search for a vehicle.

The air was becoming unbearable and the ghouls were now on the move again. The survivors had maybe a minute tops before they would be overwhelmed yet again.

While Val searched with the keys in her hands, a female ghoul lunged for her from the shadows. This one had already been on the main floor and hadn't come out yet until now. Val gasped in shock when the dead woman latched onto her arm with two pale hands, the death grip like a vise. Before she could do anything, the woman's yellow teeth clamped down on her left forearm, breaking the flesh like it was paper.

She yelled out and punched the woman in the face with the hilt of her sword and when the ghoul stumbled backwards, she sliced down hard, severing the head from the shoulders in one massive swipe, the blow fueled by anger. The pale head lopped off and rolled away, the ghoul dropping to the ground. Val only glanced at the wound, knowing there was no time to deal with it now. Pulling her sleeve down more to cover it, she began pressing car alarms, desperately trying to find a vehicle they could use.

It was Karen who called out excitedly from the corner of the garage, her coughing fit making it hard for her to talk.

"I found one, here; this one's huge!"

Rob, Jeremy and Val turned and ran to her, the shadows dancing thanks to the flickering light from the burning Pinto. The ghouls were right behind them, an army of dead faces with only one purpose, to kill and devour the survivors.

Karen was jumping up and down as she pointed to the large, four door, pearl white, Lincoln Navigator she found. As Rob approached the massive vehicle, he wondered how the owner had managed to get the massive machine inside the garage. The clearance height must have been down to centimeters.

Karen was opening the driver's door and climbing in as the others ran to her. Right behind them the undead came, and Rob spun, fired three shots at the closest ones in line, then turned back and dashed for the vehicle.

Val and Jeremy were right behind him. A ghoul lunged for Jeremy and he whacked it with his club, cracking the skull like a pineapple. He pushed the body away and ran after Rob.

When they had all reached the Lincoln, Karen was already starting the engine, the beep, beep of the dashboard telling her to buckle up sounding loud in the enclosed garage.

Rob and Jeremy jumped for the back door, and after Rob opened it, the two men leaped inside, closing the doors as bodies bounced off the metal.

Val kicked a zombie waiting for her as she rounded the front end of the Navigator and then she climbed inside, sitting next to Karen in the front seat.

"Now what do we do?" Jeremy gasped as he stared at the rotting faces pounding at the tinted windows. The Lincoln was rocking back and forth on its shocks as the undead pushed it back and forth. The staccato of fists on metal and glass was unbelievable, despite the sound dampening and the acoustic and tinted laminated windows. The din was so loud the four of them had to yell to be heard by one another.

Despite the size of the vehicle, Rob was beginning to worry the dead might be able to tip it over.

"I don't know yet. Give me a second to think, will ya?" After a moment he said, "Well, we can't stay here, that's for sure." Rob was staring at the face of a woman in a filthy power suit and a bloody name tag pinned to her breast. Even in death, Rob could see the woman had been beautiful; though now that beauty was distorted into something unholy.

"Okay, that's a given, but what do we do now exactly?" Val asked. "It's a fair question given our situation." She coughed a few times, the air inside the Lincoln growing rank from both their own gore-covered bodies, the undead bodies outside the vehicle, and the growing smoke filling the garage.

"We have to try and break through the gate again," Karen said as she gripped the steering wheel.

"How? The gates made of solid metal and there's all the zombies out there," Jeremy said.

Karen spun in her seat and glared at Jeremy. "If you have a better idea, I'm all ears, otherwise quit shooting everyone else's ideas down!" She was angry, but not just at him. She was scared and needed to vent and Jeremy was as good an excuse as any.

"Hey, don't you yell at me, it's a fair statement! So what, you're just gonna crash through 'em like we're living in an action movie? This is real life, Karen. If you try and break that gate all you're probably gonna do is get us killed."

Rob listened to them both and decided now was the time to add his opinion.

"Look, guys, you both make good points, but in the end we need to do something." To illustrate his point the Lincoln groaned on it axle, the zombies pounding and banging without tiring. It was when a ghoul on Val's side picked up a chunk of brick left over from construction and began banging it on her window that the decision was made.

"Karen's right, we don't have a choice. Fuck him, Karen, you're in the driver's seat, just go!" Val screamed as the brick struck her window again. She gripped her sword handle tighter, but felt helpless with nothing to fight.

Karen turned to Rob who only nodded, though Jeremy looked like a spoiled kid who wasn't getting his way. He didn't seem to understand if he was proved right, then they would all probably end up dead.

Karen put the transmission in drive and stepped on the gas, gently at first. She'd never driven such a massive vehicle before, and though she tried to be gentle, the engine surged to life and the Lincoln jumped forward, driving over five ghouls who had been standing in front of the SUV.

With large thumps to match the pounding, the bodies were driven over, the chassis pulverizing heads and torsos. With an almost apologetic face plastered on her visage, Karen pressed the gas pedal again and the 310 horsepower engine surged to life, breaking the Lincoln free of the bodies pounding on all sides. Karen had picked the right vehicle; there was no doubt about it. The Lincoln Navigator was as close to a tank as a civilian could get to owning, the 365 pounds of torque and 5.4L SOHC V engine more than powerful enough to overcome the frail, rotting corpses trying to hold on to the bumpers and frame.

With a squishing sound, the vehicle moved forward, gore and blood spraying into the tire wells as bodies were smashed into puree.

"Keep going, Karen, you're doing it!" Val encouraged her.

The bodies were ten thick, but they were only flesh and bone. The Navigator was solid metal and power and there was no match in the end.

Turning on the headlights, Karen swung the vehicle around and slowly, foot by gore-filled foot, made her way back to the ramp leading to the outside world.

By the time she reached the ramp, the air inside the SUV was unbearable and all had taken to trying to breathe through their shirts. The black smoke was so caustic to breathe in even the slightest amount would cause a coughing fit and Val turned on the air conditioning, hoping it might help.

It didn't and she turned it off just as fast.

But ten minutes later, the Lincoln was facing the ramp, the light from the early morning sun piercing into the darkness.

There had to be over a hundred ghouls at the gate, all shaking it and banging against it. The ones in front were smushed into paste, the weight of the ones behind forcing the ghouls into the mesh until they had large marks on their faces from the pressure.

"So what do I do? Just drive into the gate?" Karen asked as she stared at their faces. The SUV was still surrounded, the zombies following the vehicle the entire time it drove across the parking garage. The rocking became almost rhythmic, like they were on a boat on the ocean. So far, no ghoul had managed to damage the SUV, the massive vehicle too strong.

"That's about all you can do, hon," Val said and cast a glance to Rob.

"She's right, Karen. Just floor it and then hold on. All we can do is try."

"I still think it's a mistake," Jeremy added, askance of Rob.

"Yes, son, you made that clear, but unless you have another idea we don't have a choice. Do you have another idea, son?" Rob asked.

"No," Jeremy said in a low voice.

"Then it's settled. Everyone put on your seatbelts. It'll help when we hit."

After donning seatbelts, Karen glanced at each of them one at a time.

"Okay, you ready?"

"Go for it, hon," Val said with confidence. "Back up a little so you have more distance, then let 'er rip."

Karen turned forward, swallowed hard and then began to back up. Bodies behind her were run down to be crushed under the undercarriage. The hiss of burned flesh on the muffler carried to their noses, overriding the other unpleasant scents already permeating the interior of the vehicle.

Swallowing hard, Karen placed the six speed transmission into drive and, with one last glance to Val for support, she floored the gas pedal and the SUV surged forward.

Bodies were swatted aside like they were made of paper as the engine of the now blood-splattered white SUV roared like a living beast. By the time Karen was a few feet from the gate, the speedometer read forty-two.

And then the front grille connected with the gate and the airbags went off, driver's side, door panels and steering column, filling the interior with noise and sound and the four people inside were pummeled like rag dolls by the very safety feature put there to save their lives.

There was a rending of metal and the SUV punched halfway through the gate, the bottom portion ripping and tearing from the impact. Undead bodies were thrown to the sides and across the ramp to lay with broken bones and bloody wounds.

Inside the SUV, no one moved, the impact knocking them around like they were tiny playthings some giant child was finished with for the day.

From the ramp and behind, the undead mob slowly closed in on the SUV once again. The tinted windows didn't show the occupants inside, but the ghouls knew they were still in there.

As for inside the Lincoln, there was no sign of life.

* * *

The engine of the Lincoln Navigator still ticked softly as the living dead surrounded it. Once more, rotting hands began to pound on the metal while palms slapped the tinted glass. Black smoke billowed out of the garage opening to rise into the sky, where the buffeting winds broke the tendrils to whispers of their former selves.

The vehicle was rocked side to side as the ghouls attempted once again to break in, but the SUV was strong, and sat high on its wheels, making it difficult for the ghouls to reach it. Only their heads were even with the dark windows, and try as they might, they just couldn't penetrate its defenses.

With the sun slowly rising in the sky, the hundreds of bodies jostled one another for the chance to have a go at the sitting vehicle.

As for what was happening inside the Navigator's interior, the dead neither knew nor cared. All they wanted was the meat within and they had all the time in the world.

* * *

Rob was lost in a memory from his past. He and his wife were walking hand in hand at the park. The birds were in the sky, the horizon a bright blue with only a few white, fluffy clouds to mar it. Children played on the grass and a young couple sat together under a large oak tree that had to be over fifty years old if it was a day.

He glanced at his wife, but she wasn't looking at him. Instead, she was concentrating on something in a few bushes that lined the edge of the park. Then, without a reason, she let go of his hand and crossed the path until she was at the shrubs. Bending over, she picked something up. It was long, at least three feet in length, and as she turned and looked at him, he realized it was a leg.

A severed, human leg.

In fact, the sneaker and sock were still on it. Maggots crawled around the festering wound where the leg was severed from whose body he knew not. Blood still dripped from the limb and his wife held it up like she had won a prize at a carnival.

Rob was about to open his mouth to tell her to put that disgusting thing down so they could call the police when she lifted the leg to her mouth and took a large bite of the flesh from right below the calf.

Rob stood transfixed as his wife began chewing on the leg like it was a large turkey leg. Congealing blood dripped from the corners of her mouth and slid down her cheeks to pool below her chin, and her eyes rolled in their sockets, she was enjoying herself so much.

Rob took a step backward, not believing what he was seeing, and when he did this, he saw the couple under the tree wasn't in the same position they were in before.

Now they were leaning over one of the children he'd seen playing on the grass. The young couple had their hands in the child's torso, tearing at it like they were digging for gold. Small, slimy entrails were pulled from the child and the young couple began devouring them, shoving as much in their mouths as they could manage. Their cheeks bulged with red meat and their lower face and chin became scarlet.

He turned back to his wife and suddenly she was standing right in front of him.

The leg was gone and she was reaching out her hands to him. Only now she looked like a ghoul. Her eyes had sunk into her head and her complexion was cracked and pale. Those same eyes he'd loved to gaze into were now bone white and her hair was a stringy mass of gore and feces.

She smelled beyond ripe, and when she moved closer, a yellow-brown maggot wiggled out of her nose to fall onto her upper lip. She slid out her tongue and pulled the little bugger in, swallowing it whole.

"Mmmm, protein," she said with an evil grin. "Come, Robert, be with me. It's not so bad being dead," she purred as she tried to take his hands again.

He shook his head back and forth, unable to accept the reality he now found himself in and he turned and began running through the park. All around him was the same bloodshed, the same carnage, as people feasted on people.

"Rob, come back, Rob, I need you," she called out. "Rob, Rob, Rob...." Her voice echoed in his head for what seemed an eternity.

"Rob, Rob, come on, wake up," the voice said from somewhere far away.

"No, leave me alone," Rob muttered, falling in and out of consciousness.

"That's it, there's no time for this shit," Val said and then she slapped Rob hard on the right cheek, rattling his teeth in his head.

He snapped awake almost instantly and looked around himself. Val, Karen and Jeremy were all looking at him, their faces and upper bodies covered in white from when the air bags had deployed.

"What happened?" he asked as he looked about himself.

"You got knocked out from the airbag," Val said. "Those damn things do as much harm as good, I tell ya."

While he came to his senses, he realized he was still in the Navigator and now he heard all the pounding still going on. If it wasn't for the noise reduction technology built into the SUV, he doubted he would have been able to stand the noise at all.

Jeremy saw him looking out the window and he nodded, pointing with his left hand.

"They can't get in, Rob. We seem to be as safe as we can be in here."

"Yes, but for how long," Karen said. "Val said one of them had a brick in his hand. If the others figure out how to use tools we're all doomed. So far the only advantage we have is how dumb they appear to be."

"Amen to that," Jeremy said. "At least we're smarter than them."

"Well, some of us are, hon," Val smiled and he made a rude face in reply.

"So what're we still doing here?" Rob asked.

"We're not doing anything. We just came around ourselves, right guys?" Val asked the others. There was a general agreement to that.

Rob sat taller in his seat, and when he caught a glimpse of a female ghoul at the window, he felt a chill go down his spine, a fluttering of his vision from the past flooding to the front of his mind. He pushed it down for another time.

"Okay, I'm fine, guys. Karen, can we get out of here or are we stuck?"

She shook her head and then shrugged her shoulders. "Don't know. The gate's bent and on the hood, but I won't know 'till we try to move."

Fists slapped the windows harder than before and Rob pointed to the ramp.

"Then let's try. The sooner we're gone from here, the better. I can't believe how lucky we've been so far."

"Hey, some people's luck is other's determination," Val said with a slight grin.

"Fair enough, Val, I won't argue with you there. Okay, Karen, get us the hell out of here," Rob said, and when Jeremy glanced at him, mouth open to comment on Rob's choice of words, Rob held up his hand in front of his face, palm out.

"Not a word, son, even I can cheat once in a while if the need demands it."

"All right, fine, just lay off the next time I slip up," Jeremy said

"Fair enough," Rob replied.

Karen put the SUV in reverse, and with a groaning of metal, she began backing away from the gate, the walking dead following like sheep to the shepherd. As the Navigator removed itself from the gate, the bottom lip caught on the bumper. Karen wasn't aware of this and she continued to back up.

Three things happened at the same time.

The first was everyone in the SUV felt a jolt when the trapped bumper and gate reached their limit. The second was the gate was pulled from its connection to the ramp, and the third was the front bumper was torn from the vehicle, the loud clatter of metal overriding the ghouls for a brief second.

"Oops, that's not good," Val said with a smile. She felt safe inside the vehicle, as it seemed the ghouls were impotent to get at them. What had been a trying, dangerous exodus was now nothing more than a car trip.

"Don't worry about it, Karen. I doubt the owner to this thing is gonna care," Rob said.

"How could he? He's dead," Jeremy added.

"Exactly," Rob agreed. "Go 'head and get us out of this place, Karen, I think it's time for a change of scenery."

She put the Lincoln in drive again and began powering forward. It was like driving through snow or mud, the bodies of the ghouls getting in her way. She drove over them, crushing them to the ramp, the tires pulping the bodies until the ramp was awash with blood and gore. The entire time the vehicle moved up the ramp, the zombies continued to pound on it. But it was hopeless. The Navigator was huge and the small bodies could do nothing. When the mob grew in size, Karen pressed harder on the gas pedal until she wasn't driving on the street at all, but just driving over body after body. The occupants inside the SUV were bounced around, the ride feeling like they were off-roading.

"Look for an opening in the crowd!" Rob yelled from the backseat as he bumped his head against the window.

"I'm trying!" She snapped back.

"There, Karen, over there!" Val yelled and pointed to the left.

Karen followed her gesture and saw a break in the crowd. It wasn't until she was closer that she saw it was the burned out wreck of another car. This one was on its side, but there was nothing left but a scarred and blackened hulk of metal.

The ghouls had to go around the wreckage and this left an opening.

"But there's something there, I can't go that way," she said as she fought the steering wheel. The windshield was covered with blood and yellow and white pus and she hit the wipers and fluid, washing some away.

"Just hit it, this baby can take it," Val said as she held on, preparing for the impact.

Karen wasn't in the mood to argue and she swung the Lincoln in the direction of the wreck, and when she was within reach of it, she crashed into it.

The wreck was knocked back onto its chassis, more than a dozen ghouls becoming trapped underneath. They wiggled and fought to free themselves, but the weight of the wreck was too much. Inside the SUV, they all felt the impact through their teeth, but then the Navigator was past the wreck and the area was relatively free of bodies.

No matter how many there were, sooner or later there would have to be an end to them and it looked like they had finally reached it.

Karen swung the Lincoln around a small knot of ghouls and then plowed over one she couldn't avoid. The dead man's head impacted the grille, flattening the face like a pancake. The rest of the body went under the front end and was torn up by the undercarriage. When the SUV was passed, the body rolled a few feet and came to a stop.

Karen glanced in her rearview mirror to see the body still moving. With its one remaining usable arm, the man was trying to drag himself off the street. Then the body was lost amongst the others and she focused her attention forward.

"This was a big mistake, guys, we need to head for the suburbs again," Rob said apologetically.

"No kidding," Jeremy said. "Did you think of that one yourself?"

"Okay, fine, but where do we go?" Val asked.

"How about Hanscom Air force base, surely they must have set up some kind of rescue station or something," Karen suggested.

"No, sorry to break the news to you," Rob said. "But before the television went out I heard they got overrun. All the obvious places, like hospitals, police stations and fire stations were overwhelmed with people in the beginning. But some were infected, and when they turned into one of them, they attacked the rest. It was a domino factor. Soon, no one knew who they could trust and the fighting began. It was a mess. That's why I stayed in my home and then found Jeremy here. It all happen so fast it was unbelievable. In less than two days everything was messed up," Rob finished, still amazed when he thought about it.

It was truly scary just how fragile civilization could be. It reminded him of a year before when an ice storm had hit northern Massachusetts. The ice had been so heavy, that power lines had gone down and people had been without power for weeks. In just one day, almost a dozen towns had been thrown into the 1800's, using fireplaces, woodstoves and generators to keep warm, some having to evacuate or risk dying of exposure.

And that was just an ice storm, what had happened now was a thousand, no, a million times worse.

"What about Gloucester?" Jeremy suggested.

"What about it, son?" Rob asked.

"Well, they got boats there, right? You know, the docks and all that. Why couldn't we just take a boat and sail away."

"Sail away to where?" Val asked.

Jeremy shrugged. "I don't know where, who cares? As long as it's not here."

Rob nodded, rubbing his chin. Karen barely paid attention. The road was clear of bodies for the moment, but she was still fighting her way through the stalled cars and wreckage littering the roads.

And now they were in a very large vehicle and places the VW had fit were now becoming a problem for the SUV.

"That's not a half bad idea," Rob said. "But first we need to get some supplies from somewhere. If we go out on the water we need to eat and drink."

"Some of the houses we passed, maybe," Jeremy suggested. "Some of them must have stuff in them we can use. Not everyone would have taken their food and water with them. A lot of people would have figured they'd get what they needed at the rescue stations."

"Karen, you okay up there?" Rob asked suddenly.

"I'm okay; it's just hard to deal with all of this. I don't want to think how many people I must have run over in the past hour."

"They're not people anymore, hon," Val told her. "Just remember that and you'll be fine."

Karen nodded, her hair falling in front of her eyes. She pushed it out of the way and concentrated on driving.

"Okay then, Gloucester it is, unless anyone else has a better idea," Rob asked.

No one did and with a smile he patted Jeremy on the arm.

"Good idea, son, that's using' your noggin'."

Jeremy, beamed with pride, finally he'd suggested an idea everyone liked.

Rob leaned forward to get a better look at the road ahead. Karen was almost out of the city itself, the road opening up more with each second passed.

"Keep going on this street and then take the exit for I-95 in about a mile or so, okay?"

"Yes, Rob, I know my way around here too, you know," she said in an annoyed voice.

"Sorry, I knew that I guess."

With a destination in mind, and this one appearing more promising, the four survivors leaned back and tried to get more comfortable. Backpacks were opened and their sparse supplies were handed out, a few bottles of water even used to try and wash their face and hands at least.

While all this activity was going on, Val covertly inspected the bite on her arm. It was already infected and it hurt when she touched it. She lowered her sleeve and put on her best smile, but she was thinking of her mother and how the old woman had suffered near the end.

She realized two things at that moment, while she watched the others as they talked and joked with one another, all of them grateful to still be alive.

The first thing was she wouldn't be joining them on that boat, and the second was that she wasn't going to end up like her mother when it came to the end.

* * *

Once Karen had made it to Interstate 95 they all breathed a sigh of relief. But where the zombies were no longer a problem, as there were now few and far between, roaming the highway like animals migrating south for the winter, there soon became another danger to fear.

Other survivors.

As Karen drove slowly down the highway, the lanes full of clogged cars and shattered glass, the Lincoln was a beacon to others.

Most of the time, as they passed by the other occasional vehicles, the drivers and passengers would only stare at them warily. Then the vehicles would pass one another and continue on their way.

But more than once danger was apparent and the last time things could have gone down very differently if it wasn't for Rob and his Magnum.

The Navigator was on the shoulder of the highway, making its way around a stalled school bus, the windows bloody and broken; when on the other side they were stopped by what appeared to be a road block.

With the bus in the way, anyone driving down the highway wouldn't know the barricade was there until after driving around the bus.

Four bedraggled men and one woman were waiting there, two of the men with long rifles, and the woman had a small pistol. The other man only carried a knife, the blade filthy and covered in something brown, and he had a long scar on the left side of his face.

It didn't take much for Rob and the others to know they were in for trouble.

One of the men walked out and raised his hand for the Lincoln to stop. Karen slowed and glanced to Rob in the rearview mirror. He nodded and told her to do as the man said, but to keep the engine running.

While Karen, Jeremy and Val watched the man with the raised hand, Rob was watching the other three people. As the man lowered his hand and stayed rooted to the spot, Rob saw the other three begin to slide to the sides of the Lincoln.

He knew what they were doing immediately. They were trying to surround the SUV and then who knew what they might do. Kill them for their vehicle or food? Maybe take the women after slaughtering him and Jeremy?

Without saying anything to the others, he slowly lowered the window next to him until it was halfway down.

"Karen, now listen very closely to me, okay?" Rob said in a low voice. "When I say go, you drive to the right and just go, hear me? Just floor the pedal and go like the demons of Hell are on your tail."

"But I..." she began.

"No, don't talk; just keep looking forward at the man out there." He hissed his words and she realized there was something more happening than she thought.

"What's up, Rob?" Jeremy asked.

"Nothing, just sit there and be quiet, please," he hissed again.

Val was watching the man in front of the SUV and she gripped her sword handle harder. The man had a gun and there was little she could do with just a sword against him, unless she was able to get closer.

"So what do we do?" Val asked out of the side of her mouth.

"Don't do a thing; just wait there until the guy does something," Rob hissed. "But be ready."

She nodded subtly and remained facing forward.

Rob now had the Magnum raised to the window, but the dark tint kept the people outside from seeing it.

Jeremy's eyes went wide and he was about to ask Rob what he was doing when the older man punched him in the arm.

"Oww, what'd you do that for?" Jeremy whined.

"I said shut up," he snapped in a low voice.

Jeremy's distraction was almost a fatal one for them all. While Rob was telling Jeremy to be quiet, the other man with the long gun was creeping up to the Navigator. Rob spotted him at the last instant, and before the man realized what was happening, Rob leaned out of the window and shot the man in the chest.

There was a loud blast and the gunshot rolled across the open highway, the sound unexpected to the other three people on the road.

As for the man who had just been shot, he was knocked to the road like he'd been stomped on by a giant foot, a large hole now in his back, a smaller one in his chest. Blood was spreading fast and the man's mouth was opening and closing like he was a landed fish.

No one saw the man die however, as the second Rob squeezed the trigger, he screamed for Karen to drive.

"Go, now! Get us out of here!"

Karen hesitated for a moment, but then she did as she was told, not thinking, but just acting. Flooring the gas pedal, the large tires screeched on the pavement and she surged forward.

The power was too much and she lost control for a second. As the man who had raised his hand to stop the SUV tried to roll out of the way, Karen inadvertently drove right for him. The man had time for one frightened bleat of terror and then was run down like a wayward dog, his body rolling across the pavement all mangled and torn.

Karen regained control and swung around the cars blocking the highway, taking the denuded dirt shoulder with two right wheels in the mud.

If it wasn't for the traction and stability of the Lincoln, they never would have made it, but the SUV powered through and they were free.

Gunshots sounded from behind and the rear window cracked, two holes appearing from whence spider-web like cracks began growing.

"Get down, keep your heads down!" Rob screamed as the SUV swerved back and forth, Karen painfully frightened. Her eyes were wide like a deer caught in the headlights of an oncoming car.

Then they were out of range of any more bullets and speeding down the road. Karen was bouncing off the other stalled cars and Val reached out and calmed her down, getting her to slow down before they had a bad crash that got them all killed, or worse, lost their transportation. It was growing more obvious with each mile that without transportation they wouldn't last long.

A mile from the ambush she pulled over and put the SUV in park. She said nothing, just stared out at the road ahead.

Val looked at Rob and Jeremy, but no one knew why she had stopped.

Suddenly, Karen began crying, long sobs that filled the inside of the SUV and made the others uncomfortable. At first no one spoke; letting her cry, but then Rob leaned over so his head was near hers and touched her shoulder. She turned and placed her face against this neck and cried some more, her sobs of pain, fear and exhaustion flooding out of her.

Val reached out and touched her hand and Karen took it. Val felt herself getting choked up and she forced it down. She was tougher than that and if she was going to cry, then she would do it when she was alone.

Jeremy sat in the back seat feeling lost and alone as no one was paying any attention to him.

Finally he spoke up. "Hey, guys, I'm scared out of my mind, too, ya know."

Rob glanced at him and smiled, and when he did, in Jeremy's eyes he saw a scared kid instead of a wisecracking young man. He reached out with his free hand and grabbed Jeremy gently by the neck, pulling him into the embrace with him and Karen.

As the three hugged one another, the adrenalin of the past few minutes slowly wearing off, even Val allowed Karen to pull her closer.

With the Navigator's engine ticking softly on the sun-drenched highway, the four scared survivors took a minute to console one another, and to Hell with the rest of the crumbling world for just a few minutes.

* * *

The Navigator slowed on the outskirts of a rural neighborhood about five miles south of the Gloucester city limits. Though in normal times the rest of the trip would have been made in under twenty minutes, at the rate they had been traveling so far, that twenty minutes would end up being hours.

The deeper they got to the coast, the more congested the roads became until I-95 had become a parking lot.

It seemed others had the same idea when everything had begun to get bad, but all the exodus had done is to cause major traffic jams all along the highway. An overturned tanker truck filled with cooking oil blocked the highway so bad not even a motorcycle would have been able to pass. Instead of trying to drive on the medium or turn around and drive the wrong way on the highway, people had simply waited for the emergency crews to come and free the road again. But instead, the undead, either from the nearby neighborhoods bordering the highway or perhaps some had been in the waiting cars, had been attacked and the vehicles abandoned.

Karen had driven over the medium to the southbound side and had then taken the on ramp down to a main road, thus trying to get by the wreckage, but once she attempted it, it was clear the lower roads were no better.

As the sun crept by over head, it was painfully obvious they wouldn't be reaching Gloucester this day and knew they needed to find a safe place to spend the night.

More cars and trucks passed them every now and then, but the occupants neither slowed nor tried to see who was in the Navigator.

That was fine with Rob and the rest of them. They had all agreed it seemed to make sense to stay just the four of them. Too many humans in one place didn't seem such a good idea at the moment. So when the cars passed them by, they never slowed themselves, but kept on moving to their destination.

"What about that one?" Jeremy asked as he glazed out the tinted windows at the dark houses lining the quaint street about twenty-two miles north of Boston.

"Nah, too many windows," Rob replied.

Jeremy nodded and kept looking as the Navigator slowly rolled down the street, the SUV avoiding vehicles and obstacles when it came upon them.

Here, the sidewalks once had grass on them and there were trees in front of every house. The gutters were once clean of litter and there would be no clunkers sitting in the driveways, dripping oil on freshly paved asphalt.

This neighborhood was once the American dream with a chicken in every pot and a two car garage with two point three kids waiting for daddy when he came home at night from a hard day at work.

But the neighborhood didn't look so good right now.

Numerous homes had been burning a short time ago and the acrid smell of burning insulation and rubber, mixed with other manmade items, blended on the wind to make it hard to breathe. Once manicured green lawns were now tinted red and brown and countless bodies and body parts were strewn around like stray trash. Many of the homes had shattered windows, jagged glass with pieces of flesh still hanging from the edges. More than one had cars sticking out of the front of them, the dead drivers still hanging out the windows after the crash, more than half their bodies now gone, eaten by the undead.

And of course, there were the ghouls.

They wandered around the roads, looking down at their feet as if they were sad.

Rob wondered if they were. Did they still feel anything? Were any parts of their former selves still in those diseased bodies? When they came back, was their soul still in there? Or had it left, leaving nothing but a shell of meat that ran on automatic.

These were the questions he wrestled with as he stared at the dead roaming the streets. And the zombies were better dressed here, too. Female ghouls wore slacks with print sweaters and the men wore Dockers with shirts with little alligators stitched on the breast. Some wore loafers and the women had on expensive shoes, no heels of course, for comfort around the house.

Many driveways still had their owners cars parked in them, the cars and sport utility trucks now sitting silently, waiting for their owners who would never return. More than one had a van, grand or mini, it didn't matter, the soccer moms now lying dead in their kitchens, their stomachs and torsos torn out to drape fancy dining sets and cover Italian tiled floors with blood.

It was the American dream gone horribly wrong and Rob found it hard to look at it.

"What about that one?" Jeremy asked, pointing to another.

Rob shook his head. "Nah, no garage."

"Well, then you pick one," he snapped, angry about getting shot down again. "I don't see what the big deal is. It's not like we're gonna live there. We'll be gone by morning."

"Maybe, but if the place isn't at least halfway strong you might wind up with one of those things in your bed."

Jeremy gave that some thought and nodded.

"Okay, good point, but still, you pick."

In the front seat Val was leaning back with her eyes closed, resting. Karen was still driving, but she was exhausted, and her head would nod forward sometimes before snapping back up.

Rob knew how she felt. They were all exhausted. It seemed like every minute of existence was now an ongoing battle to survive and he longed to be able to close his eyes for a moment without worrying about something trying to attack him.

He jumped in his seat when a ghoul walked into the SUV, the body bouncing off the fender as it fell to the road.

Before it could rise, the Lincoln was ten feet away and still moving.

"Right there, Karen. Pull over, that one's good!" Rob exclaimed as he touched her shoulder. All eyes went to the house as Rob pointed excitedly.

It was a duplex, with both sides having a two car garage. On the left side however, the garage was partially open, no more than half a foot, but it was something. If they didn't have to break into the house that would mean the locks would remain intact as well as they wouldn't make any noise that could attract unwanted attention.

The windows were all intact, too, and the front door was closed. There was no car in the driveway either, though that could mean it was in the garage.

At the end of the day, the house still looked normal, like the owner had left for work that morning and would be returning promptly at five or so.

"Go right up to the garage, I want to pull this monster inside so we can do whatever we need to in private."

"Private? Hell, Rob, there's no one around to see us," Jeremy stated. Val was awake now and she stared at the house like she was visiting an old friend.

"No one's around, huh? What about them?" Rob queried and pointed to the half dozen or so shambling figures in the street.

"What about 'em?"

Rob sighed heavily. Sometimes the boy could be so obtuse.

"Look, son, if even one of those things sees us go into the house, they'll follow. More will see those and before we know it there'll be more than we can handle. Understand?"

Jeremy nodded, comprehension dawning on his face.

"Good," Rob said and turned back to Karen. "Just pull in the driveway and I'll make sure the garage is clear. Then you can drive it in and we can close the door."

"Okay," she said and swung around a putrefied corpse in the road as she aimed for the driveway. She was a little off and the left tire drove over the hand of a corpse. Little snapping sounds could be heard as bones were crushed by the weight of the vehicle. Inside the SUV, the soundproofing was good as the day the vehicle was made, so none of them heard it.

Karen pulled into the driveway and stopped in front of the garage door. Already in her rearview she could see three ghouls approaching, the others also now focused on the Lincoln.

"They're coming," she said flatly, her voice void of emotion. She was emotionally and physically exhausted and just wanted to lie down and sleep for a week. They had been on the go constantly since last night and it seemed like it had been months since she'd last slept.

"I'll take care of them," Val said simply, and before anyone could object, she opened her door, the bulb going on in the overhead, and stepped out into the light of the day with her sword in her hand.

She rubbed her wound gently, the arm now feeling a little stiff, but she knew she had time before it would get bad. She remembered her mother and how a few days had passed before the older woman had fell sick.

The first ghoul was almost on top of the SUV and Val moved around to the side of the Lincoln until she was facing the shambling body.

It had once been a middle-aged man, with graying hair and a few pimples on his forehead. Despite the rot and bloated stomach, the man was relatively still intact and she could see what he'd looked like before he had become a member of the dead team.

The man was wearing a pair of gray slacks and a sweater, but his feet only in socks. Val's eyes went to the gold cross hanging from the man's neck, as if the small emblem was mocking her. A low groan issued from the dead man's mouth and Val decided she needed to get moving before the body was too close to use her sword.

Stepping back a foot, she brought the blade up in a defensive move and then lunged forward, slashing downward at a right angle.

The man's stomach was sliced and the bloated gas within escaped to fill the air with putrid decay and noxious gas. Maggots and roaches poured out of the wound to splash on the driveway, while ropy, gray intestines splattered the pavement to steam in the sun.

Val forced down her need to want to vomit, the sight more than even she could take, and then prepared to finish the job.

The man never slowed after receiving his wound, but merely stomped through the concoction of filth, his socks squirting and squishing as they absorbed the viscous liquid. As he raised his arms level to grasp Val, she swung the sword in a forward arc, slicing the blade into the man's neck. But the man had muscle there and the blade only went partially through.

Pulling her sword free, black ichor and spots of red coated it. She almost expected the blade to begin to steam, as if the liquid would be like acid and etch her blade. As for the dead man, his head was lolling to the side, the thick skin and tissue keeping it from falling off. He looked like a cookie jar with a hinge on one side, the container left open by a child too lazy to close it.

The man stumbled for a few more seconds and then collapsed to the driveway, the head smacking the cement with a sickening thump.

Val ignored the body and moved on to the next one.

A teenager with her hair still tied in a pigtail was next, her braces flashing in the sun. As the female zombie attacked Val, she sidestepped the grasp and stabbed her sword into the girl's abdomen. With a hard uppercut, she sliced upward, eviscerating the body and allowing organs and blood to spill out to splash on the street. She yanked her sword back, swung it around and then jammed the tip into the girl's left eye. Steel met orb and orb lost.

She continued on to the other five walking corpses, hacking and slashing like a woman possessed. By the time the others were down, she was sweating heavily, the blood splatter covering her face and upper body so bad she looked like she had donned another meat suit.

Wearily, she lowered the blade and trudged back to the others who had been busy. Rob had opened the garage door, and after checking to see it was clear, the SUV was pulled inside. He stood there now, his hands over his head as he held onto the bottom of the garage door.

When she was closer, he spoke up.

"You okay?"

"Yeah, Rob, I'll live," Val answered while wiping a gobbet of meat from her cheek.

"Great job out there," he added.

"Thanks," she mumbled

He nodded and stepped back so she could enter.

As she stepped into the gloom and shadows of the garage, he pulled down the garage door, then locked it.

* * *

Across the street, on the lawn of a quaint, one family, a ghoul with useless legs dragged itself along the grass.

Val had taken the shambling dead down fast, but she hadn't made sure this ghoul was truly dead.

She had managed to sever its spine, its legs and left arm now useless, but the rest was still working fine.

Slowly, with its legs like two thick tree branches, and its arm like a loose noodle, the ghoul began to crawl across the lawn and into the street with its remaining right hand, only the fingers able to pull it along.

It would take hours before the zombie made it to the house where the humans had disappeared, but that was all right.

After all, the ghoul was dead and had all the time in the world.

* * *

There was a flurry of activity inside the garage as Val entered. Karen was ransacking a clothes dryer and hamper for fresh clothes while Jeremy stood by the gas cap of the SUV, a red, five gallon gas can in his hand. He was pouring what was left in the container into the fuel tank. The gas had been there to be used for the lawnmower in the corner and the chainsaw in the shed outback, unbeknownst to the four survivors.

Jeremy smiled when Val looked his way but she only nodded back.

Karen came back holding a hamper full of clothing.

"It was in the washing machine," she said. "It never got washed, but compared to what we have on its practically fresh off the assembly line."

"It'll do," Rob said as he reached for the towel Karen handed to him. There were five towels in all so each of them got one to use for cleaning themselves.

Val went in a corner on the opposite side of the Lincoln, that when she removed her shirt, she was able to hide her wound from the others.

Not that she had anything to worry about. The others were chatting together as they cleaned up, a few precious water bottles being used sparingly.

They talked and joked and no one paid attention to Val.

She touched her wound again and winced when sharp pain filled her body. Deciding there was nothing she could do at the moment; she ripped a piece of the towel that wasn't too filthy and wrapped her arm with it. She chuckled internally at the condition of the towel.

Sterile bandages were the least of her troubles at the moment.

Ten minutes later, they were all relatively clean and wearing new clothing.

Rob's shirt and pants were a hair too tight, but Karen's and Val's fit them perfectly. Jeremy did okay, too, the clothes almost a perfect fit.

The men had been gentlemen and had turned around while Karen had dressed, though Jeremy had snuck a peek when he thought no one was looking.

What he saw surprised him.

Under Karen's clothing was a well rounded body with curves in all the right places.

She was a milf if he'd ever seen one before.

Once she was dressed, loose clothing like before, the shape and curves were lost under the folds of material once again. Jeremy decided to not judge a book by its cover from now on when it came to women.

When they were all clean, Rob took the lead with the Magnum and entered the home through the garage door. Once again the door was unlocked, though closed.

That gave Rob hope. If any ghouls had wandered in from outside, he doubted if they would have been polite enough to close the door behind them. The kitchen was just off the garage, and as they entered the gloomy room, there was no smell of decay, no scent of rotten meat.

Feeling hopeful, Jeremy and Rob went off to search the house while Val stayed and watched over Karen.

In five minutes flat the two men returned with the good news. The house was empty, neither living nor dead occupying it.

After locking up and taking extra care to make sure all the windows and doors were secure, the four weary survivors began ransacking the kitchen and pantry.

Though it wasn't overly stocked, there was plenty for a few dozen meals, and they sat around the small, four-chair table and ate canned food and stale pretzels and chips.

No one complained, just glad to be somewhere relatively safe again.

They chatted about Gloucester and about what they would do once they got a boat, and when they were through, they gathered as much food, juice, beer, and water they could find and loaded it into the Lincoln so they would be ready to go in the morning.

When they were finished, it was pitch-black outside, and with them all exhausted from the work they'd accomplished, they all decided to go to bed, wanting to be refreshed in the morning.

Rob considered having one of them stay up and keep an eye out for trouble, but with one glance out the front window to see only an empty street, he decided against it.

What he didn't see was the prone ghoul, crawling right below the window on the lawn. If he had, he may have reconsidered that idea.

Val had been silent most of the time, eating little and talking less.

No one noticed, all too caught up in the slow letdown of a hectic day and previous night.

As they all headed to a bedroom, Jeremy stopped Val in the second floor hallway.

"So what do ya say we get together like we did at the mall?"

Val smiled wanly, but shook her head no.

"Sorry, hon, but I'm wiped out, I'll take a rain check, okay?"

Dejected, Jeremy could only nod.

She felt bad, so she reached up and touched his cheek.

"Hey, it's not you, really. Actually, how can you even be thinking of sex at a time like this?"

He shrugged. "Hell, Val, that's all I do think of. I'm nineteen for Christ's sake."

"I heard that!" Rob called from a nearby room.

"Shit, that man had ears like an elephant," Jeremy hissed.

"I heard that, too. Don't make me come out there!"

Jeremy mumbled under his breath some more and Val chuckled. She leaned forward and kissed him softly on the lips.

"Just go to bed, you horndog, we'll talk about it more tomorrow."

"Okay, but if you change your mind, you know where I'll be."

She sighed like she was talking to a child who wouldn't say no.

"I won't, now good night." She disappeared into her room and closed the door.

Jeremy leaned against the doorframe of the room he was going to sleep in as he stared at Val's closed door.

Rob's head poked out from his room.

"What's the matter? She turned you down?"

"Yeah, what's it to you, old man?" Jeremy replied with annoyance.

Rob let the comment slide.

"Aww, hang in there, champ, there's always tomorrow."

"Yeah, but I'm horny now," he sighed. "Oh, well." He raised his right hand to his face like he was talking to it. "At least there's always you, Five Finger Mary."

Rob made a disgusted face.

"Holy cow, son, too much information, now go to bed, will ya?"

Jeremy grinned, and with a wave good night, entered his room.

Karen exited the bathroom after using a toothbrush and brushing her teeth. She had found a few new ones still sealed in the packages in a hall closet, though even if she hadn't, she wasn't picky at the moment. She would have used one of the ones sitting on the sink if necessary.

Jeremy had and he was no worse for wear. Rob had taken one of the new ones and it was unknown to the others what Val had done.

Karen had washed with a washcloth and felt infinitely better, and was now heading back to her room. They had decided to use the toilet and would only flush once when it was full sometime in the night.

There was only enough in the tank for one more flush so it was rarer than gold, unless they wanted to go in the bushes in the backyard.

None of them did if they didn't have to.

"'Night, Rob," she said when she passed him, and he grinned to her in greeting. But then she stopped and backed up a few steps, and when she was even with him, she kissed him on the cheek. It wasn't meant to be romantic, just a thank you for being there for her.

He said nothing, holding still, and as her lips left his cheek, she slowly let them slide across his skin until her lips were over his. She kissed him again, soft and slowly.

At first he did nothing, his heart beating fast in his chest. He hadn't been with a woman for a very long time since his wife had passed and this was strange, yet familiar, territory.

Karen dropped the cup with a few sips of the remaining water she was holding, the water seeping into the throw rug on the hall floor, and wrapped her arms around his neck, and this time Rob began to reciprocate. Reaching out for her, he took her in an embrace and the two began kissing with more passion, exploring one another's mouths with the tip of their tongues.

Rob felt his pants becoming tighter and he began breathing hard as Karen pushed her groin against him.

When they finally broke free of one another they were both gasping for air.

"Want to come inside with me?" Rob asked as he gestured to his bedroom.

She nodded slowly, a mischievous smile on her lips.

"I'd like that a lot, Rob."

He took her by the hand and led her into his room, closing the door behind them.

"I hope you're a patient woman, Karen, 'cause I'm a little rusty," he said as he began to close the door.

"Don't worry, Rob, you have all night to get back into the swing of things, she grimed seductively."

When the door had clicked shut, Jeremy's bedroom door opened again and he poked his head out into the hall. He'd heard everything and now he could hear Rob and Karen talking and giggling together in the bedroom.

He frowned slightly. "Oh, well, at least someone's gettin' some tonight." Then he closed the door and prepared to go to sleep, but not before having a little fun himself, though he would be the first to admit it was even more fun when there were two under the covers.

* * *

Later that night, as the moon watched over the small neighborhood, two things happened of relevance.

The first was Val woke in the middle of the night after having a terrible nightmare. Her heart was beating fast and her arm throbbed from pain.

After getting up, she went to the bathroom, and after lighting a candle found in the hall closet with others, all the companions now having one in their room, she inspected the wound on her arm over the sink.

Yellow pus was seeping around the edges and the aroma of gangrene came to her nose.

The same thing had happened to her mother in the same time line.

She knew by tomorrow she would begin to feel weak, dizzy spells affecting her at unexpected times. She wasn't looking forward to the next few days.

After cleaning the wound with antiseptic, despite knowing it was a wasted effort, she bandaged it with gauze found in the medicine chest over the sink. She used a bottle of water to wash her face, wiping it dry on the towel hanging on the wall. After rummaging through the medicine chest, she found some aspirin and she popped four into her mouth, washing them down with a sip from the water bottle.

As she headed back to her room, she paused at Jeremy's bedroom door. She stood in the gloom of the hallway and stared at his door for more than five minutes before making her decision.

For all she knew, this might be her last night on earth where she was still healthy and fit. She decided not to waste it, and after going to her bedroom to disrobe, she walked back to Jeremy's room.

Opening the door, she slid in, the shape under the sheets of the twin bed easy to see from the moonlight seeping around the window shade. The room was filled with toys and posters, and even in the darkness she could see this was a child's room.

She padded across the floor, the cool air feeling good on her bare flesh and then lifted up the bed sheets and slid in.

"Huh, what?" Jeremy said and then realized Val was next to him.

Wiping sleep from his eyes, he blinked at her in astonishment.

"But you said you weren't interested."

She shrugged, her dark skin making her harder to see in the gloom.

"Can't a girl change her mind?"

"Uh, sure, I mean, hell, yeah." He shifted in bed. "But I thought you..."

She cut him off, kissing him passionately as he made mumbling sounds, wanting to finish his sentence. She didn't let up and eventually he forgot what he was going to say.

When she came up for air he was smiling.

"Wow, what's gotten into you tonight?" he asked breathlessly.

"Life, hon, that all, just life." And she crawled on top of him and made love to him like there was no tomorrow. Because in her mind, she truly believed there wasn't one.

* * *

The other thing of interest to happen this night while the four survivors paired up and sought comfort in one another's arms, was the crawling ghoul Val had left behind was still outside the house. Now on the front walk, it had reached the front door and began to scratch at it pathetically. Like a dog pawing to get in, the one-armed ghoul did nothing to alert the occupants of the home, but did get noticed by other zombies moving about the street like insomniacs out for a walk.

Slowly, one at a time, the living dead spotted the prone ghoul and moved in to investigate. In their dull brains or by some unconscious telepathy, they each knew when another of their kind had found prey.

Like molasses trickling from a spilled cup, the undead began moving towards the house. As the hours passed and the moon rose high and then began to descend after another long night of ruling the sky; ten, twenty, and then fifty rotting forms arrived. Soon the entire street would be filled with them, all moving to surround the house.

And all the while, the occupants slept silently, unaware of the coming doom.

* * *

Crashing glass pulled Rob from a deep sleep.

Looking around the room, he could see just a hint of the rising sun peeking through the curtains. At first he didn't know what had awoken him, but a second later the sounds of more glass, followed by what sounded like a lamp being knocked over downstairs, came to him.

He glanced to Karen next to him. She was still sleeping softly, a satisfied grin on her peaceful face. Despite alarm bells going off in his head, he still couldn't help but feel a sense of pride that he'd been a good lover to her.

But then more crashing and pounding came to his ears and he threw off the covers and began dressing.

"Karen, get up, there's something going on downstairs," he snapped, getting the woman to roll over and blink up at him. At first her eyes were groggy from sleep but then she heard shattering glass and adrenalin flooded her system.

"What was that?"

"Don't know, but it can't be good," he said while he finished dressing. Picking up his Magnum, he double checked to make sure it was loaded, though he knew it was. After making love to Karen twice, the woman falling to sleep, he'd gotten up and cleaned it thoroughly with some rags and other items found around the house. He knew the revolver working properly could be the difference between life and death.

Rob didn't wait for her to finish dressing, but moved to the door, opened it, and stepped into the hallway. Both Jeremy and Val greeted him, both in a state of undress, but dressing while they entered the hallway, and Rob noticed casually they were both in the same room. Evidently Val had changed her mind about Jeremy's proposition. Val was dressed in the same clothes as the night before, and by the look of it, she'd probably slept in them.

"You guys hear that?" Rob asked them.

"Oh, yeah, and I know what it was, too," Jeremy replied.

"So, spill it," Rob said, though he had a pretty good idea what was making the crashing, but he prayed he was wrong.

"Come in here and see," Jeremy said and pulled Rob into the bedroom.

Rob entered and immediately detected the scent of sex hanging in the room.

Jeremy moved to the bedroom window, the one facing the front of the house, overlooking the street, and when Rob joined him his jaw dropped in astonishment.

Below, on the trampled lawn, sidewalk and street, there had to be over a hundred zombies. They moved about the house, banging on the walls, and a few had managed to break the windows on the first floor.

All the windows on the first floor were high and the ghouls could only reach them with their fists, their heads below the frame. The shattering glass had been those same rotting hands breaking the window panes, but at the moment they couldn't enter. But Rob knew sooner or later they would either figure out a way or simply crawl over one another like stepping stools to reach the now open windows.

Rob opened the bedroom window and gazed out below. The redolence of rot and purification was unbelievable. Not that it surprised him.

He remembered when a dead skunk had been found under his den a few years ago. The animal had been dead for about a week, maybe a little longer. The state of decay had been unbelievable. The main part of the body had actually been bubbling as the internal gases of the rotting insides tried to escape. Maggots had been crawling in the eye sockets, ear and nose canals and all the soft tissue was gone. Ants had been there, as well, devouring what they could find. And the scent had been atrocious which was how he'd found the small carcass in the first place

That same odor struck his olfactory senses now, only times a hundred.

He waved a cloud of flies away from his face, as there were thousands feeding on the walking dead, and slammed the window closed.

"We're screwed," he said simply.

"Why?" Val asked. "All we have to do is drive out of here. We'll just drive over them like before."

Karen had joined them and she listened silently, her arms around her body, like she was hugging herself. She'd heard them talking and could hear the mass of undead outside.

"Maybe, but first we have to get out of the garage and they're stacked up nut to butt out there. The weight of all those bodies is too much."

"Well, we can't stay here, sooner or later they'll get in," Val said.

"We can take them, hell, we've done it before," Jeremy added.

"Yeah, but we were in the SUV then and moving. Now we're trapped and surrounded."

"There has to be a way to get out of the garage," Val said.

"What about a distraction?" Karen suggested softly, but with Val, Jeremy and Rob arguing, she wasn't heard.

"We could shoot a bunch away from the garage door," Jeremy said, gesturing to Rob's gun.

"Can't, son, not enough bullets to do the job. I'm really low now."

"I said, what about making a distraction?" Karen asked, a little louder this time so they could hear her.

All eyes turned to her.

"What'd you say?" Rob asked.

"I said, if you would listen to someone else for a change, what about a distraction? You know, do something to get all of them away from the garage. Then we can drive out and get away from here."

"Hey, that's not a bad idea," Jeremy said. "But what could we do?"

Rob was thinking and rubbing his chin while he mulled some thoughts over.

The others had seen this look before.

"You got something already, don't you," Jeremy said.

"Maybe, but it depends."

"On what?" Val asked.

"One whether luck is with is. Come on, I need to get to the garage. Jeremy, you're with me. You two ladies gather as much of the stuff we didn't load last night into the SUV and then get ready to leave. And hurry, I don't think we have much time before they get inside."

"What are you gonna be doing?" Val asked, not enjoying being delegated to the same duty as Karen. She was as good as any man and she knew it.

"We're gonna go get that distraction." They took off then, leaving Val and Karen alone.

"You all right, Val? You look a little pale," Karen said.

Val frowned, annoyed. "That sounds like a black joke, Karen. Are you trying to be funny?"

"No, no, of course not. I really mean it. You don't look so good. Are you sick?"

Val pushed past Karen to gather her belongings from her room. Luckily, she had retrieved her clothes in the middle of the night or else would have been caught buck naked in Jeremy's room.

"I'm fine; now let's get a move on. If Rob's right, we don't have much time to waste."

* * *

Rob and Jeremy dashed down the stairs to the first floor and were shocked at the sight that greeted them. Every window in the house was now broken, flailing, bloody hands reaching and grasping while twinkling shards of glass littered the floor like confetti.

A loud crash came from the back of the house and both men turned and ran to investigate.

There was a large window in the den, but this one had easier access from the ground outside as there was a small bulkhead leading to the cellar below it.

As the two men stood in the doorway to the room, two ghouls were even now attempting to climb inside the house.

Rob raised his Magnum and shot one in the chest, the force of the round punching the body back and out the window to fall on its brethren below.

The other made it into the den and Jeremy acted quickly. There was a large bookend, made of brass or some other heavy metal on a shelf to his left, and he grabbed it, ran to the ghoul, and smashed the zombie over the head before the dead man could so much as try to bite him. The heavy bookend caved in the soft skull and the ghoul dropped to the floor, gray brain matter seeping from the wound.

"Help me with this!" Rob yelled as he moved to the corner of the room where a large, wooden bookcase sat. With Jeremy's help, the two of them moved the bookcase across the floor, scratching the polished hardwood in the process as hardcover books tumbled to the floor.

"There, that should hold them long enough for us to get out of here," Rob said as he admired the large barricade.

Jeremy nodded, agreeing with his assumption, but when the bookcase shifted from the force of the bodies behind it, he went and began pushing the armchair and desk that were also in the room towards the bookcase.

"Let's put these there, too," Jeremy suggested.

Rob nodded and helped him push the chair and desk against the bookcase, the added weight now holding the bookcase in place. They picked up a lot of the books that had fallen from the shelves when they had moved it, hoping any extra weight would slow the undead down.

"Okay, to the garage," Rob said and they were off. As they moved through the house, daylight began spilling in through the open windows. Drapes and curtains were pulled from their hangings as rotting and deformed hands attacked whatever they could grab hold of. It was a surreal scene, moving through the house with hands and arms waving and squeezing the air, most of them bloody and more than half with missing digits.

But then the two men were at the garage, and Rob charged inside, pleased to see it was still safe and secure. Heavy pounding on the garage door made it shake, but it was strong enough to hold the dead off...at least for the moment.

Rob went to the gas can in the corner of the garage and picked it up, shaking it.

It was empty.

"Great, empty," Rob yelled over the noise of the slapping fists. "Did you have to use it all?"

"What was I supposed to do? Of course I used it all, what a stupid thing to say," he snapped back.

"Yeah, you're right, sorry, son, just rack it up to stress." He began looking around the garage again, hoping to find something he could use as a substitute, but there was nothing. No turpentine, paint thinner or even paint. Whatever the man who lived here did for a living, he wasn't a carpenter or handy man.

Then Rob spotted the lawnmower in the far corner, a sheet draped over the engine.

Without saying anything to Jeremy, he ran to it, slid the sheet off it and checked it to see if it had fuel.

It did.

He looked around the room again to see if there was something feasible to drain the gas into, but there was nothing in view. Once again he cursed the man who lived here. If this had been his house, there would have been empty coffee cans for storage of nail, nuts and bolts, paint thinner, all kinds of odds and ends. And now that he thought of it, there wasn't even so much as a hammer in sight.

Deciding there was no time to mess around, he called Jeremy to him.

"Here, help me carry this back upstairs."

"The 'mower? Why, what're you gonna do, cut the carpet?"

"Just shut up and help me and spare me your comments. In case you haven't noticed, we're about a heartbeat away from dying very messily."

"Okay, okay, relax, I'll help you," Jeremy said and picked the lawnmower up from the front.

Rob got the metal handle and the two of them carried the machine through the house, the undead filling the home with a cacophony of noise. Flies were buzzing everywhere, carried with the diseased bodies, and they crawled on the walls and ceilings, looking for food.

Waving them away from their faces, the two men carried the lawnmower back up the stairs and set it down in the hallway.

"We need to get to the room that's right over the garage," Rob said.

Val appeared from her room, and when she saw the lawnmower, she shook her head.

"I'm not even gonna ask what that thing's for."

"Good, 'cause there's no time to explain it," Rob replied. "We need to find a window over the garage."

Val gesture over her shoulder. "My room does, I think. Why, what do you have planned?"

"Nothing you need to worry about. Do you and Karen have everything you're gonna take with you?"

"Yeah, we're good." She turned to the room Karen was supposed to have used for the night, but had spent it with Rob instead. It had been a little girl's room, all pink and full of My Little Ponies and stuffed animals. It was easier not to think where that little girl might be right now.

"Karen, the boys are back, you ready to go?" she called.

Karen appeared holding a sheet with items wrapped inside it. "Ready, just say the word."

"I am," Rob said. "Both of you get back to the SUV and wait for us. One of you has the keys, right?"

Both women began searching their pockets and for a second their eyes lit up with alarm.

"Oh, no way, you've got to be kidding me," Jeremy said when he saw the look on their faces, thinking they had lost the car keys.

Then Karen reached deep into her back pocket and came out with the keys, the tag from the parking garage still attached.

"Got 'em, I forgot I put them in my back pocket."

With a relieved sigh, they all breathed out, then Rob pointed to the stairs.

"Okay, good, now both of you get going. And Val..."

"Yeah?"

"Leave the dead people alone; just get to the garage and wait for us. We'll be right behind you."

"Fine, but if a few get too close to a window, I have the right to take their heads off."

"Fair enough," he replied and then began rolling the lawn-mower down the hallway. The connection for where the grass catcher would connect to the bag scraped the hall molding and bits of dried grass dropped off to land on the floor.

"Come on, Jeremy, I still need you," Rob told him as he kicked in the bedroom door Val had used, then dragged the machine inside.

Rob pulled the lawnmower to the window and ripped the shade and curtains off without a care, tossing them to the side. After taking the screen out of the window, he used the Magnum to break the glass, the pieces falling to the ground below, more than one shard piercing an upturned face. He ran the barrel of the revolver up and down the sides, needing it to be clear of obstructions, and when he was finished, he grunted and turned to the lawnmower again.

As he began unscrewing the gas cap on the small fuel tank, he pointed to the sheets lying messily across the bed.

"Rip me a small piece of that sheet over there, will you? I need to make a wick."

"Okay," Jeremy said and got to work while Rob inspected the mower better. The tank was almost full and the machine itself looked to be in good shape. Whoever the man had been who lived here, at least he'd taken care of his lawnmower.

By the time he was done checking everything, Jeremy had the sheet ripped. Rob took it from him, twisted it into a roll and then shoved the end into the fuel tank.

"You got a lighter still, right? I used mine to blow up Val's car," Rob said.

"Yeah, here, ya go," Jeremy said and handed Rob a Zippo similar to one he'd used before.

"Thanks, okay, when I tell you to, you get the left side, by the engine, and I'll get the right, then out the window it goes. Got me?"

"Ah, okay, yeah." Jeremy said perplexed. He still didn't understand what Rob was doing. Out the window? Why?

"Relax, son, just do what I say, when I say it, and it'll all be over in a second."

Jeremy said nothing.

Rob grabbed the rip cord and pulled, the lawnmower sputtering once then dying. Frowning, he primed the engine with the small press button, and then pulled the cord again. This time the engine roared to life, a cloud of black smoke appearing out the exhaust. It idled rough for a second or two and then leveled out.

"Okay, get ready," Rob said as he leaned down and lit the wick sticking out of the gas tank.

It caught fast, the fumes of the gas already rising, and the sheet was soaked. The two men had less than three seconds before the gas blew.

"All right, now, pick it up and help me toss it out the window!" Rob yelled over the growling engine.

Jeremy did as he'd been instructed and he picked up the mower on the side of the engine, while Rob did the same. The blade was spinning like a helicopter rotor and he was very aware of how close his legs were to the razor-sharp blade.

"Okay, on three," Rob yelled. "One... two," they pulled back to give them reach. "Three!" And they tossed the lawnmower out the window.

The lawnmower arced straight out into the air, missing the window frame by less than an inch on each side, before gravity took over and it began to spiral down, the blade spinning the entire time.

Just before it hit the ground, about head level with the mob of ghouls, the gas ignited, and a small fireball appeared in front of the garage.

The spinning blade of the mower was detached in the explosion and it sliced through bodies like a scythe. At neck level, more than a dozen ghouls had their heads chopped from their shoulders in the blink of an eye before the blade lost momentum and embedded itself in the torso of an old woman. As for the rest of the lawnmower, when it exploded it was like a large grenade going off.

Shrapnel went off in all directions, slicing and cutting into the undead mob.

When the fireball had dispersed, there was a large hole in the crowd a few feet in front of the garage. Bloody bodies were scattered across the driveway, the wounded ghouls already beginning to rise with missing eyes, limbs or open torsos.

Rob and Jeremy saw none of this, however. The instant the mower went through the window; the two men were running through the house again, their destination, the garage.

When the explosion sounded through the house, shaking the very walls, both men were dashing down the stairs and were soon in the garage again.

Val was in the driver's seat of the blood-splattered SUV, and Karen was next to her. The back door was open and Rob and Jeremy jumped in.

The only problem was the SUV was facing forward, the rear bumper at the garage door.

Now Rob regretted not backing it in, but at the time, he thought it best to get inside the garage and out of sight as soon as possible.

They would just have to make do.

Jeremy was first into the vehicle and then Rob, who slammed the door shut while yelling, "Go, Val, go! I just hope my plan worked!"

Val put the transmission in reverse, and with a, "Hold on to your hats, boys and girls," she slammed her foot on the gas pedal.

The rear of the Lincoln crashed through the garage door, wood splinters and paint chips flying everywhere. The bodies weren't as heavily packed now, thanks to Rob's makeshift Molotov/grenade. The zombies in the driveway were flattened by the collapsing door and then again when the SUV drove over them.

The mob was spread out, but was closing fast yet again. The rear bumper of the Lincoln slammed into bodies, flattening faces and crunching torsos.

Then they were free and Val skidded in a circle, slammed the transmission into drive, and took off down the road, now the front bumper striking bodies and sending them flying twenty feet to land in heaps of mangled meat.

As Val swerved around a large knot of walking dead, Rob leaned forward and grinned.

"See? What'd I tell ya, piece of cake."

All eyes went to him, but no one said anything. Rob frowned, expecting congratulations, but when one wasn't forthcoming, he slowly leaned back in his seat.

"Heck, I thought that went great," he said sadly.

Jeremy patted his arm.

"It did, it did, just don't get too full of yourself, old man."

Rob turned to face him and raised his right index finger to point at Jeremy.

"Yeah, yeah, I know, don't call you that," Jeremy said and then turned away to look out the tinted window.

The dead were falling away and open road, such that it was with wrecks and corpses everywhere, was coming up.

With the four survivors gazing out at the devastation around them, Val pointed the front bumper to Gloucester, and hopefully safety.

*   *   *

"This is ridiculous," Jeremy said from the back seat. "We're going so slow I can see them behind us."

Val glanced in the rearview mirror from the driver's seat.

"Well, if I could go any faster, hon, I would. In case you haven't noticed, the tow trucks don't seem to be out today."

"Now, guys, please don't fight. We're doin' good. They're behind us and we're inside this vehicle. We're fine. Besides, we're almost there, anyway."

"Still," Jeremy added. "What's the point of escaping if the people you're running from can catch you? I mean, they're makin' better time than us."

Val opened her mouth for a rebuttal, but Karen touched her shoulder, shaking her head not to. With a grumble of anger, Val nodded and concentrated on trying to get through yet another ten car pile up on the road.

But Jeremy had a point.

Since leaving Interstate 95, and then reaching Route 128, the last leg to get them to Gloucester by Route 133, the highway was a mess, the road choked with cars and other vehicles, all either burned or wrecked. There were places where Val had to use the Navigator as a ram and force her way through, and other times she had to drive on the shoulder and grass, and then when they entered the city, the sidewalk.

Once she'd reached downtown, it became worse with places where she truly believed they would be trapped with barricades of metal in front and hordes of the undead behind them.

She had taken to knocking over mailboxes and ornate metal trash cans, the latter put out by the city, to get by whenever possible, and one time she drove halfway through an antique store.

They were down to walking speed now and sometimes not even that. And all the while the undead were behind them, slowly following.

One reason they maintained their speed was they never seemed to pause or hesitate. When an obstacle blocked their path, they went over and around it. As they were walking, they would just squeeze through tight spaces, the same spaces Val had to work and fight to get through.

But the Navigator was still the safest place to be.

As walking dead appeared in front of the Lincoln, the vehicle protected the four humans from the continuous attacks. If they had been on foot, they would have been surrounded and overwhelmed hours ago.

The sun was high in the sky and they still had miles to go as they attempted to crawl down Pleasant Street in the middle of downtown Gloucester.

Miles that became even longer thanks to the difficult path they had to use.

The docks were only a few miles away, but it felt like it could have been days or weeks before they made it there by the speed they were traveling. No other human life had been seen for hours, as well. Either any survivors were hiding in a hole somewhere or had headed for the hills.

Only the dead ruled the land at the moment, as the four survivors slowly made their way through a world that was familiar and yet wasn't.

Val halted the SUV and everyone glanced up from what they were staring at for the moment, waiting to see why the woman had stopped. Karen knew immediately as she was in the front seat, but both Jeremy and Rob had to lean forward and ask.

"What's up? Why'd you stop" Rob asked, and when his eyes scanned forward out the front windshield, he saw the reason.

A fire truck was blocking the road, the long ladder truck jammed in tight against a bakery on one side and an antique store on the other. Here in downtown Gloucester, all the natural charm that had made the place a destination for tourism was apparent. Red brick sidewalks, old fashioned street lamps, and historic buildings lined the street. Rob had been here only a few years ago with his wife, before she'd become too sick to leave the house.

They had gone on a whale watching tour and had strolled along the boardwalk together arm in arm.

He remembered the exact same street he was on now, the antique shops and the free library only a few things they had admired that day.

But now the street was utter devastation. The fire truck had arrived to put out a four alarm blaze, but had been hopelessly out matched. Bloody firemen's uniforms could be seen scattered near the truck and an unraveled firehouse lay like a massive dead snake on the road, a few parts of it draped over parked cars.

The acrid smell of old smoke filled the interior of the Lincoln and to the right was the reason why. A large building had gone up, and as old as it was, it was like kindling to the flames.

More than a quarter of the block had been destroyed before the fire had finally petered out.

It looked like there was no way through.

All around the SUV, the dead were moving, coming out of buildings, alleyways, and from behind cars and open doorways.

"We need to go, Val," Rob said quickly, watching the bodies moving towards them. More than one was nothing but a charred mess of burned meat and clothing. Some had no eyes, the empty black eye sockets absorbing the sunlight like two dark pits. They stumbled along blindly, a few holding on to one of their brethren, like a helpful stranger assisting a blind person across a busy street.

"So then tell me where to go and I will," Val said as she looked around her on all sides to try and find a way through.

It was Jeremy who spotted a likely spot.

"What about if you try to get around the front of the truck?" He suggested.

"How? It's tight against the building," Val told him.

"Nah-uh, look again. There's a glass storefront there and it goes all the way to the sidewalk. Can you drive into the store and then get around it?"

The first ghoul had reached the Navigator and began pounding on the side fender, followed by another who was at the rear window. They all jumped inside the SUV, but tried to ignore them, knowing as long as they were inside they were safe.

"I don't think it'll work," Val said. "We could get stuck in there." She'd done the same thing before, but this time the building looked trickier. There was a small lip near the sidewalk, about two feet high and it was possible the undercarriage could get caught. Jeremy couldn't see it from where he was sitting.

Then three more ghouls arrived and one had a brick in its hand.

Before any of the survivors could do or say a thing, the brick crashed against the rear side window, right where Rob was sitting. Bits of safety glass splattered both Rob and Jeremy and Rob found a pale, dead face glaring at him.

Picking up the Magnum from the seat next to him, he shoved the barrel of the weapon into the ghoul's mouth, breaking a few of its teeth in the process, and shot the upper part of its head clean off its shoulders.

The tongue was still there and it flapped around as the body fell away from the vehicle.

"Give it a try anyway, Val, we're all out of options. We can't go back the way we came," Rob said to Val.

Val glanced in her rearview mirror and saw that he was correct.

The road was filled with bodies, the dead gathering behind the SUV like the Pied Piper and his rats. There was a parade of the dead out on the streets of Gloucester this day and the SUV was the Grand Marshall.

"Okay, but don't blame me when we get stuck," she said to them all.

"Just go!" Rob said as he fought off another ghoul.

Karen sat in the front with eyes wide, hands on the dashboard as she watched the dead come for them. Her heart beat fast and she wondered if she would live to see the next hour, hell, the next five minutes!

Val floored the gas pedal and swung the Lincoln to the left, knocking bodies to the side like they were made of dried paper. In seconds she was at the large window and the front of the SUV crashed into the plate glass, the shattering glass raining down across the hood in a hailstorm of sound.

Val turned the wheel to the left again and nudged the Lincoln, the front of the SUV moving deeper into the store. Chairs and tables inside the small shop were knocked over and pushed aside as she tried to make her way around the front bumper of the fire truck. Screeching metal and squealing tires filled the air as she fought to drive a large SUV through a store.

Rotting corpses were in the store, decaying and melting into the floor. She looked away, concentrating on getting them through this last leg of their journey. If she could get them past the fire truck, they should be home free to the seaport.

And then it happened just as more of the dead got close enough to harass them. The undercarriage got caught under the protuberance of the wall where the glass had slid into it.

The Lincoln's engine roared in protest, but it wouldn't move.

"What are you waiting for?" Jeremy yelled. "Go already!"

"I'm trying, you idiot, but I told you we might get stuck and now we are!" she snapped back while trying to spin the wheel.

"Try backing up and going at it from another angle!" Rob yelled.

She took his advice, having no other idea, and the SUV bucked to the side, all of them thrown forward. Karen whacked her head on the dashboard and cried out.

"You all right?" Val asked quickly.

"I'll be better when we get outta here," was her reply. She had a large bruise on her forehead and she could feel it swelling almost immediately, but it was the last thing she cared about at the moment. Val managed to back up two feet and then she swung the wheel again and put the transmission in drive.

Always believing power and brute force was the answer to every problem, she did the same this time, flooring the gas pedal and burning rubber on the linoleum floor of the store.

The Lincoln shot forward, and just as she thought they were free, there was a jarring impact that had them all shooting forward in their seats. The sound of metal tearing metal filled the cabin and the exhaust now sounded so loud it resembled a dozen Harley Davidson's with bored out mufflers.

"You ripped the exhaust off the car!" Jeremy yelled as he tried to sit back up.

Val ignored him, because though they had lost their exhaust system, the SUV was free and she was swinging out of the store and back onto the road.

"Yeah, it worked!" she screamed, pumping her free hand into the air.

No one spoke, all too shook up.

Val saw there was an open road ahead of her, the fire truck having halted all traffic on this side of town, and she stepped on the gas, the sound of the engine unimaginable.

"We're almost there, now!" she yelled and the speedometer shot up to fifty, then sixty, before she realized it, the power of the eight cylinders finally being allowed to be used to their full potential.

"Slow down, Val, we're going too fast!" Karen screamed, not liking the speed. They had come across too many things to slow them down for them to go this fast.

"Relax, hon, we're okay. We did it, we made it," she said, seeing a sign for the historic seaport on a post to her right declaring one more mile to go.

But as she took the next corner hard and fast, she didn't see the roofing truck lying on its side to her right. But that wasn't the problem. The truck was out of her path, so she never thought to hit the brakes and slow down.

Just before she passed the truck however, her eyes spotted a thousand twinkling silver reflections in the road.

When the roofing truck had overturned weeks ago, roofing nails had spilled out of shattered boxes to cover the street from one side to the other.

Val didn't realize what the twinkling items were, assuming they were just glass pieces, until the SUV drove over them and all four tires blew at once.

One second they were taking the corner at sixty miles an hour, the next the SUV was spinning out of control and rolling end over end.

Inside the vehicle, the four survivors were tossed around like rag dolls, the windows shattering and items tossed every which way. Rob's gun jumped from his hand and struck him on the cheek, leaving a small gash. Karen's head smacked the doorframe and she saw stars before the lights went out all together.

With the airbags expelled, there was no added protection from the abuse of the crash for fragile human bodies made of flesh and bone.

The SUV rolled three times before coming to a stop against a shattered storefront on the left side of the road, the engine steaming, the flattened tires still spinning. Red transmission fluid leaked from the undercarriage like blood, the Lincoln resembling a massive animal that had been shot and killed by poachers.

The engine sputtered and died, not able to continue running on its side and the world seemed to descend into silence.

Nothing stirred but the creaks of the metal from the wrecked Navigator, and inside, there wasn't a thing stirring. From the shattered side window a limp hand could be seen, a trickle of blood dripping off it to fall to the road.

Then there was movement all around the smoking wreck as dead feet slapped the road, stepping on roofing nails and glass and puncturing their foot soles without a care. One female ghoul, who was barefoot, stepped on dozens of nails until her feet resembled pin cushions, the sharp points sticking up through the skin on the tops of her feet. The woman neither noticed nor cared; only having eyes for the Navigator.

One at a time, the dead slowly approached the crashed vehicle, the ones far behind now having the chance to catch up.

Five minutes, ten minutes, fifteen minutes passed, as the dead moved to surround the Lincoln.

And all the while, no life stirred inside its destroyed interior.

* * *

The hand dripping blood stirred and consciousness slowly returned to Rob as he and the others lay crumpled and hurt inside the wrecked Lincoln.

One tire still spun lazily and Rob could hear the squeaking of it.

He heard something else, as well, though he couldn't put his finger on it.

As he lay there in a place between consciousness and unconsciousness, his mind tried to piece together what had happened and where he was.

Another three minutes ticked by before he was jolted fully awake by a pair of dead, pale hands trying to grasp his arm and pull him from the SUV. He punched the hands with his fist and they retreated with multiple digits now broken.

Spitting blood, he shook his head and immediately regretted it. He gazed up to the sky to see nothing but blue. Turning his head to the left, he saw five rotting countenances glaring back at him.

"Oh, no," he mumbled, his memory flooding back to him in an instant. For the moment, the dead couldn't get at him and the others, the vehicle on its side protecting them. The front windshield was shattered, though still there, but it wouldn't be long before the dead realized they could push it in and get them that way. The back window was entirely gone, but it had ended up facing a store. There wasn't much room for bodies to get at them that way, but it was also not an escape route either.

Moving about slowly, Rob's hand rested on something metal and hard. Looking down, he was pleased to see his Magnum had survived the crash with him. Picking it up, he checked to see the safety was on and then went to Jeremy who was curled upside down next to him. The moans outside the vehicle and the fists on slapping metal came to him, but he blocked it out.

One thing at a time, he thought.

Jeremy was coming to, as well, and Rob grasped the young man, helping him to a sitting position.

"You okay?" Rob asked.

Jeremy nodded. "Yeah, wow, what happened?" Then he shook his head. "Forget it, stupid question. Are Karen and Val all right?"

"Gonna check them now," he said and crawled to the front of the vehicle.

Val was lying on her side and her sword was in between her arms. Instinctively, she must have reached for it when the crash began, like a drowning man would a life preserver. He touched her neck and felt a steady pulse. She would live it seemed. Karen was next, and when he touched her, she stirred slowly, a low groan issuing from her lips.

"Karen, honey, you need to wake up. We have to get outta here," Rob prodded.

She stirred slightly, but didn't move.

Mumbling a few words under his breath, he went back to Val.

Shaking her gently, he got her to moan softly this time, and when he shook her again, her eyes fluttered open.

"Oh, what happened?" she asked in groggy words.

"We crashed, that's what. Don't know why it happened, and it doesn't matter right now. We need to move and fast."

She looked around herself and at the way she was lying and realized the SUV was on its side. Moving in her seat, she winced when her right leg sent pain shooting through her body. Glancing down, she saw there was a large gash on her thigh dripping blood on the seat.

Tearing a piece of her shirt off, she tied the wound as best she could, wincing at the sting.

Great, she thought, *that's all I need.*

Karen was coming to and she moaned again, holding her hands to her head. Beside the lump on her forehead, she now had a large gash on the top of her scalp. It was bloody, but harmless, and she would live. But the wetness of her hair made her scared, especially when she pulled her palm away covered in red. Her thoughts were muddled and it was possible she had a concussion.

Rob was busy as he waited for the others to regain their faculties. He'd managed to gather everything worth taking with them, and when he was finished, he pushed two packs to Jeremy.

"What?" The younger man asked.

"You're the least hurt by the looks of things, son, so you get to carry two packs."

"Fine," Jeremy said and jumped as more hands slapped the vehicle. A few were on the side of the undercarriage, but most were on the roof side, slapping the roof. Then one found the shattered windshield and began pushing on it.

"Aww shit," Val said as she stared at the dead face through the cracked glass.

"I know, tell me about it," Rob said. "If you're up to it, we need to go before we can't get away. I don't think there's too many of them out there yet," he added.

"Yeah, let's go," she replied.

Rob pointed to Karen. "Help me with her and then get the packs," he said as the two of them began lifting Karen to a sitting position.

When she was in a better position, Jeremy was volunteered by Rob to climb out the top of the SUV, which was now the passenger side.

"Check it out, son, and let me know how safe it is," Rob told him.

Jeremy didn't want to do it, but knew someone had to, so up he went, climbing up the seats. When he stuck his head out through the broken window, he saw dozens of ghouls, but most were on the roof side and weren't quite there yet, their stiff legs only letting them move so fast. They had been following the SUV for hours and now their tenacity had paid off. They had less than three minutes before the initial wave of the dead was upon the wrecked Lincoln and there would be no way for the four survivors to break free.

Jeremy dropped back down, sorry he'd looked.

Apparently he'd made it through the crash unscathed.

"Well?" Rob asked.

"We got more of them than I wanted to count," he said. "But they're a little ways down the street. There's only a few right outside. If we go now, I think we can make it."

Rob nodded and turned to Val.

"Hear that? It's not over yet."

"Then let's go," she said and the two of them, along with Jeremy, helped Karen up.

"Are we there yet? Are we safe yet?" Karen asked in a dazed voice.

"Almost there, hon, a little more," Val said. "First we need to go for a little walk."

"I like walks," Karen said, dazed and confused.

Jeremy climbed up to the top and Rob and Val handed him Karen. The moment her head broke into the air and she saw the dead approaching she snapped back to herself and let out a yelp.

"Yeah, know what ya mean," Jeremy told her.

Val and Rob climbed up next, handing Jeremy the backpacks and gear.

Then they were all on the side of the Lincoln, or rather the top thanks to the wreck. Deciding there was no time for messing around; Rob used the Magnum and shot six zombies who were the closest danger to them. One at a time he fired from a few feet away and the bodies dropped to sprawl across the road, brains and gore spreading out to mix with the glass and nails.

"Okay, let's go. Val, you up for a fight?" Rob asked her.

"Just try me," she said and winced when she moved her leg. Rob didn't see this and they slid off the side of the SUV, using the undercarriage like a ladder.

A ghoul came at them and Val slashed it in the face, blinding it in an instant. When the ghoul came back again, she pushed it away and it stumbled off in the wrong direction.

"Figured I don't have to kill 'em all, just get them to leave us alone," she said as Rob watched the ghoul move away.

"Good idea; now let's move."

There were ten more ghouls in their immediate path and Val took down three herself, while Jeremy picked up some rubble off the sidewalk and took out two on his own. That left five for Rob, and after reloading the Magnum while Val watched his back, he shot all three in the head from no more than six feet away.

He thanked God the ghouls were slow. If they moved faster than a slow walk, the survivors wouldn't have been able to stop them all.

He wondered why this was and figured it had something to do with rigor mortis. If the bodies were dead, then the muscles must be atrophied and stiff.

They headed out, Val limping as she favored her wounded leg. From behind them, the dead parade swarmed around the Lincoln and continued on after them.

Rob and the others tried to move faster, but they didn't have the energy. Exhausted from their long ordeal and two days of nonstop running and fighting, they were already beat. And the crash had sapped whatever reserves of energy they had left.

As they limped down the middle of the street, taking out the ghouls that came for them, they were ever wary of the growing mass of walking corpses at their backs.

By the time they had covered a half mile on their one mile trek through the dead city of Gloucester; all four of them were breathing hard and sweating profusely.

Behind them, the undead were closing and it was a chilling vision.

The entire street was filled from one end to the other with nothing but rotting bodies in different stages of decay. Some appeared fresher, with only pale skin and bloody wounds, but others, who had been dead since the outbreak first began, were bloated and blue, more than one with burst stomachs, their abdomens now exposed with handfuls of intestines that tripped them up as they walked.

Flies hovered over the diseased crowd like a black cloud of smoke, feeding on the diseased corpses, and Rob realized there was no way they would reach the seaport in time.

With each foot they made of progress, the ghouls made two more, and it wouldn't be long before they were finally run down and torn apart.

But they continued on, and by the time the seaport came into view, the sails of some of the closest ships and boats seeming to beckon to them, the undead horde was only twenty car lengths away and closing.

Rob turned and shot the rest of his rounds at the mob as they hobbled down the street, picking off the closest ones. That bought them some time, but not much.

He did make sure to save four bullets for each of them, knowing if the time came and they knew it was hopeless, he could shoot each of them, and then himself.

It wasn't a happy ending, but it was a better one than the alternative.

So they trudged on, with the moans and wails of the dead filling their souls with dread; tickling their spines with the threat of their coming doom.

It was when they had only four hundred feet to go that it became apparent they weren't going to make it.

The distance and time, plus how close the ghouls were, now less than five car lengths, proved they weren't going to make it.

They had done their best, but it wasn't enough.

"It's no good, I can't go anymore," Karen gasped as she fell to her knees."

"Yes, you can, come on, Karen, we're almost there!" Rob yelled, trying to get her up. "Jeremy, give me a hand with her."

Jeremy did as he was told, though he was as tired as the rest of them. But his lack of wounds gave him that extra edge.

Val stood next to them, her eyes glancing to the seaport and then to the undead, the first of the crowd moving forward, wanting to reach them before the others.

The four survivors began moving again, and when they did, Val kept turning around to see the dead faces of the crowd, then she would look at the festering wound on her arm, then her leg, which was bleeding badly despite her attempts to staunch the blood flow.

She wondered if she had nicked an artery or something which made sense as she was feeling lightheaded.

She knew she was in a bad way and even if she reached the seaport with the others, she was already dead, so with one last glance to the dead army following them, she moved up to Jeremy and kissed him hard on the mouth, taking him completely off guard.

"It's been fun, hon, don't you forget that," she said.

Jeremy looked at her, not understanding what she was talking about, then Val looked to Rob and waved.

"You promise me you'll make it, ya hear me? I didn't go through all this shit for nothing. Someone's got to make it."

"What're you talking about? You're coming with us," he said as they walked, hopped, and almost crawled along, slowly losing ground as the undead came closer.

"No, I'm not," she said. "I got this the other day." She held up her arm and pulled her sleeve back to expose the bandaged wound to him. "Plus, this leg is slowing me down. I can barely walk now. But this is the deal breaker," she said as she grinned wanly to Rob.

"Don't worry 'bout me. I'll get to see my mom again."

"I know you will. She's probably in Heaven right now waiting for you," Rob said in a low voice, his breath coming in gasps as he carried Karen with Jeremy, hobbling along like an old man with arthritis.

"But Val..." Jeremy said.

"No, hon, there's nothing more to say, now don't go all chick on me and start gushing and shit, just keep moving. I'll slow the fuckers down for you to give you the time you need."

Jeremy's eyes were tearing and he fought it off, wanting to be strong for her. She wasn't one for emotional outbursts and he wanted his last memories of her of seeing him being a man.

Val gave Karen a kiss on the cheek, as well, and the woman only nodded.

Then Val raised her sword and stopped walking as the others continued on.

"Just keep going. Don't look back, keep going forward. You better make it, or I swear to God I'll give you so much shit in Heaven when you find me."

"Good luck," Rob said to her and she nodded.

Jeremy took one last look at her, wanting that memory forever. Though he didn't love her, at nineteen he felt something very close to it. He was too young to separate sex and love, and after being intimate with her more than once, he felt he could have loved her if she'd let him.

Not that it mattered now.

She waved one last time to him, and then blew him a farewell kiss.

Jeremy let one tear roll down his cheek now that he was away from her and then he turned forward, needing to face that way so he could help carry Karen.

Rob was looking at him.

"You all right?"

"No, I'm not all right, for all purposes my girlfriend is about to die very badly," he said angrily. "Just shut up and walk, we owe her that much."

Rob said nothing, leaving his outburst alone. He knew how Jeremy felt, that same sense of loss had been with him when his wife died, only this was a little different.

As they three of them continued walking, Rob snuck one brief glimpse over his shoulder, his curiosity getting the better of him.

He saw Val standing in the middle of the street, sword held high, and as the first ghouls in line came at her, she brought the blade down, severing the ghoul's hands at the wrists; she followed that up with a slice to the Achilles tendon, the ghoul dropping to the pavement. She ignored it, not concerned with killing it, only slowing it and its brothers down. The next one she slashed across the eyes, the next in the neck, then danced around another and stabbed the sword in its right eye, piercing the brain. She was a whirlwind of action, adrenalin fueling her actions, but there were far too many for her alone to hold out forever, and with more than twenty bodies at her feet, one got under her guard and wrapped its filthy arms around her legs. She stabbed at it and her sword became stuck in its torso and as Rob turned to watch for one last second, he saw the warrior woman go down under an avalanche of bodies, the woman kicking and scratching the entire time.

Then she was lost from sight and he turned forward again.

Jeremy hadn't looked back again and Rob decided the young man didn't need to know Val's fate. He was sure he knew it already.

With added determination now thanks to Val's heroic sacrifice, they pushed onward, the smell of the ocean breeze tantalizing them with its hope of safety.

*　*　*

Ten minutes later, they reached the seaport, the ghouls only a few feet behind them. There wasn't much time to pick which boat to take, but Rob knew he needed an older one.

"Why. A newer one would be better," Jeremy had gasped, his face covered with sweat and grief for Val. Karen was getting a little better and was walking on her own. Her head wound had stopped bleeding and her foggy mind had cleared a little.

"No, it wouldn't," Rob said. "Unless there's keys in your pocket for one of those ships, we need something old that I can hotwire. The older ones should be easy, but the newer ones are gonna have a security system, too. We need a fishing or lobster boat."

They continued on, stepping onto the wooden dock with a little relief. The boats were lined up on the left and the dead were only seconds behind. If Rob turned around, he could see them just behind him. He tried not to. Knowing how close they were only added to his terror.

As they moved along, the waves pushed the hulls of the boats against the dock and Rob studied each one as they went.

It was the fifth boat in, as he wasn't about to take his time in choosing, that he saw a lobster boat that had seen better days. The words painted on the side read, **The Pacific Princess**, and it had peeling paint and old tires on its hull to protect if from damage when it was moored.

"There, that one will have to do! And hurry, we don't have any time left!"

Jeremy wasn't about to argue with him, and with both their help, Karen was the first over to the boat. Jeremy and Rob were next and Rob pointed to the mooring lines.

"Get those off, hurry up; we need to get away from the dock!"

Jeremy ran to the right line while Rob did the left. They were heavy ropes, but someone had tied them with an easy pull knot. In seconds, the ropes were off and the boat was free of the dock.

"Quick, help me push us away from the dock! Hurry, damn you, we don't have any time!" Rob screamed, the first ghoul only a few feet away from them and Rob with only four bullets left.

Both men leaned over, grabbed the dock and then pushed as hard as they could. At first it didn't seem to be working, and as they strained as hard as their muscles would allow, Rob worried his back was going to go out, the first ghoul reached them, followed by hundreds more.

Then the boat began to move inch by inch, and Jeremy lost his balance, but Rob grabbed his shirt and prevented the younger man from falling into the water.

As the boat moved away from the dock, three ghouls managed to get aboard while the fourth, fifth and sixth tumbled into the water, their feet coming down where the boat was a moment ago

Rob and Jeremy punched and kicked the bodies and Jeremy picked up an oar lying on the deck and smashed a ghoul in the face. Weathered wood pulped its nose, and as the ghoul tumbled to the side, Jeremy used the oar and pushed it overboard, the body sinking the instant it struck the water.

Rob was fighting two at a time and he was losing. Karen was behind him and he would protect her at all costs, even if he had to sacrifice himself by grabbing the ghouls and pulling them overboard with himself. He was contemplating this very idea when Jeremy went to his aid, and with a *whack* to the head, he sent another ghoul over the side.

Rob ducked out of the way of the last one, rolling across the deck. When the dead man turned to follow, Jeremy slapped the man in the chest with the oar, the man losing his balance and following his brethren into the drink.

The boat had floated a few feet from the dock, but Rob could see the current would push them back in a few minutes.

"We need to get this clunker running or we're dead," he said.

Karen was on the side of the port deck and she moved forward wanting to be as far away from the dock as she could.

The dock was now packed with corpses and the ones in front were being forced into the water, the weight of the ones behind pushing them forward.

Bodies sunk and others floated, but they couldn't reach the deck of the boat. There was a four foot hull from the waterline, but a few were already slapping the hull with waterlogged hands. They were harmless.

"Watch her, I'm going to the wheelhouse," Rob said about Karen and took off forward, down the deck and up the ladder to where the controls would be.

Karen stared at the dead people on the dock and a chill went down her back, she was so past terrified it almost didn't mean anything anymore.

"You okay?" Jeremy asked.

"Ask me in a minute after Rob starts the engine," she said as she hugged herself. She jumped when a zombie slapped the hull below her and she decided to sit in the middle for a while.

That was when Jeremy spotted something that made his blood run cold.

Pushing through the undead crowd and making her way to the front was Val. But she wasn't Val any longer. She was one of them.

Her sword was still held in her right hand, the death grip firm, and there was a large bite wound on the left side of her neck. Her arms and legs were also torn apart and there were spots where bone could be seen. Her torso was ripped open and her insides glistened in the sun, though there wasn't that much to glisten at the moment. Her once dark face was now a pale gray and her eyes were bone white.

"Oh, shit, no," Jeremy gasped as he stared at the woman he'd cared so deeply for.

Karen heard him and when she followed his gaze, she let out a gasp upon seeing Val.

The warrior woman stood at the front of the line, sword still held tightly in her hand, eyes glaring at Jeremy with anger and hate.

Jeremy had to turn away; he couldn't take looking at her any longer.

The boat was getting closer to the dock again and Jeremy began to get worried.

He moved forward and called up to Rob

"Uhm, Rob, it's now or never, buddy!"

Rob didn't hear him as he was under the dash board in the wheelhouse. He was pulling wires and he thought he almost had it when he felt something tug at his feet. At first he thought it was Jeremy, but when he ducked his head lower to see what was happening, his eyes went wide to see a ghoul pulling him out from under the dashboard.

The ghoul wore the overalls of a deck mate and its hands were now wrapped around Rob's legs! Before he could do anything, he was dragged out from under the dashboard to sprawl on the deck of the wheelhouse.

His Magnum was above his head, out of reach on the dashboard, and he stared up into the face of his own death, as there was no way he could get away while he lay on the deck, vulnerable to attack.

The ghoul raised wrinkled hands and opened its mouth wide, prepared to fall on Rob and tear him apart, when suddenly, there was a loud clank.

The ghoul wobbled on its feet and then tumbled to the side, and behind it was Karen, a red fire extinguisher in her hands, bits of blood and scalp now stuck to the bottom from where she had cold-cocked the ghoul.

"Jeremy said you need to hurry, the boats floating back to the dock. Now quit screwing around and get that engine started."

He blinked up at her, shocked he was still alive, and then he rolled over and crawled back under the dashboard.

"Thanks," he said, his voice muffled as he worked.

"Just get us out of here and that's thanks enough," she replied.

Rob got back to work, and thirty seconds later, there was a dull rumbling coming from under their feet and the engine surged to life.

"Oh, yeah, never had a doubt," he said with a grin as he pulled himself out from under the dashboard.

Standing tall, he pushed the throttle forward and the boat slowly began to move forward.

"Uh, before we get too far, you need to go down and see Jeremy," she said.

"Why?"

Karen shook her head, not wanting to say what was waiting for him on the dock.

"Just go, please."

"Okay, fine," Rob said bringing her to the wheel. "Here, hold the wheel like this. It's like driving a car. If you need to turn, then do it the same way you would if you were driving."

"Fine, just go, before we're too far away from the dock."

He nodded and did as she asked, not understanding her last comment. Picking up the Magnum, he went aft to see to Jeremy.

When he got there, Jeremy grabbed his arm and dragged him to the edge. He pointed to Val and Rob's face went white.

"Oh, God no," he said in shock,

"Yeah, and do you remember what she said? She said she didn't want to be one of them. Shoot her, Rob! Shoot her fast before we're too far out!"

"You're sure?"

"Goddamn it, old man, just fucking shoot her!" Jeremy screamed, tears in his eyes.

Rob nodded, and ignored the man's swears. This was one time it was okay with him.

He raised the Magnum.

Knowing he only had four bullets left, he lined up the shot. The boat was rocking gently on the waves and he didn't want to waste the last of his precious ammunition, but he'd already decided in an instant he would gladly use all of them to put Val to rest if need be.

He let out a breath and slowly calmed himself, and when he was ready and he thought he had the feel of the waves as the boat chugged away from the dock, he squeezed the trigger.

Across the water on the dock, Val's head snapped back, and because of the bodies behind her, she didn't fall backward, but instead went forward.

Her body tumbled into the water where it floated face down. The sword sank, the arm holding it being dragged downward. With her torso open, water seeped inside the body, and with her sword as an added weight, her body sank from view.

"A burial at sea. Hell, Rob, she got better than a lot of other people," Jeremy said softly.

"Yeah guess she did at that." He patted Jeremy's shoulder and then turned away.

The sun was high in the sky and a few seagulls were overhead, catching the warm air currents. The fresh open breeze wafted over their bodies, drying the sweat and calming them. Filling them with hope for the future.

They didn't know where they'd be going next, but they had packs full of food and water, and an old but sturdy boat under their feet.

Wherever they went, they would survive, together.

And in a dead world, sometimes that was all anyone could ask for.

Epilogue

The Pacific Princess was sitting idly in the middle of Massachusetts Bay, about ten miles off the shore of Cape Ann.

In the wheelhouse, the blood stain from where the ghoul had been killed by Karen still remained, but the body was long gone, tossed overboard with the rest of the trash.

Down below, on the aft deck, the three weary survivors were relaxing, letting the engine rest as they enjoyed the ocean breeze and just being alive.

They had been lucky when Rob had picked this boat. In the small kitchen below decks, they had found a decent supply of food stores as the boat was well stocked, the crew probably preparing to go out on a run, but never had the chance when the dead began to walk. They had also found detailed maps of the area, and the boat's well-maintained navigation system would see them wherever they wanted to go. Rob guessed they had enough food and water for more than a month. Longer if they wanted to ration some. The engine was clean and had just been serviced and though the outside of the boat was beat-up, it was obvious the captain had loved his ship and had treated it with respect.

They had talked about Nova Scotia, but hadn't made up their minds yet. Jeremy wanted to go to Cape Cod, but Rob figured if Boston and the surrounding states were like where they had come from, then the Cape would be no better, though it was more isolated.

Rob and Karen were sitting on a bench where nets were stowed while Jeremy fished off the aft end of the boat. He didn't know if he would catch anything, but it was still fun. It reminded him of when he used to go deep sea fishing with his father when he was eleven. One time he had been so sick he couldn't even fish, his father, too, but all his father had done was vomit over the side when the need came and then continue fishing. He had paid for the trip and he'd be dammed if he was going to waste it sick. He wanted flounder!

"It's food for the fish, son," his father had told him about the vomit. "It attracts them."

Jeremy had vomited twice as hard after hearing that.

So with the sun high overhead, a few gulls hanging about looking for hand outs, the three survivors enjoyed the day.

"What do you think'll happen to us?" Karen asked while she played with one of Rob's fingers resting on her lap.

He shrugged. "Don't know, and right now, I really don't care." He turned to her and kissed her softly on the forehead. "Let's just live in the moment for a while, okay? Whatever's left of the world will still be there when we're ready to go back."

She nodded and leaned her head against his shoulder, happy for the first time in she didn't know how long.

"Hey, hey, I got something! I caught a fish!" Jeremy yelled. "Whoa, it's a big one, too!"

He began wrestling with the rod and reel and Rob sat up.

"Need any help?"

"Nah, you just sit there and rest those old bones, I got it," he said cockily. "Mmmm, I can't wait, for fresh fish for dinner."

He began backing away from the aft end, and when he moved forward, he would reel the line in. He did this for quite sometime and he was beginning to wonder if maybe he'd caught an old boot or something worthless. The line was top of the shelf and he was sure it wouldn't break. Even if he had caught a small shark he was sure the line would hold.

Suddenly, the line went slack and Jeremy lowered the rod, thinking it had broken after all.

"Aww, tough break, kid," Rob teased from behind him. Karen slapped him on the arm, not wanting the two of them to start teasing one another again. They had in the past, the two like father and son.

Jeremy was about to give up and just reel the rest of the line in and start over when he was surprised to see a bloated and blue hand slap the edge of the boat, followed by a pale, water-drenched face. Karen and Rob stood up; both gasping at the sudden appearance of what was obviously a zombie.

But how? Way out here? These and other unspoken questions were on all their lips.

Jeremy stared at the ghoul as it tried to pull itself onboard, but it couldn't seem to reach over the edge. As the ghoul struggled, Jeremy studied it more. The red hair was still bright and in the pale white and blue skin he could still make out what had to be freckles. Though dark from water saturation, the ghoul was wearing what could only be called hospital scrubs, the color green where seaweed wasn't covering it.

The name **SMITH** was stitched on the shirt, just over the ghoul's left pocket, and when the ghoul belched loudly, a miasma of decay and rot flooded over him before the breeze washed it away.

The ghoul managed to get a leg over the side and the body dropped to the deck with a thump. As it began to rise, Rob pulled his Magnum, the three bullets still remaining, but Jeremy held his right hand up for him to stop.

"Don't waste the ammo, I got this," he said with a grin, and with a heavy sigh like he was doing unpleasant chores like vacuuming or taking out the trash around the house, he picked up the oar lying on the deck, the same one he'd used before to save Rob, and raised it over his head like it was an axe and he was going to chop wood.

"Oh, well," he said jovially as he stepped towards the zombie, the oar already coming down to crack the waterlogged ghoul's head like a soft watermelon.

"Here we go again."

NOTES FROM THE AUTHOR

This is something new for me, adding notes at the end of one of my books, but this story needed it; at least in my eyes.

You see, why I was writing it and the main characters wound up in a shopping mall, I kept feeling like I was being repetitive.

I take great pride in knowing that every story I write about zombies is in some way original. Now, whether that is a situation like in Dead Morning with a serial killer, or with Dead Freeze, where the zombies are frozen; each story is slightly different from the others and has a different feel.

Back in Dead City, I had Henry and his companions in a shopping mall, so to me, the whole mall thing was finished, but when I was writing this story, quite by accident, the heroes ended up in a shopping mall.

Here's a little history about this book you hold in your hands and how it came to be.

I was honored to be asked by A.P. Fuchs, author of Blood of the Dead, to pen a short story about zombies for his soon to be released anthology titled Dead Science.

But as I wrote the story, the story wouldn't end, and I ended up going way over the amount of words A.P. needed.

So I wrote him another, shorter one and put this one aside to finish later figuring I could make a decent short story out of it.

Then I finished Dead Reckoning which I had put on hold for a few days so I could bang out the short story for A.P.

Once that was finished, I picked up the book you have in you hands and kept going, liking the characters enough that I felt I could make a fun novel out of them instead of merely the short story.

So, about the shopping mall. Sorry, I can get off track. Think I'm bad here; you should talk to me in person.

In the scene where the heroes are getting into the Honda Civic, and Rob accidentally backs up and crashes through the glass doors of the shopping mall, he was never supposed to do that.

In my original story, he was going to drive away, leaving the shopping mall behind, and he and the other survivors were going to end up at a junkyard, where other survivors had holed up, and true to form, no one would get along, despite their lives depending on it.

But as so many times it would happen, the story tells itself and I'm just here to put it on paper. So instead of driving away, Rob crashed into the mall and Karen gets pulled out the broken rear window and attacked by zombies.

And that is when Val shows up, right?

Up until that exact second when Karen was yanked from the car, Val did not exist in the story, nor did I have any plans for her, but then she was there and she saves the day and now there were four.

Another thing you may have noticed and found kind of weird was how there were no chapters in this book. The explanation for that is easy. As I was originally writing this as a short story, I only had pauses, not actual chapter breaks. So I decided to just go with it for the entire story.

As you could tell at each break, the book could be put down and then picked up again anytime.

So, though this story doesn't break any new ground in the zombie world of literature, I hope you enjoyed it, and will keep coming back for more, because I'll tell you a little secret, I have more ideas than I know what to do with, and I plan on writing these stories for a long time to come.

Anthony Giangregorio
January 2009

KINGDOM OF THE DEAD
by Anthony Giangregorio

THE DEAD HAVE RISEN!

In the dead city of Pittsburgh, two small enclaves struggle to survive, eking out an existence of hand to mouth.

But instead of working together, both groups battle for the last remaining fuel and supplies of a city filled with the living dead.

Six months after the initial outbreak, a lone helicopter arrives bearing two more survivors and a newborn baby. One enclave welcomes them, while the other schemes to steal their helicopter and escape the decaying city.

With no police, fire, or social services existing, the two will battle for dominance in the steel city of the walking dead.

But when the dust settles, the question is: will the remaining humans be the winners, or the losers?

When the dead walk, the line between Heaven and Hell is so twisted and bent there is no line at all.

THE DARK
by Anthony Giangregorio

DARKNESS FALLS

The darkness came without warning.

First New York, then the rest of United States, and then the world became enveloped in a perpetual night without end.

With no sunlight, eventually the planet will wither and die, bringing on a new Ice Age. But that isn't problem for the human race, for humanity will be dead long before that happens.

There is something in the dark, creatures only seen in nightmares, and they are on the prowl.

Evolution has changed and man is no longer the dominant species.

When we are children, we are told not to fear the dark, that what we believe to exist in the shadows is false.

Unfortunately, that is no longer true.

DEAD UNION

by Anthony Giangregorio

BRAVE NEW WORLD

More than a year has passed since the world died not with a bang, but with a moan.

Where sprawling cities once stood, now only the dead inhabit the hollow walls of a shattered civilization; a mockery of lives once led.

But there are still survivors in this barren world, all slowly struggling to take back what was stripped from their birthright; the promise of a world free of the undead.

Fortified towns have shunned the outside world, becoming massive fortresses in their own right. These refugees of a world torn asunder are once again trying to carve out a new piece of the earth, or hold onto what little they already possess.

HOSTAGES

Henry Watson and his warrior survivalists are conscripted by a mad colonel, one of the last military leaders still functioning in the decimated United States. The colonel has settled in Fort Knox, and from there plans to rule the world with his slave army of lost souls and the last remaining soldiers of a defunct army.

But first he must take back America and mold it in his own image; and he will crush all who oppose him, including the new recruits of Henry and crew.

The battle lines are drawn with the fate of America at stake, and this time, the outcome may be unsure.

In a world where the dead walk, even the grave isn't safe.

DARK PLACES

by Anthony Giangregorio

A cave-in inside the Boston subway unleashes something that should have stayed buried forever.

Three boys sneak out to a haunted junkyard after dark and find more than they gambled on.

In a world where everyone over twelve has died from a mysterious illness, one young boy tries to carry on.

A mysterious man in black tries his hand at a game of chance at a local carnival, to interesting results.

God, Allah, and Buddha play a friendly game of poker with the fate of the Earth resting in the balance.

Ever have one of those days where everything that can go wrong, does? Well, so did Byron, and no one should have a day like this!

Thad had an imaginary friend named Charlie when he was a child. Charlie would make him do bad things. Now Thad is all grown up and guess who's coming for a visit?

These and other short stories, all filled with frozen moments of dread and wonder, will keep you captivated long into the night.

Just be sure to watch out when you turn off the light!

SOULEATER

by Anthony Giangregorio

Twenty years ago, Jason Lawson witnessed the brutal death of his father by something only seen in nightmares, something so horrible he'd blocked it from his mind.

Now twenty years later the creature is back, this time for his son.

Jason won't let that happen.

He'll travel to the demon's world, struggling every second to rescue his son from its clutches.

But what he doesn't know is that the portal will only be open for a finite time and if he doesn't return with his son before it closes, then he'll be trapped in the demon's dimension forever.

DEAD TALES: SHORT STORIES TO DIE FOR
by Anthony Giangregorio

In a world much like our own, terrorists unleash a deadly dis-ease that turns people into flesh-eating ghouls. A camping trip goes horribly wrong when forces of evil seek to dominate mankind. After losing his life, a man returns reincarnated again and again; his soul inhabiting the bodies of animals. In the Colorado Mountains, a woman runs for her life, stalked by a sadistic killer. In a world where the Patriot Act has come to fruition, a man struggles to survive, despite eroding liberties. Not able to accept his wife's death, a widower will cross into the dream realm to find her again, despite the dark forces that hold her in thrall. These and other short stories will captivate and thrill you. These are short stories to die for.

ROAD KILL: A ZOMBIE TALE
by Anthony Giangregorio
ORDER UP!

In the summer of 2008, a rogue comet entered earth's orbit for 72 hours. During this time, a strange amber glow suffused the sky.

But something else happened; something in the comet's tail had an adverse affect on dead tissue and the result was the reanimation of every dead animal carcass on the planet.

A handful of survivors hole up in a diner in the backwoods of New Hampshire while the undead creatures of the night hunt for human prey.

There's a new blue plate special at DJ's Diner and Truck Stop, and it's you!

DEADFREEZE
by Anthony Giangregorio

THIS IS WHAT HELL WOULD BE LIKE IF IT FROZE OVER.

When an experimental serum for hypothermia goes horribly wrong, a small research station in the middle of Antarctica becomes overrun with an army of the frozen dead.

Now a small group of survivors must battle the arctic weather and a horde of frozen zombies as they make their way across the frozen plains of Antarctica to a neighboring research station.

What they don't realize is that they are being hunted by an entity whose sole reason for existing is vengeance; and it will find them wherever they run.

DEADFALL

by Anthony Giangregorio

It's Halloween in the small suburban town of Wakefield, Mass.

While parents take their children trick or treating and others throw costume parties, a swarm of meteorites enter the earth's atmosphere and crash to earth.

Inside are small parasitic worms, no larger than maggots.

The worms quickly infect the corpses at a local cemetery and so begins the rise of the undead.

The walking dead soon get the upper hand, with no one believing the truth.

That the dead now walk.

Will a small group of survivors live through the zombie apocalypse?

Or will they, too, succumb to the Deadfall.

ANOTHER EXCITING CHAPTER IN THE DEADWATER SERIES!
BOOK 5

DEAD HARVEST

by Anthony Giangregorio

Lost at sea and fearing for their lives, a miracle arrives on the horizon, in the shape of a cruise ship, saving Henry Watson and his friends from a watery grave. Enjoying the safety of the commandeered ship, Henry and his companions take a much needed rest and settle down for a life at sea, but after a devastating storm sends the companions adrift once again, they find themselves separated, exhausted, and washed ashore on the coast of California.

With each person believing the others in the group are dead; they fall into the middle of a feud between two neighboring towns, the companions now unknowingly battling against one another.

Needing to escape their newfound prisons, each one struggles to adapt to their new life, while the tableau of life continues around them.

But one sadistic ruler will seek to unleash the awesome power of the living dead on his unsuspecting adversaries, wiping the populace from the face of the earth, and in doing so, take Henry and his friends with them.

Though death looms around every corner, man's journey is far from over.

UNDEAD PRESS
UNDEAD PRESS
Where the Dead
Never Sleep
UNDEADPRESS.COM

VICTORY OF THE DEAD
ANTHONY GIANGREGORIO

CLAN OF THE BIGFOOT
BY ANTHONY GIANGREGORIO
LIVING DEAD PRESS.COM

RAT WAR
A HORROR ANTHOLOGY
EDITED BY
ANTHONY GIANGREGORIO

CREATURE FEATURE
A MONSTER ANTHOLOGY

EDITED BY
ANTHONY GIANGREGORIO

THE BOOK
OF
CANNIBALS
KISS
THE
COOK
Longoria Grill
EDITED BY
ANTHONY
GIANGREGORIO

SUNSET
OF THE DEAD
ANTHONY GIANGREGORIO